D0477387

000000753734

A
KILLER
PAST

A KILLER PAST

MARIS SOULE

ROBERT HALE · LONDON

ISBN 978-0-7198-1490-7

Robert Hale Limited
Clerkenwell House
Clerkenwell Green
London EC1R 0HT

www.halebooks.com

2 4 6 8 10 9 7 5 3 1

Typeset in Sabon
Printed in Great Britain by Berforts Information Press Ltd

CHAPTER ONE

MARY HARRINGTON KNEW she was in trouble the moment the old Chevy gave its last gasp. She'd seen the two boys sitting on the sagging porch steps of an abandoned house. From the distance, she could only guess their ages, but they looked to be in their late teens.

As her car coasted to the curb, the boys kept their gazes on the roach they were sharing; nevertheless, Mary knew they were aware of her presence. Having car trouble was bad enough, but being stuck in this neighborhood late at night was double trouble. It didn't matter that her house was only two blocks away. A woman her age, out on the streets by herself, was way too tempting.

'Damn,' she muttered. She should have left her granddaughter's birthday party earlier. That or she should have let her son drive her home.

But no, she'd told them she wasn't feeble, not yet, and that she could take care of herself.

She hoped like hell she wouldn't have to test that statement.

Although Michigan's economy was recovering, this part of the neighborhood had been hit the hardest by the housing slump and still had a long way to go. Only a few homes had lights on, more 'For Sale' signs displayed than Halloween decorations. People had moved away in search of work, leaving their abandoned houses for the gangs and drug dealers. Those who didn't leave, locked their doors and remained inside once the sun went down.

One of the boys on the porch steps turned slightly and said something to his friend. The second boy glanced her way, then back at his friend.

She couldn't remain in the car forever. They would come over, sooner or later. Better to be prepared.

They wouldn't get much from the car. No GPS, stereo, or CD player. The tape deck had jammed years before, and the AM/FM radio wasn't worth the effort. Even the tires needed to be replaced. Her son had been telling her to buy something newer, but up until now the Chevy had served her well.

Without being obvious, Mary slipped her credit cards, ID, and house keys out of her purse and into the inside pockets of her windbreaker. If the two punks on the steps wanted her purse, they could have it. She never carried more than twenty dollars. If she was lucky, it would be a snatch and run. She'd give the expected yelp of surprise and indignation, and that would be it.

She didn't want trouble.

For a moment she considered simply locking the car doors and calling her son. Maybe the boys on the porch steps would leave her alone until Robby arrived. He could be there in ten or fifteen minutes, depending on how fast he drove. But speeding could get him in trouble. She'd seen him down three martinis as they celebrated his daughter's eighteenth birthday. No telling what his blood-alcohol level might be.

Besides, Robby wasn't a fighter. He took after his father. Dear sweet Harry always said he was a lover, not a fighter. He didn't even fight the cancer. 'I'd rather have quality of life,' he'd told her after the doctor gave them his options. 'Six months of being able to do things with you is better than a year or two of chemo and radiation.'

As it was, they had nine months together, and then he was gone.

'You'll be fine,' he'd said that last night, before the morphine eased him to sleep. 'You're the strong one.'

Maybe so, but she wasn't as strong and agile as she'd been in her teens and twenties. The article that had appeared in last month's *Kalamazoo Gazette* had made her sound like an Amazon, but Mary knew the truth. Her workouts at the gym kept her arthritis at bay and helped her retain some muscle tone, but she was no spring chicken. A seventy-four-year-old shouldn't have to fight.

'Play it safe,' she muttered to herself as she opened the car door.

She clutched her cellphone in the palm of her right hand, but kept a light hold on her purse. When the boys did grab it, she wouldn't resist.

Sergeant Jack Rossini was on his way home when he heard dispatch call for a cruiser. Although he was off duty, he flipped on his lights and made a U-turn. Lately there'd been an increase in gang violence in that part of town, and the mayor had been pressuring the chief to get the problem under control. In the last ten years, Rivershore's image had plummeted. Once viewed as a model of small-town living, the area now matched Detroit's record for unemployment and robberies. Way too many young people had nothing to do but get into trouble.

Rivershore's police force had shrunk along with the town's population. Jack knew the two officers responding to the call wouldn't object to his presence. Backup, when it came to gang violence, was always welcome.

He passed an old, gray Chevy parked by the side of the street. The cruiser, its red and blue lights flashing, was about a half-block farther on. Residents had come out of the surrounding houses and stood on their lawns, on the sidewalk, and in the middle of the street. Whatever they were looking at was blocked by the cruiser.

An elderly black woman wearing a bathrobe and slippers and holding a drink in her hand stood in the path of his Dodge Durango. Jack rolled down his window and yelled at her to move.

The woman turned and raised her free hand to shield her eyes from the glare of his headlights, then staggered toward his vehicle. 'Serves 'em right,' she slurred, her breath strong enough to tell him the liquid in her glass wasn't water.

'Them?' he repeated.

'Dem two.' She waggled a finger toward the cruiser. 'Dey's been hanging around dat house all night, jest waitin' fer trouble.'

Jack was sure she wasn't referring to the officers who had responded to the call, but he still couldn't see anything. 'Did you witness the shooting?'

'Didn't see nuttin',' she said, then smiled. 'Nuttin' at all, 'til I heard 'em screamin'.'

'How many shots were fired?'

'Shots?' She shook her head. 'None dat I heard.'

'So you didn't see anything … didn't hear anything?'

'Saw her leave. Dat's what I saw. And she were limpin'.'

'There was a woman, a girl involved?' One way or another, there usually was.

'Yeah, guess so. She shore didn't waste any time gittin' out of here.'

'Which way did she go?'

His question seemed to confuse the woman, and she looked both ways before finally pointing east.

'We'll want a description of this woman,' he said, though the way she was squinting at him, he doubted a description would be much help. 'Where do you live, Mrs…?'

'Black. Cora Black,' she said and pointed at the house behind her.

'All right, Mrs Black, if you'll step out of the way, someone will talk to you later.'

Jack eased the Durango by her and parked just past the cruiser. As soon as he was on the sidewalk, he could see the victims. The two males were in their late teens or early twenties and were seated on the grass in front of the responding officers. One of the boys held a towel to his face, while the other kept rocking back and forth, clutching his arm and moaning.

With the nearest street light out, and the flashing red-and-blue lights distorting colors, Jack wasn't immediately sure if the two were Caucasians or Latinos, but as he drew nearer, he saw Towel Holder had a blue bandana tied around his wrist. The bandana, along with the baggy jeans, hooded sweatshirts, Air Jordans, and an RB tattoo on the side of Arm Holder's neck – the R touching the B so the B looked like a heart on its side – clearly identified the boys as members of the River Boyz. The gang saw themselves as an offshoot of one of the Mexican cartels, though Jack wasn't exactly sure which one. He wasn't even sure the gang members knew.

Over the last two years, Jack had dealt with several of the gang's members, but these two were new to him. 'What happened here?' he asked the two officers he'd come to assist.

Stewart VanDerwell, who'd been on the force for five years,

glanced his way. 'Hi, Jack. Seems, according to these boys, we have a little old lady going around beating up our young citizens.'

Jennifer Mendoza, the only female on Rivershore's police force and a rookie, grinned. 'They insist they were doing nothing wrong, that they offered to help her, and she just started hitting and kicking.'

'The bitch broke my arm,' Arm Holder said, glaring up at Jack before resuming his rocking.

'Broke my nose,' the other one added, lowering the towel from his face.

The twisted bridge of the boy's nose, along with the blood seeping from one nostril, verified his statement.

'Think she broke my knee, too,' he said, groaning as he tried to move his leg.

'We've called for an ambulance,' Officer VanDerwell said, glancing back toward the direction Jack had driven. A siren could be heard in the distance.

'You catch this "old" lady's name?' Jack asked the two on the lawn.

'Naw, she just came at us,' Arm Holder said.

'Like a crazy woman.'

'Crazy,' Arm Holder repeated.

Jack smiled. 'And just how old is old?'

The two boys glanced at each other, and then back at him. Arm Holder answered. 'I dunno. A hundred, maybe.'

'A hundred.' Officer Mendoza laughed. 'Sure, she was.'

'She was,' Towel Holder insisted. 'She had wrinkles. Lots of them.'

'And it's the night before Halloween,' Officer VanDerwell said. 'You punks ever think she might have been dressed up like an old woman? Could have even been a guy in drag.'

Again, the boys looked at each other. Towel Holder shrugged but shook his head. 'It weren't no fuckin' costume.'

Mary limped into her living room and sagged into Harry's La-Z-Boy. Her heart hadn't stopped pounding since she'd left the two boys. Even though pain radiated up her leg, the adrenalin racing through her body overrode the sensation. Excitement clashed with fear. My God, what had she done?

The boys hadn't been content to simply take her purse and run. Oh no, they wouldn't leave it at that. The short one blocked her escape while the tall one looked inside her purse. He said a twenty wasn't enough, wanted to know where she'd put her credit cards, where she lived. They'd threatened her.

When the tall one grabbed her arm and reached for the lapel of her jacket, she didn't even think before she reacted. Forty-four years might have passed, but her body automatically responded with ingrained moves. A shift of position, one step back, and she had her assailant off balance. She used her cellphone as a weapon, jamming the edge hard against the bone of his forearm. As she applied pressure, a sweep of her foot, along with a twist to her side, had him falling forward. The moment he hit the ground, she dropped down and slammed her knees into his back and ribs. Before he could react, she used the edge of the cellphone to cuff his ear, then grabbed his arm and gave a violent twist. He started screaming right after she heard his shoulder pop.

A quick roll to the side put her on her back. The short one stared down at her, his mouth open and his eyes glazed with confusion. She knew she didn't have much time, but springing to her feet was not an option. Her joints might remember the moves, but age had robbed her body of its elasticity. What once had taken a single maneuver now required three stages, but she was on her feet before Shorty truly understood what was happening.

She used the cellphone in her hand to deliver the blow to his face, a sidekick took out his knee, and a chop to his neck put him down on the ground. In the past, she would have finished him off then, finished both of them off. She knew the killing points. Two strategically placed jabs, and both of the boys would be eliminated, no more threatening old ladies.

But that was in the past.

'You stay where you are,' she demanded over their whimpering.

She retrieved her purse from where the tall one had dropped it, gave the pair one last glance, and turned away. Breathing hard, she hoped she wouldn't have a heart attack before she reached her house.

CHAPTER TWO

THE TOWN OF Rivershore had been built along the banks of the Ash River back in the late 1800s, and for a time was a way-stop for travelers going from Kalamazoo to Lake Michigan. Its population decreased after a better road was developed farther south, then grew again when a national brand company built a factory to process and package the blueberries, grapes, and apples that local farmers grew. By the early 1990s, the town had attracted several small companies, along with residents who preferred living in a small town and were willing to drive to Kalamazoo or Grand Rapids for their jobs. Then came the economic downturn in 2008.

The town still hadn't recovered, not completely, but early Friday morning, as Jack drove west along Main Street, heading for the police station, he noticed a sign in the window of what had been an empty storefront. One of those fancy coffee shops was coming soon.

Just what we need, he thought, wondering how many restaurants and coffee shops a town of 5,000 could support.

So far, along the six blocks of Main Street that paralleled the river, there were three restaurants, two bars, and three ice cream shops. In the summer, two more huts opened up next to the city park, both selling soft drinks and snacks to the tourists who came to kayak and canoe down the river.

Of course, in addition to the eating places, Rivershore had the usual businesses that sustained a population, ranging from grocery and hardware stores to banks and credit unions. Most of the cloth-ing stores, however, had gone bankrupt when the economy turned down, only two having managed to stay open.

There were gas stations and repair shops at both ends of town, and the town's new fire station had been built on the west end, next to the hospital and what was, before an electrical fire, the police department. After the fire, the city council decided to hold off building a new police station until the economy improved. Jack had a feeling he'd be retired before that happened. For way too many years now a warehouse one block south of the fire station had been

Rivershore's 'temporary' police station.

Jack parked in back of the warehouse but walked around to the front of the building and unlocked the door. This early, only the night shift officers were on duty, 911 calls going to county dispatch. The regular receptionist and day officers weren't due in for another hour.

The building had an empty, cold feel, and Jack noticed a musty odor that probably meant there was mold in hidden areas. He immediately went over and turned up the heat. If the city council wanted to complain about the high gas bill, let them spend eight or more hours a day in this building.

A large window that looked out on First Street helped give the front area a light, cheery feel. Once beyond the ceiling-high dividing wall behind the receptionist's area, only the harsh glow of halide lights illuminated the officers' cubicles, two temporary holding cells, and a booking area. There was one enclosed office in the far back corner, probably originally built for the warehouse manager. The chief now used that room. It had the only other window in the rectangular building.

Jack, with twenty-four years' seniority in the Rivershore Police Department, had been given the largest cubicle. His desk and file cabinets were back by the chief's office. This was the coldest part of the building, as far as Jack was concerned. He turned on his space heater as soon as he reached his area.

From his desk, he could see the cubicles of Rivershore's other sergeant, six full-time patrol officers, and two part-time officers. He knew the moment officers Stewart VanDerwell and Jennifer Mendoza came into the building.

'You're here early,' Jennifer said as she headed for her desk.

'I wanted to catch you two before you headed home, see what the status was with those teens from last night.'

'You mean the ones in the shoot-out at the trailer park?' she asked, slipping off her leather jacket.

'No.' That gang fight had been on the eleven o'clock news. 'County boys got that, didn't they?'

'We offered our services,' Stewart said. 'They said they had it under control.'

'Glad to hear that. No, I'm talking about the mugging on Archer Street.'

'They're not pressing charges.' Stewart walked back to Jack's cubicle and dropped into the chair next to Jack's desk. 'Neither one of them. They're now saying they simply tripped and fell.'

'You tell them you didn't believe them?'

'We told them,' Jennifer answered, her voice easily carrying in the near-empty building. 'I asked the one with the dislocated shoulder if he was always that accident prone. He just glared at me.'

Jack looked at Stewart. The officer was at the end of an eight-hour shift, but he looked like he'd been up for days. 'You getting enough sleep?'

'Not yesterday. Had to take my kid to the doctor.'

'Anything serious?'

'Asthma attack. Valerie thinks we should move somewhere warmer.'

Jack knew Stewart's wife didn't like Michigan winters and had been pushing him to apply for a job with one of the police forces on the west coast. Once the economy picked up and the job market opened, Rivershore would probably lose him.

'Go on home,' he urged. 'You can write up your report tonight.'

'I think I will.' Stewart yawned as he pulled out a notebook. 'Here's what we have so far. Names of the two victims are Manny Ortega and Carlos Perez. Ortega is the one with the dislocated shoulder; Perez has the broken nose and dislocated knee. Both age nineteen; both new to the area. Ortega had a green card. Perez said he was born in LA, and he does have a California driver's license. No warrants for either, as far as I could tell.'

'They say why they were in that area late last night?' Jack asked.

'Said they were looking at a house, thinking they might buy one,' Jennifer said, coming over to stand beside her partner.

Stewart glanced up at her, then looked back at Jack. 'One of the neighbors we interviewed said the two had been sitting on the steps in front of the house for at least an hour, smoking weed.'

'Maybe that's why they tripped and fell.' Not that Jack believed that story.

'Yeah, right,' Stewart scoffed. 'By the way, they had a couple of "friends" visiting them when we arrived at the ER to interview them. Those "friends" left as soon as we stepped into the room.'

'Fellow gang members, I'm sure,' Jennifer added. 'No one said as much, but both had the RB tattoos and blue scarves.'

'Which explains why the two aren't pressing charges,' Jack said. 'They're going to take care of this situation without our help.'

Jennifer nodded in agreement. 'Worst part is, we still have no idea who the woman was or even if it was a woman. I interviewed Mrs Black, the woman you talked to.' She chuckled. 'You said you smelled liquor on her breath.... Well, she was absolutely out of it by the time I got to her. Best she could give me was "It looked like an old woman, she wasn't very tall, and she limped."'

'Did she say if the woman was white or black? Color of hair? Anything?' Over the years, Jack had learned every detail could help.

'She said with that street light out and the person walking away from her, she couldn't really tell, but she thought the person had dark hair. That or she was wearing a dark hat. Mrs Black was sure the woman had on a dark-colored jacket, dark slacks, and shoes.'

Jack leaned back in his chair. 'We need to find that person.'

'Radio and TV newscasts are asking anyone with information to call.' Jennifer rolled her eyes. 'But you know how likely that's gonna happen.'

'With them not pressing charges, I don't see what more we can do,' Stewart said.

Jack knew Stewart was right, but he also felt, if they didn't do something, they'd be investigating a homicide in a very short time.

'I think a few extra passes through that neighborhood tonight might be a good idea. Any sign of gang activity, give me a call.'

'Will do, Sarge.' Stewart stood, gave a mock salute, then headed for his desk. Jennifer stayed where she was.

'That gray Chevy was still there this morning,' she said. 'It's not illegally parked, but I checked the plates.' She paused and smiled. 'The car is owned by Harry Harrington, who just happens to be in his eighties and lives on Maple Street ... two blocks away.'

*

The telephone rang and Mary groaned as she pushed herself away from the kitchen table and the cup of tea she'd been nursing. Although she'd taken a hot bath and downed two aspirin before going to bed, she'd had a rough time getting to sleep, and so far had accomplished little since waking. She would swear every muscle in her body ached, and even though her ankle wasn't swollen, a large black-and-blue area was forming where her shin had hit the tall one's legs. She also had a bruise on the side of her hand, on her wrist, and partway up her right arm. The long sleeves of her bulky black turtle-neck sweater, along with her orange-colored sweatpants, covered most of the discoloration, but the areas were super-sensitive to the touch.

And here she'd thought she was staying in shape.

All those hours she'd spent at the gym working out on the weight machines and fast-walking – never running – on the treadmill certainly hadn't prepared her for last night. Or maybe they had. She smiled and slowly limped toward the phone. She might be hurting, but she'd bet those boys hurt even more.

'Pick on an old lady, will you,' she muttered as she lifted the receiver.

'What?' a high-pitched, quavering voice asked on the other end of the line. 'That you, Mary?'

'It's me, Ella,' Mary answered and eased herself onto the stool she kept near the telephone.

Ella Williams lived two doors down and across the street from Mary, and a call from her always turned into a long ordeal, which was why Mary kept the stool by the phone. Today she was glad she did.

'Did you hear what happened last night?' Ella said, slightly breathless.

'No ...' Mary's stomach tightened. 'What happened?'

'A couple of kids got beat up on Archer Street. Beat up bad, they say.'

'How bad?' Mary asked, hoping she hadn't delivered any fatal blows or inflicted damage the boys couldn't recover from.

'Bad enough to put them in the hospital.'

'They're in the hospital?'

15

'Were,' Ella paused and yelled. 'Cleopatra, get off the counter.'

Mary flinched as Ella's voice pierced her ear. Ella yelling at her cats, of which she had way too many, was a common occurrence during their telephone conversations. Best to wait, Mary had learned, until Ella took care of whatever problem the cats were causing; otherwise, she'd be talking to dead air.

'Now, where was I?' Ella said when she came back on the line.

'You said the boys were in the hospital. They're now out? They're OK?'

'I guess. Nancy's the one who told me about the incident. I stopped at the hospital for my flu shot, and she asked if I'd heard what happened.'

Nancy had been one of the nurses who had helped during Harry's last days. She was a sweet woman, very caring, and she and her husband lived in the neighborhood, on the next block over. 'Did Nancy say who attacked the boys?' Mary asked, afraid that was the reason Ella was calling. If Ella knew she'd been involved, the whole world would soon know.

'She said they kept changing their stories. First they said a woman attacked them, then they said it was a ninja, a guy all dressed in black.'

'A ninja?' Mary laughed and glanced toward the front door, where she'd hung her black windbreaker on one of the hooks.

'It's not funny,' Ella snapped. 'This neighborhood's not what it used to be. Nancy said these guys were gang members, that she was scared just being near them. If they're on Archer Street, how much longer before they're on our street? I won't even drive through that area anymore. It's just blacks and Mexicans.'

'Ella, your prejudices are showing.'

'I don't care. Things were better when you and I first moved here. People took care of their places, kept up their yards. You could go for a walk at night and not worry about gangs. I'm afraid to even turn on my light tonight for trick-or-treat. Did you see on the television there was another gang-shooting in the trailer park across the river?'

'I saw.' She'd been watching television all morning, waiting to see if there was anything about the boys or if anyone had recognized her. One reporter on the 6.30 news said there'd been a gang fight on Archer Street, and anyone with information should call the police, but that was it. From seven o'clock on it was all about the gang-shooting in the trailer park.

No mention of her, and she certainly wasn't going to call the police and tell them anything.

'Aren't you afraid?' Ella asked.

'Afraid?' Mary repeated and thought about the word. For years she'd been afraid someone would recognize her, but time had eased that fear. And growing up she'd lived with fear: fear that her mother would leave her, and she'd be all alone; fear that she'd end up like her mother; and then, in her twenties, fear for her life. But somehow she'd survived. Now that she was in her seventies, she didn't even fear death. Not that she wanted to die, but with Harry gone, the idea didn't seem as terrifying. 'Afraid of what?'

'Being mugged,' Ella said. 'I mean, if it could happen to two teenagers, it could happen to us. Who knows who's going to be on the streets tonight? I hope mothers are wise enough to go trick-or-treating with their children.'

'I just hope I have enough candy.'

'Speaking of children,' Ella went on, 'I see your car isn't in your driveway. So did Robby drive you home last night?'

Mary avoided a direct answer by telling the truth. 'He's sure his mom is getting too old to take care of herself.'

'Well, he's got a point,' Ella agreed. 'I tell you, it's not safe for someone our age to be out after dark. Not safe at all. How was your granddaughter's birthday party?'

'Good.' Mary smiled, remembering. 'Seems like just yesterday she was a baby, now she's all grown up. I still can't believe she's a high school senior. Most of the talk last night was about where she'll go to college.'

'What did you get her for her birthday?'

'I gave her that pin, the one you saw the day you helped me take Harry's clothes to the Salvation Army. And, of course, money. What else can you give a teenager nowadays? Shannon has definite ideas of what's cool and what's "Oh, so last year."'

'Did she like the pin?'

'I think so. I....' The sound of her doorbell stopped her, and Mary felt her heart start racing. 'Someone's here,' she said, suddenly very tense. 'I'll ... I'll call you back later.'

CHAPTER THREE

THE FRONT DOOR opened a-ways, a safety-chain holding it in place. Through the opening, Jack could see a white-haired woman on the other side, wrinkles etching the corners of her blue eyes and around her mouth. 'Yes?' she said, frowning slightly.

'I'm looking for Harry Harrington,' Jack said. 'Is he home?'

The woman's frown turned into a smile. 'He's in his eternal home.'

'Eternal...?'

'He's dead,' she supplied. 'My husband died two years ago.'

'Oh.' It was Jack's turn to frown. He turned slightly and pointed to the west. 'The car. It's registered to him.'

'Oh, yes, the car.' She sighed and cocked her head to the side. 'And you're?'

'I'm sorry.' He pulled out his identification. 'Sergeant Jack Rossini. And you are...?'

'Mary Harrington. I know I should have gotten the registration on the car changed, but ...' She shrugged. 'I don't know, seems like every time I was going to do it, something came up. But I will get it moved. I—'

'Could I come in?' he asked, interrupting her. 'I'd like to ask you a few questions.'

'You want to come in?' She hesitated, making him wonder if she might say no, then she pushed the door shut.

He was about to yell at her through the door when he heard her disengage the chain. Once again the door opened.

Jack wasn't quite sure how to categorize the woman standing in front of him. Her outfit – the bright orange sweatpants, black turtle-neck top, and fluffy pink bedroom slippers – reminded him of the attire worn by some of the residents at the local nursing home, and her long, white hair could certainly use a good brushing, but the way she was looking at him indicated an alert mind. He guessed her height around five-five or -six, and she didn't slouch, as so many older women did. She also didn't have a midriff bulge and probably didn't hit a hundred and twenty pounds soaking wet.

Although she wasn't wearing any makeup, and gravity had turned one chin into two, he had a feeling she'd been quite stunning in her younger years, and he wondered how old she was.

'Come on in,' she said and motioned toward the kitchen. 'I was just having a cup of tea. Would you like some? Or maybe coffee?'

A wooden table with orange jack-o-lantern-shaped placemats sat to the side of a marble-topped counter. He saw a mug on one of the placemats, an ice pack next to it. A few feet away, one of those single-cup coffee makers sat on the counter. Since he didn't like tea, his decision was easy. 'Coffee would be great.'

'Light roast, medium, or dark?' she asked, pointing at a carousel with a variety of small containers.

'Oh, I don't care.' He watched her limp over to the coffee maker. 'Did you hurt yourself?'

She gave him a quick glance, and for a moment he thought he saw a look of fear, but then she shrugged and smiled. 'Tripped coming down the stairs.'

He could see a staircase, just off to the right of the entryway. 'Those are pretty steep stairs. Are you all right?'

'A little bruised up,' she said. 'That's all. Go ahead. Sit down. Take off your coat.'

Jack pulled out the wooden chair on the side of the table opposite the placemat with the mug and ice pack. He shrugged out of his overcoat before he sat down, and from the inside pocket of his wool jacket removed a three-by-five notebook and the stub of a pencil. 'Is there a reason you parked your car on Archer Street?' he asked as her coffee maker began spewing coffee into a purple mug.

'It stopped running,' she said.

'And what time was that?'

'Hmm....' She brought the mug over and set it on the placemat

19

in front of him. 'I'm not sure. Do you take milk or sugar?'

'Neither.' He shook his head, all the while watching her. 'Morning, noon, or night?' he asked, even though he already knew from reading the interviews of the neighbors that the car hadn't been there until after dark.

'Around ten, I guess. Ten or ten-thirty.' She sat across from him and smiled. 'At night.'

'Really.' Ignoring his coffee, he sat back and stared at her. The boys had said an old lady beat them up, but he hadn't believed them, and he still couldn't fathom how someone Mary Harrington's size and age could take on the boys. 'Two, ah…. Two young men were attacked in that area last night. Would you know anything about that?'

'My neighbor called and told me about it,' she said, looking him directly in the eyes. 'In fact I was on the phone with her when you rang my doorbell.' She shook her head. 'Ella said a ninja beat them up. Is that true?'

'Where'd she hear that?'

'From one of the nurses at the hospital. Are the boys all right?'

'They'll survive. And no, I don't think it was a ninja.' Jack glanced at the ice pack on the table. 'The incident happened about the time you say your car stopped running.'

'Oh, my.'

'Where were the boys when you left your car?'

She smiled. 'I don't know. I didn't see any boys.'

'You're sure?' According to the report Jennifer had handed him before she left the station, more than one of the neighbors said the boys had been sitting outside of the abandoned house for over an hour. From where the Chevy was located, they would have been easily visible. 'The boys were wearing sweatshirts. Hoodies.'

'I guess I was simply focused on getting home.'

'When I arrived last night, the boys said a woman beat them up. An old woman.' He kept his gaze fixed on her face, waiting for her reaction.

'Not a ninja?'

'No. An old woman.'

She gave a stilted laugh. 'And what where *they* smoking?'

'How did you know they were smoking anything?'

She shook her head. 'I didn't, but really, an old woman beat them up?'

'This woman might be in danger.'

'How's that?' Her voice and eyebrows lifted slightly.

'They're members of a gang.'

'Ah.' She nodded. 'Ella ... my neighbor ... and I were just talking about gangs. Wasn't there another gang-shooting last night?'

'Different gang,' he said, unwilling to allow the conversation to be diverted. 'This gang, the one the two boys belong to, is a particularly nasty group. Image is very important to them, and they would think nothing of killing someone they felt didn't show respect. They wouldn't want it getting around that a woman, much less an old woman, beat them up.'

'So why aren't they in jail?'

'So far no one's willing to testify against them.'

She gave a slight nod and then shrugged. 'Well, from what you've told me, the ones doing the testifying would be the gang members. They were the ones beat up. Right?'

'But maybe there was a reason for the beating.' He waited, hoping she'd give him one.

'Maybe,' she said and lifted her mug of tea and took a sip.

'Such as?'

She shrugged and set her mug back down. 'I guess you won't know until you find who did it.'

'I think you know who did it,' Jack said, irritated by her casual attitude.

'Me?' Again she shook her head. 'No.'

He studied her for a moment, trying to figure out why she would hide the truth; finally, he decided it was fear. 'You're not going to get into trouble, you know. Even if they did press charges, no judge would believe you went out of your way to attack those boys. And, as of this morning, they're not pressing charges. But if we could get them off the street....'

He let the idea hang out there.

'I'd like to help you,' she said, oh so sincerely, 'but I'm afraid I can't.'

He pointed at her right hand. 'I think that's where you got those bruises, why you're limping this morning.'

'Oh, come on.' She leaned back in her chair and folded her arms across her chest in a protective – or maybe defensive – manner. 'I'm seventy-four years old. I have arthritis. Do I look like someone who could beat up two boys in their prime?'

He had to admit, the woman seated in front of him looked more like a grandmother than a fighter, but he knew things weren't always as they appeared. 'Have you ever studied the martial arts, Mrs Harrington?'

'I've done a little tai chi at the gym,' she said. 'They say it's good for your balance.'

'I'm not talking about tai chi. The way the boys said it went down, you were delivering kicks and karate chops like a pro.'

'Well, I can assure you, I've lived in this town for forty-four years and not once have I taken a class in martial arts.' She pushed her chair back. 'Is there anything else, Sergeant? If not, I need to call my son and see if he can come over and get my car running.'

'I told you the boys aren't pressing charges,' Jack said and stood, 'but that doesn't mean they don't plan on retaliating.' He reached into his inside pocket and pulled out his business card. 'Keep your doors and windows locked and give me a call if you see anything unusual.'

'Unusual like…?'

'Like groups of boys hanging out on the street corner, or cars going by your house real slow. Whatever you do, don't open your door for anyone you don't recognize.'

She took his card, gave it a glance, then slipped it into the pocket of her orange sweatpants. 'There is one problem,' she said and smiled.

'And what's that?'

'It's Halloween. I'm going to have lots of little strangers at my door tonight.'

'You know what I mean,' he grumbled and grabbed his overcoat.

CHAPTER FOUR

ROBERT HARRINGTON DIDN'T arrive until 12.15. By that time, Mary had brushed her hair back into a twist, put on some makeup, and had downed enough tea to feel halfway decent. She didn't, however, change out of her turtleneck, sweatpants, and slippers. Not only was the outfit comfortable, it covered most of her bruises.

She smiled when she opened the door and saw both her son and granddaughter. 'Trick or treat, Grandma,' Shannon said. 'Dad's taking me to lunch. Do you want to come, too?'

'Oh, honey, I would love to, but I had a late breakfast,' Mary lied. No need to chance Robby or Shannon noticing her limp or bruises. 'No school today?'

'Just this morning,' Shannon said. 'Teacher in-service this afternoon ... or something like that. Are you sure you can't come with us?'

'I'm sure.' Mary looked at her son. 'Did you see the car?'

'Not yet. What I need to know is what do you want me to do with it?'

For Mary, the answer was obvious. 'Get it running.'

'You know I don't know anything about cars. That was Dad's forte.'

'Then have it towed somewhere where they can fix it.'

'Mom, why beat an old horse to death? Get a new car. Or a new used car. They say that's the wisest way to buy a car.'

'Get something sporty, Grandma,' Shannon added. 'Something red, like mine.'

'Or purple?' she asked, knowing how her son would react.

Robby rolled his eyes. 'Please, no.'

She grinned. The older Robby got, the more he looked and acted like his father. As the town dentist, Harry had always been aware of the image he projected, and their son had adopted the same attitude. At the moment, Robby was wearing a tailor-made pinstriped suit that emphasized his height and slender physique and gave him an aura of self-assurance. She knew, as a financial advisor, image was

23

critical. If you were going to handle a client's money, you needed to look like you knew what you were doing. And it undoubtedly helped if your mother appeared respectable.

'OK, no purple cars,' Mary said. 'Let's see if we can get the old Chevy fixed.' She pointed the direction of Archer Street. 'It's just two blocks over. Call Triple-A, they'll tow it somewhere.'

'Don't you have a Triple-A card, Grandma?' Shannon asked.

'I do, but you have to be with the car, and I don't feel like walking over there.' She didn't want to chance someone recognizing her from the night before, and her ankle still hurt.

Robby caught her hand as she brought it back to her side. He gently pushed her sleeve back from her wrist, but Mary couldn't help flinching as the bulky knit rubbed over her bruise. 'Now what have you done, Mom?'

'I sort of ran into something.'

His gaze immediately went to the stairway behind her. 'You didn't fall down the stairs again, did you?'

'No ... I ... I just sort of hit something.'

'Like what?'

'Something. It was dark.'

Her son gave a deep sigh. 'Mom, what are we going to do with you?'

'You don't have to do anything.'

Again he looked behind her, at the stairway leading to the upstairs bedrooms. 'It's not safe for you to live here alone.'

'I'm fine.' She grinned, remembering her experience the night before. 'I just ran into something I didn't expect.' To change the subject, she turned to her granddaughter. 'I see you're wearing the pin I gave you. Do take care of it.'

Shannon looked down at the small, diamond-encrusted gold box pinned to her sweatshirt. 'Oh, I will. I love it.'

'That was quite a gift,' Robby said. 'After you left last night, Clare looked it up on the Internet. You were right. It is called Pandora's Box, but it's not made by that company that makes the charms.'

'Mom was really impressed,' Shannon added. 'She said it's quite valuable.'

24

Robby looked at the pin on his daughter's sweatshirt and then at Mary. 'I don't remember ever seeing you wear it.'

'I haven't. Not for years.'

'Did Dad give it to you?'

'No,' she admitted, remembering the day her former partner gave her the pin, along with a passionate kiss. 'It was a gift from a man I knew years before I met your dad.'

'I'll take good care of it,' Shannon said. 'I promise. I'll treasure it for the rest of my life.'

Mary smiled. Those were almost the same words she'd said more than forty-four years ago. Back then, after that kiss, she'd wondered if she'd been a fool to keep David Burrows at arms' length, if there might have been a chance for them. Two years later, she met Harry Harrington and knew she'd made the right decision. David would have given her passion and excitement; Harry gave her love and security, along with a child ... and years later, a granddaughter.

Such a precious grandchild.

In many ways Shannon reminded Mary of herself. Whereas Robby had his father's brown hair, brown eyes, and lean physique, Shannon had inherited Mary's ash-blonde hair, blue eyes, and willowy figure.

Well, Mary thought, her hair used to be blonde and her figure used to be willowy. Over the years the color had faded to white and gravity had caused some of those curves to sag. Not that she cared at her age.

'Did you two want to come in for a minute?' she asked and took a step back.

The moment she put weight on her bruised ankle, pain shot up her leg, and she grimaced.

'Are you OK, Mom?'

'I'm fine,' she lied, forcing herself not to groan. 'It's just my arthritis kicking in. And I suppose you two do want to get going so you can have lunch.'

Robby glanced at his watch. 'It is getting late.'

'So will you have time to call Triple-A today? I hate to leave the car parked on the side of the street for long. Especially tonight. Who knows what might happen to it.'

'I've taken the afternoon off,' he said. 'After we have lunch, Shannon and I will take care of the car.'

'Just let me know where it's towed, and I'll take it from there.'

Her son sighed. 'Mom, why don't you simply move into Shoreside? Then you wouldn't need a car. They have vans that take residents wherever they want to go.'

They'd had this argument before. 'I am not moving into a nursing home and taking a van wherever I want to go.'

'It's not a nursing home, it's a—'

'Forget it.' They could call it a residential facility if they wanted, but she knew what Shoreside was, and she didn't want to go there.

'Mom, if it's the idea of riding in the van that bothers you, one of us could always drive into town and pick you up.'

She shook her head. 'Honey, I'm just not ready to go into one of those homes. They say today's seventies are yesterday's fifties.'

'Maybe so,' he said, 'but you weren't bumping into things in your fifties, and now that Dad is gone, I worry about you.'

Mary appreciated his concern, but thinking of the night before, she smiled. 'Thank you, Rob, but I think I can still take care of myself.'

Back at the station, Jack tried to put Mary Harrington out of his thoughts. No charges had been filed by the two teenaged gang members, so there was no case to follow up on. And it wasn't as if he didn't have anything to do. As the town's one and only special investigator his caseload didn't allow time for pet projects.

But something wasn't right.

Call it a gut feeling, intuition, or the result of thirty-four years of interviewing people, but Jack couldn't shake the idea that Mary Harrington was involved in what had gone down the night before.

But how?

In a fight, guys in their teens or twenties could easily inflict the damage those two gang members had suffered, but a woman Mary Harrington's age and size? It didn't make sense. Yet she had those bruises, and her car was in the area where the boys had been attacked, left there according to her, just prior to the attack. Add in the testimony of Cora Black – iffy as that might be – and the evidence certainly pointed to Mary Harrington being involved in some way or another.

During his lunch hour, just out of curiosity, he started searching through his computer for information about Mary Harrington. That's when he came across the article and pictures of her in the *Kalamazoo Gazette*. She was one of three women profiled in the article. At age seventy-four she was the youngest of the three, the other two in their eighties. The picture of Mary showed her in Spandex shorts and a halter top lifting barbells, and Jack realized the bulky black sweater and orange sweatpants she'd had on when he interviewed her had hidden a well-toned body. Maybe gravity had added a sag here and there, and time had turned her hair white, but looking at the picture, he would have taken her for a much younger woman. Maybe not a twenty-year-old, but someone around forty or fifty. A well-conditioned forty or fifty.

The article touted how exercise could slow the aging process and ward off dementia, and how senior citizens who regularly exercised had fewer medical problems. There were quotes from each of the three women. The one attributed to Mary Harrington caught his attention. 'Working out with the weights has improved my balance, as well as my strength.'

He grunted and looked back at her picture. She'd said she'd fallen down the stairs, that the fall had caused the bruising on her arm and was the reason for her limp. 'You lied to me,' he murmured to the picture.

'What?' the officer in the cubicle across the aisle asked, leaning back in his chair to look at Jack.

'Nothing,' Jack said and bookmarked the article. 'Just talking to myself.'

He continued his search into Mary Harrington's background by checking for a military record. Lifting weights wouldn't have given her the skills to take down the two last night, not with her being a good six inches shorter than one of the boys and the other twice her weight, but military training might have.

He found no record of her ever having been in any branch of the service.

He also found no record of any arrests, no outstanding warrants, and her driving record was clean, not even a parking ticket. Going back two years, he found an article announcing the death of Harry Harrington, a retired dentist. It listed Mary (Smith) Harrington as his wife, Robert Harrington as his son (married to a Clare Worthington), and one granddaughter, Shannon Harrington, all living in Rivershore. Harry also had a sister in Montana, and an uncle in Chicago.

The next mention of Mary Harrington was in a short article announcing that Robert (Rob) Harrington, son of long-time residents Harry and Mary Harrington, had joined a brokerage office in Rivershore. As far as Jack could tell, that was the last mention of Mary's name until forty-two years earlier, when he found the record of her marriage to Harry Harrington. As in her husband's obituary, Mary's maiden name was listed as Smith.

Mary A. Smith.

Again he grunted. How common a name could you get?

Using her social security number, he narrowed his search for Mary down to the Mary A. Smith who opened a bookstore in Rivershore forty-four years ago. He found only one article about the store's opening. There were quotes from Mary Smith, a picture of the storefront and another picture showing a mother and child looking at shelves of books, but there were no pictures of Mary herself. Six years later, a blurb appeared in the paper stating the store had been closed. Again, no pictures.

Other than the photos in the article on aging and exercise and on her driver's license, Jack found absolutely no pictures of Mary A. Smith *or* Mary A. Harrington. And when he looked for anything about Mary prior to opening the bookstore, he came up empty-handed.

It was as though Mary A. Smith, later to become Mary A. Harrington, sprang to life at the age of thirty.

Witness Protection, he wondered.

Jack leaned back in his chair and considered the possibility. Forty-four years ago Rivershore was primarily rural: blueberry, apple, and grape crops were the area's main source of income. Over the years the town had grown, but it was too far away from Lake Michigan to attract many tourists, and too far away from any major interstate to lure major industry. Only recently had an environmental group cleaned up the river, bringing kayakers and canoers to Rivershore.

If Mary A. Smith did indeed witness a mob murder or political corruption, the government might have decided Rivershore was a safe place to hide her. She'd certainly kept a low profile. If he hadn't stopped by her house that morning, he never would have known she existed.

CHAPTER FIVE

BY MID-AFTERNOON, MARY had downed a half-dozen pain pills, taken another hot bath – laced with Epsom salts – rubbed arnica lotion on her bruises, and used a heating pad on her back and hip. Nothing truly took the pain away, and she couldn't relax. Her mind kept replaying the events of the night before along with the questions Sergeant Jack Rossini had asked. She could tell he didn't believe her story. For all she knew, someone had seen her leave her car, had watched the boys approach her, and had seen what happened. He'd said the boys weren't pressing charges, which was probably why she hadn't been arrested, but it didn't mean she was home free.

Damn, she should have let them take her keys and credit cards. Ella had a spare key to the house and once home she could have reported the cards stolen. Within a day she could have had the locks changed, and the car keys wouldn't have done the boys any good. She wouldn't have been there to begin with if the Chevy had been running.

If only the tall one hadn't grabbed her arm.

Mary closed her eyes and leaned back in Harry's old recliner, letting the heat from the pad behind her warm aching muscles. Who would have thought she'd still remember the moves? It had been at least forty-five years since she'd been in a situation where she'd had to defend herself physically. More than half a century since she'd been taught how to use her body as a weapon. Her instructors had told her repetition was the key, that once her body knew the routine, she would never forget it. Over and over they'd made her practice the kicks and blows, forced her to spar with men and women of all sizes. 'Use their weight against them,' Carl had preached. 'Get them off balance. Keep them off balance.'

Evidently they'd been right. She hadn't forgotten the moves. What she'd forgotten was how much bone against bone could hurt, that inflicting pain didn't mean you avoided pain. Back then she'd hurt like this, but then pain had been a badge she wore with honor. 'No pain, no gain.' My God, how many times had she heard that old cliché?

Every night that first month after she'd arrived at the training compound, she went back to her room sore and exhausted. More than once she'd told them where they could take their damn program, and more than once she'd thought they would tell her she'd failed. Some nights she wished they would tell her to leave.

But after a while, the bruises disappeared and her muscles grew stronger. Slowly she began to understand the purpose behind her training. As her body changed into a lean killing machine, her daily instructions expanded to include foreign languages and customs, proper protocol, international business, cooking lessons, and wine tasting. They gave her cosmetics and clothes that accented her beauty, along with lessons on how to walk and talk. Little did the men who gazed at her shapely legs realize one strategically placed kick could end their sex lives … or their lives altogether.

Should she have killed the boys?

Sergeant Rossini had said the two she took down were members of a gang. He'd as much as come out and said she was in danger, and she understood why. No gang member could let it be known he was beat up by a little old lady. She would have to be taught a lesson. Someday, some way, they were going to get back at her.

She should have let them have their way with her.

Mary chuckled. What a quaint phrase: 'Have their way with her.' Gads, when did she get so old?

What would her granddaughter say today?

Shannon would probably use the F word and a few more expletives. Those boys certainly had.

Fuck you, the short one had said.

Well, it wouldn't be the first time for her, but she doubted that had been their intention last night. They'd seen her as prey, had considered her an easy mark. Maybe they would have knocked her around a little, but rape? Mary didn't think so.

Then again, the first time she was raped she didn't expect it either, never thought her mother's latest boyfriend would do such a thing. Worst part was she'd actually liked him, thought maybe he would marry her mother, and that they would be a family ... a family like she dreamed of. How naïve she'd been back then. What a dreamer.

Mary forced those memories to the back of her mind. In a way her dream had come true. She did end up with a wonderful husband, did have a child, a home ... love. She wouldn't think of what came before those times. Not now, not ever.

She left the comfort of Harry's chair to stand in front of the plate-glass window that looked out on the street. 'Leave me alone,' she muttered to no one. 'Forget I exist.'

Somehow or other she had to keep her past a secret.

Jack spent the afternoon writing up a report on a robbery and testifying at a domestic violence trial, but he couldn't shake the image of Mary Harrington sitting across from him at her kitchen table. The way she'd answered his questions, smiled, and scooted him out of her house had him certain she was involved, but why wouldn't she admit it?

He'd told her the boys weren't pressing charges. She shouldn't be afraid of being arrested. He'd told her she might be in danger. Most women would find that frightening, yet she'd merely shrugged off the idea. Maybe he hadn't stressed that point enough.

Or maybe there was a reason she wasn't frightened.

After work, he headed for the local gym. At one time or another most of the area's residents ended up at the Shoreside Gym, built one block away from the Rivershore hospital. Some came for physical therapy, others to workout and take classes. The first thing Jack did was pay a visit to the director.

'Mary Harrington?' the director said, skimming through computer files. 'Ah yes, here she is.' He looked up from the monitor and smiled. 'She's the one that reporter wrote about. After that article came out, our senior membership doubled.'

'She said she's taken some classes in tai chi,' Jack said. 'What about martial arts classes? Has she ever taken any of those?'

The director shook his head. 'We've never offered anything other than tai chi.'

'So, if she wanted to learn martial arts, where would she go?'

The director shrugged. 'Probably Kalamazoo or Grand Rapids, they offer a variety of classes. Tae kwon do. Karate. Aikido. Just about anything you can think of.'

'Thank you,' Jack said, knowing both locations were close enough that Mary Harrington could have driven there, especially when she was younger. The question was, how long would it take him to find the location where she'd learned martial arts ... or was it worth the effort?

As long as he was at the gym, a workout seemed a good idea, and Jack went from the director's office to the men's locker room. He was changing into sweats when one of the local doctors came into the area.

'Hey, Doc,' Jack called, stopping the man from going to his locker. 'You got a minute?'

Sam Schell was in his early fifties, a sprinkling of gray in his dark sideburns giving him a distinguished look. Tall and slender, the doctor was often at the gym the same time Jack worked out, and had been giving Jack tips on what weight machines would best help him with his back pain. Jack knew the doctor's specialty was geriatrics, which made him the perfect person to question.

'You see old people all the time,' Jack said. 'By any chance is Mary Harrington one of your patients?'

Schell frowned. 'Now, Jack, you know I can't talk about any of my patients.'

'Is that a yes or a no?'

Schell chuckled and shook his head. 'You know what's terrible, I'm not sure. The name sounds familiar, but I see so many patients....'

'About a month ago she was featured in an article about staying fit.'

'Oh yeah, I do know the one you mean.' He shook his head. 'No, she's not one of mine.'

'But you've seen her picture. Right? Do you think she could beat up two boys in their late teens?'

'Using what for a weapon?' Schell asked.

'Nothing as far as I can tell.'

'When you say "beat up", what exactly do you mean?'

'Dislocated shoulder on one, broken nose and dislocated knee with the other.'

'Wow.' Schell came closer. 'Isn't she in her seventies?'

'Seventy-four.'

'She didn't look very big in the picture.'

'She isn't.' Jack held his right hand up just past his chin. 'I'd say she's around five-five or five-six. Maybe a hundred twenty pounds.'

'So why did she beat up these boys?'

'I don't know. I don't even know for sure that she did. It's just that her car was in the vicinity of the incident, she admits she was there around the time of the incident, and she has bruises on her arm, wrist, and hand and is limping. But ...' He paused, thinking how to explain everything. 'She says she wasn't involved, saw nothing, and got the bruises when she fell down some stairs.'

'And what do the boys say?'

'At first they said they were attacked by an old woman, then they said it was a ninja.'

'A ninja?'

'Yeah, like we have a lot of them around here.' Jack chuckled. 'Anyway, now they're saying they simply fell.'

'Which, of course, wouldn't have caused those injuries.' The doctor set his gym bag down on the bench and ran a hand through his still thick hair. 'Where did this all happen?'

'Over on Archer Street. Our once peaceful neighborhood. So what do you think? Could she have done it?'

'I don't know. With most people, there's a loss of about a half a per cent of lean muscle mass every year between age twenty-five and sixty, and a corresponding decline in muscle strength. From age sixty on, the rate of loss doubles to about one per cent, then doubles again at age seventy, and again at age eighty, and ninety.

We call it sarcopenia. I know that article was about how she and other seniors have slowed the decline by staying physically active, but for a seventy-four-year-old woman to take on two teenagers in their prime...?' He shook his head. 'I doubt it.'

'She says the only martial arts training she's had is tai chi.'

'So you think she's lying?'

'I don't know,' Jack said. 'But if she did take down those boys, I'd sure like to know how she did it.'

'And you don't know who her doctor is?'

'I did a little research on her today, but that didn't come up.'

'I'll ask around, see what I can find out.' Schell smiled. 'Meanwhile, what about you? Have you been doing those exercises I suggested?'

Jack considered lying, then shook his head. 'Haven't had time.'

'And...?'

Jack knew what Schell wanted to hear. 'Going to start today.'

CHAPTER SIX

I HAVE LIZARD skin, Mary thought, staring at her legs. The drier air of fall always brought dry skin. Add more age spots that she could count, and the surface of her legs did resemble a lizard's hide. As if that wasn't ugly enough, her right leg was one big bruise from the middle of her foot up to a point below her knee.

She applied a liberal amount of lotion to both legs, flinching slightly as her hands passed over the bruised area.

As a child, she'd acquired her share of bruises, most of them from being slapped around by her mother. Over time she'd learned to keep her mouth shut, do what she was told, and stay out of the way. All she wanted to do was survive until she was old enough to be on her own. In her dreams, she would leave the cruddy apartment she shared with her mother, would meet a rich and handsome man, get married, and live happily ever after.

Even after being raped by her mother's boyfriend, she refused to give up the dream. It wasn't until her mother died that she discovered a girl could starve on a dream. Fifteen-year-olds didn't attract rich and handsome men except for one thing, and a proposition was not the same as a proposal.

Raphael became her savior ... and her pimp. Her mother had worked for him, so when she came to him for help, he willingly took her on. He sent her to the johns who were willing to pay the big bucks. She was seventeen the day she was sent to Carl Smith's hotel room. She'd thought the man was crazy when he said all he wanted was for her to take an IQ test and talk to him, but she did as he asked. Back then she'd been amazed at what got men off.

Short and pudgy, with thinning blond hair, Carl definitely wasn't handsome, but he did have the money. For two hours after she finished the IQ test, he asked her questions. Some were stupid, like who was the president and what did she think about Russia. Others she had to think about. Should someone who'd threatened to detonate an atomic bomb in the United States be assassinated before he did it? Did she believe in an eye for an eye?

When she asked him why he was asking her all these questions, he said a couple of people had told him she was way too intelligent to be a prostitute. She'd laughed, and told him she made more money in a week than most seventeen-year-olds made in a year. He left after that, and it was a month before she saw him again.

The second time he paid for her services, he offered her a job. He said he couldn't tell her what she'd be doing or who she'd be working for, but he promised she'd make a lot more money than she ever could as a prostitute, and she'd be using her intelligence. She told him he was crazy, that even if she wanted the job, the only way she could quit was over Raphael's dead body.

Two days later, Raphael was dead.

Mary set the bottle of lotion on the table. Enough reminiscing. That seventeen-year-old no longer existed, hadn't for fifty-seven years. The day she boarded the plane bound for Washington DC and sat next to Carl, she had no idea what lay ahead. She certainly didn't think thirteen years later she'd be living in a small, midwestern town and be known as Mary Smith, or that by the age of seventy-four all of her childhood dreams would have come true:

that she would marry a kind and handsome man, have a son she was proud of, and a granddaughter she loved dearly.

For the last forty-four years she'd kept her past a secret. She wasn't about to reveal it now, especially since she knew what the consequences would be.

Damn that sergeant for being so nosy.

If she were twenty years younger, she might be flattered by Sergeant Rossini's concern for her welfare. In spite of a Roman nose, the guy wasn't bad looking. He certainly had a nice, full head of silver-gray hair, and his pot belly wasn't as pronounced as most middle-aged men's. He was about the same height as Harry had been, but Rossini was broader in the shoulders. In a way, he reminded her of David.

Damn, she hadn't thought about David for years, and now, twice in one day, he'd come to mind. *David and Pandora.* They'd made quite the pair back then. She wondered what he was doing nowadays, or if he was even still alive.

The doorbell rang, startling her, and Mary glanced at the kitchen clock. It was a bit early for trick-or-treaters, but with all the news about gangs and shootings, mothers might want to get their young chicks home before the older kids hit the streets.

Time to stop thinking about the past, she told herself. David was probably dead by now, and Pandora no longer existed.

She pushed her pant legs down so they covered her bruises, eased out of the chair, and limped over to her front door.

The bell rang a second time, and Mary looked through the peephole. She smiled when she saw Shannon's heavily made-up face on the other side. Quickly she released the safety chain, and opened the door.

The exaggerated mascara, eyeshadow and lipstick were combined with a frilly pink prom dress that accented her granddaughter's small waist. Clear-plastic high heels, a rhinestone-studded tiara, and a plastic wand completed the costume.

Mary laughed. 'Don't tell me you're out trick-or-treating?'

'Nope.' Shannon gave her a quick kiss on the cheek before flouncing into the house, the netting of her dress crackling as she passed. 'I came to help you give out treats.'

*

After his workout, Jack headed for the Shores Bar and Grill. The building was one of the oldest in town, dating back to the early 1900s, and wasn't much more than a hole-in-the-wall, but as far as Jack was concerned, they made the best burgers in Michigan, and the beer on tap was always frosty-cold.

Michigan's no smoking law, and a good clean-up by the staff, had eliminated the tobacco smell but not the odor of spilled beer and sweaty bodies. Favored by construction workers as well as off-duty police, the place was jammed, and at first he didn't see Officer Jennifer Mendoza sitting back at a corner booth. If she'd had anyone with her, he would have simply taken the one empty stool at the bar, but she was alone. 'Mind if I join you?' he asked the younger woman.

She looked up and smiled, a hand gesture toward the opposite side of the booth indicating her agreement.

'So how's it going?' he asked as he slid onto the bench. 'Stewart treating you all right?'

'Considering some of the stories I heard at the academy about what rookies go through, Stewart is a dream of a partner. Doesn't even seem to mind that he's been paired with a woman.' She leaned forward, resting her elbows on the table, her chest nearly touching her half-finished salad. 'Is it true I'm the first woman ever hired on the Rivershore Police Department?'

'First in my twenty-four years here.' Jack motioned to the waitress to bring him a beer, then looked at Jennifer. 'You drinking?'

'Just iced tea. I'm on duty tonight.'

'You must be racking up the hours, what with the overtime you put in this morning.'

'Stewart wanted to follow up on those boys,' she said, 'and I wanted to get my paperwork started while everything was still fresh in my mind. Did you follow up on that car parked on Archer Street? The one owned by Harry Harrington?'

'I talked to the owner this morning. It was left there by a little old lady.'

Jennifer's eyebrows rose, and she sat back. 'You're kidding.'

'Not at all.'

'So were the boys telling the truth last night? Do you think an old lady did that to them?'

Jack started to shake his head, but shrugged instead. 'I'm not sure what to think.'

'Stewart thinks they were so high they probably did it to each other.'

'Hospital tested them, didn't it? What did the tox screen show?'

'Traces of coke, but mostly marijuana. We even found a bag in the tall one's shoe. They were definitely flying, but I don't think they were high enough to make up a story like that.'

'This old lady's in her seventies. About your height. Think you could have taken them on? Both of them?'

'Wow. I don't know.'

Jack watched her chew on her lower lip, then take a sip of her iced tea. He knew she was remembering the boys from the night before and the injuries they'd sustained. He liked the way Jennifer Mendoza's mind worked. In the two months since she'd been hired, he'd watched and listened as she learned the routine and worked with Stewart VanDerwell. She asked questions, followed up on leads, and wanted facts. No jumping to conclusions. No taking the easy way out.

She was young and enthusiastic, and he envied her that. She also knew how to take a joke. She might consider Stewart a dream, but so far her partner had played two pranks on her ... or tried to. One was the old standby of having a friend lay in a casket in the local funeral home, and then having someone call in a 10-34. From what Stewart said the next day, when they went to investigate the open door, Jennifer had no idea what was going on and screamed like a banshee when the guy sat up in that casket.

It was the second prank Stewart tried that backfired.

Jack sat back in the booth as the waitress brought his beer. 'Same as usual?' she asked, and he nodded, then added, 'Easy on the onions.'

Once the waitress left, he looked at Jennifer. 'That day you said you had a terrible headache and couldn't drive, did you know Stewart had put Vaseline on the cruiser's door handle?'

She grinned. 'When he made such a big deal about me driving, I knew something was up. And to squelch a rumor, I did not wet my pants that night at the funeral home.'

'Well, you wouldn't be the first if you had,' Jack said. 'That's one of the oldest pranks around.'

'What about you?' she asked. 'When you started, did they give you a rough time?'

'Not here. When I was hired here, I'd already put in ten years in Chicago. I think they were afraid to pull anything on me.' And he knew they felt sorry for him back then. Losing your partner in a shoot-out was one of the worst things an officer could go through.

'What brought you here?'

He chuckled. 'You mean to Mayberry?'

'This town isn't that backward.'

'And it never has been, but Rivershore also never has had the same level of crime as Chicago. Still doesn't. Our stats may have gone up over the years, especially regarding gang violence, but it's still a nice place to live. And that's why I applied here. In Rivershore there was a good chance my boys would have a father as they grew up, and my wife would have a husband, one who wasn't so stressed out from the job and so cynical about mankind that he turned into a drunk. Also, my wife grew up in Paw Paw, and we decided Rivershore was close enough that we could easily visit her folks when we wanted, but far enough away that my in-laws wouldn't always be over.'

Jennifer said nothing for a moment, then nodded. 'I can't imagine what it would be like to lose a partner ... to have something happen to Stewart. I mean, he's got little kids.'

Jack did know what it was like. 'My partner, Craig, had four. Two boys and two girls. His wife remarried after a few years, but she said things were never the same after he died.'

'So do your boys live around here?'

'No. Johnny's in Virginia with his wife and daughter – he works for the FBI – and Richard is somewhere in the Middle East.' At a location he couldn't reveal, Richard had said last time Jack talked to him. 'He's a general in the marines.'

The waitress brought his hamburger and asked Jennifer if she wanted dessert. Jennifer shook her head. 'Just bring me my check, please.'

As Jack grabbed the catsup bottle, Jennifer pulled out her wallet. 'I'm afraid I've got to take off. I want to pick up some candy to take in the patrol car. I figured it might help make a good impression with the kids.'

'Might give Stewart something to nibble on around midnight.' Jack watched her stand and brush crumbs off her uniform. 'Be careful tonight. Halloween seems to bring out the worst in some kids.'

CHAPTER SEVEN

'I HAD TO get away from Mom,' Shannon said, wandering into the kitchen and opening the refrigerator. 'She is absolutely driving me crazy.' Shannon grabbed a can of soda and popped it open before facing Mary. 'Was your mother ever like that?'

Mary thought back to her childhood – her real childhood – and grinned. 'We had disagreements.' Out-and-out fights, she remembered. Especially when Mom was high on drugs. 'So what's the problem?'

'School.' Shannon flounced back past Mary, into the living room, where she flopped down on the couch. 'You heard her last night. All she can talk about lately is college. She wants me to apply to the University of Michigan, Harvard, Yale. Every college in the universe.'

'Those are good colleges, and you have the grades.'

Her granddaughter looked at her as if she'd just joined the enemy, and Mary realized she'd missed something the night before. 'I thought you were excited about going to college.'

'Like, yeah.'

'OK.' Mary tried another approach. 'What would you like to do?'

'What you did.' Shannon sat up straighter and faced her grandmother. 'After I graduate, I want to travel. You didn't go to college right after you graduated from high school, and you did fine.'

'Don't use me as an example.' *Please,* Mary prayed. 'I was lucky. If my parents hadn't died and left me money, I wouldn't have been able to move here and open a bookstore, wouldn't have met your grandfather.'

'Are you sorry you traveled?'

Mary sank into the easy chair opposite her granddaughter. How to answer? What to say? 'No,' she admitted. 'I'm not sorry I traveled. I enjoyed going to foreign countries.' *At least I did when I wasn't afraid of being caught.* 'I enjoyed learning about other cultures.' *Even when the lessons and training went on and on, day after day, until they were sure I wouldn't make a mistake.* 'But things could have turned out different.' *I could have been the one who was killed.* 'I'm sorry, but I think your mother's right. You should go to college first. Get that degree. Then, after you graduate, if you still want to travel, I'll see to it that you have the money to do so.'

'Maybe you could travel with me.'

Mary chuckled. 'Honey, I'll be eighty ... or close to eighty by then.'

'I mean now. Next summer. We could go to France. Dad said you speak perfect French, better than the teacher he had in college. I've always wanted to go to France. You could take me places you went, show me what you saw.' She leaned forward, excitement dancing in her eyes. 'We'd have a wonderful time.'

Mary leaned back in her chair and closed her eyes, flashes of memory taking her back fifty years to a mansion just outside of Paris where she seduced René LeMond. She remembered the look of surprise on his face when she inserted the needle and injected the aconitine, remembered how close she'd come to being caught, and the headlines the next day.

'Don't you want to go back?' Shannon asked, a note of concern in her voice.

Mary opened her eyes and looked at her granddaughter. 'What's the saying? "You can't go back." That's how I feel about France. It was an exciting time, but I was in my twenties then. I fell in love with Paris, with the countryside and the people. It wouldn't be the same now, and it wouldn't be the same for you if I were along.'

Especially if I were along. She wondered if anyone over there would remember her … recognize her. Would she be considered a hero for eliminating one of France's vilest sex offenders or simply remembered as a murderer? Whichever, she wouldn't want Shannon knowing.

'So you'd make new memories. Please,' Shannon insisted.

The doorbell rang and both Mary and Shannon looked that way. Shannon moved first, hopping off the couch. 'I'll get it.'

The girl was at the door before Mary could rise to her feet.

'Trick or treat' she heard tiny voices sing out.

'Oh, aren't you two adorable,' Shannon responded.

Mary watched Shannon scoop a handful of candy from the bowl near the door and drop it into the two pumpkin-shaped plastic baskets the children held. Shannon had the door closed and was halfway back before Mary took two steps away from her chair.

'Weren't they the cutest ever?' Shannon said.

Mary shook her head and eased herself back into her chair. 'I don't know. I barely saw them.'

'Well, they were. Absolutely adorable.' Her granddaughter plopped herself back on the couch. 'You know, you don't have to get up. I'm here so you don't have to exert yourself. Dad worries about you. He thinks you fell down the stairs.' Shannon looked toward the steep staircase that led up to the second floor. 'Did you?'

'No, I did not fall down the stairs.' At least she could be honest about that. 'I just bruise easy.'

'Well, Dad worries. That's all he talked about during lunch, how you shouldn't be alone, that you'd be a lot better off if you went into that retirement home.'

The doorbell rang again, and again Shannon was on her feet. 'Just stay where you are. I'll get it.'

The next time she came back to the couch, Shannon took a gulp of her soda, then sighed. 'I told him you weren't ready to go into a retirement home, that you're too active for something like that. I mean, didn't he read that article about you? You work out more than most of my friends do.'

Mary didn't even start to move the next time the doorbell rang. Her body ached and her lack of sleep the night before had her content to sit in the chair and watch her granddaughter bounce up and down, oohing and aahing at costumes, and giving out candy. Between trick-or-treaters Shannon's conversation skipped around from one topic to another. School. Her friends and what they were doing. Her boyfriend, Aiden. How he didn't want her to get her hair cut short, but why should she listen to him, because she'd wanted to go to a party tonight, but he was off with his dad, up north some-where, so what right did he have to tell her to keep her hair long?

'What does he think of your idea of traveling around Europe?' Mary asked.

'He thinks it's a neat idea. He's already signed up for a European biking trip next summer, and when that ends, he's going to stay over there until he runs out of money. We figured we could meet up in Paris.'

'Aah.' Now Shannon's plan made sense. 'And if you aren't there?'

'It will be a real bummer.'

The doorbell rang again, and Shannon took off to answer it.

'Mom's dead set against me going,' Shannon said when she returned, 'but if you went with me, I think I could talk Dad into it. And it would be good for you, too.'

Mary chuckled. 'How's that?'

'Dad would see you aren't feeble, so he'd stop harping about the retirement home.'

Shannon was working every angle, which reminded Mary of her own mother. Samantha Coye was a user of more than drugs. She used the johns who paid for her services, the government programs that paid for their food and housing, and even her daughter.

'What did your parents say when you told them you were going to Europe?'

Shannon's question brought Mary back to the present. *Her parents?* Shannon meant the made-up, loving couple who gave their daughter everything she ever wanted, loved her dearly, and tragically died just before Mary Smith turned thirty. The parents who had the money Mary 'inherited,' the money she used to move to Rivershore and open a bookstore forty-four years ago.

She needed to be careful what she said. She not only had to make sure she didn't say anything that didn't match past stories, she also needed to phrase her response in a way that didn't give Shannon the wrong idea. Although she didn't always agree with her son and daughter-in-law, in this case she thought Robby and Clare were right. Shannon should go to college after she graduated from high school. A trip to Europe and joining up with her boyfriend were not in her granddaughter's best interest.

'They were very upset,' she said. 'Begged me to reconsider. And now that I look back, I realize they were right. I should have gone to college first, and then traveled.'

'But once you took off, were gone, they supported you, right?'

'They ...' Mary wasn't sure what to say. 'They were very upset.'

'How did you get over there? Fly? I've been checking. Every so often they have cheap tickets. How much money did you take with you?'

Mary thought of the private jet that took her on her first journey to Europe, the elegant clothes she was given to wear, and the fine hotel they booked her in. Her job was to seduce a man, get him alone, and allow her partner to eliminate him. She didn't need money. Everything was taken care of for her. All she had to do was play her part.

'I ...' Funny, no one, not even Harry, had ever asked her how much it cost her to go to Europe. 'I don't remember,' she finally said.

'I've been saving my babysitting money, along with what you gave me for my birthday.' The doorbell rang again, and Shannon rose to her feet. 'I have almost five hundred. I know it's not enough, but by the time school's out, I'll have more.'

'Shannon, I don't think you should go, not until—'

The moment Shannon opened the door, the chatter of the children ended Mary's advice. She knew she couldn't be heard over the youngsters' excitement. 'Here you go, now,' Shannon said. 'No fighting. There's enough for everyone. Hey, you guys better get home. It's getting dark.'

Mary saw Shannon start to close the door, then hesitate. Her granddaughter was looking at something outside.

'Grandma, do you know anyone who drives a black car?'

'A black car?' A frisson of fear brought Mary to her feet.

'I keep seeing one go by, real slow. At least, I think it's the same car.'

'Let me see,' Mary said and limped over to the doorway.

Clouds darkened the sky, and a chilling breeze brushed against her cheeks. Standing beside her granddaughter, Mary watched a black sedan drive slowly by, its tinted windows up so she couldn't see who was in the car.

'I guess it could be a parent,' Shannon said and grabbed a piece of candy from the basket by the door for herself.

'I suppose it could be,' Mary agreed, but she closed the door and turned off the porch light. 'I think that's enough for tonight. The little ones should be heading home to bed, and the older ones shouldn't be bothering an old lady. Right?' She forced a smile and steered her granddaughter toward the kitchen. 'How about a cup of hot chocolate?'

CHAPTER EIGHT

JACK PASSED A group of teenagers walking along the side of his street. He couldn't tell if the bandana tied around one boy's head and the patch over his eye was supposed to be a costume or if the kid had been injured in a fight. One of the girls was dressed like a hippy, and another one wore a crown on her head. He supposed they were out trick-or-treating, but he drove by slowly, just to let them know he'd seen them, and also, if any cars were damaged during the night, he could identify them.

Most of the houses along his block had turned off their porch lights, the glow of televisions and some upstairs bedroom lights the only signs that people were at home. 'One more Halloween down,' he said to himself as he pushed the remote for his garage door.

He hoped VanDerwell and Mendoza had an easy night. Twenty-four years ago, when he was a rookie assigned to Halloween night, he'd had it easy. Back then they didn't have the gangs and gang fights. Waxed windows and egged cars made up the bulk of the night's mischief. Nowadays the chief doubled up patrols and had even asked Jack to be on standby. Considering how many beers he'd downed at the Shores Bar and Grill, he hoped he didn't get called.

His house was dark when he went inside, but he didn't bother snapping on a light until he reached the living room. After twenty-four years of living in the same house, he had no problem finding his way around in the dark. With a sigh and a burp he sank down onto his couch and lit a cigarette.

He'd stayed at the bar long after Officer Mendoza left but had moved to a stool at the counter. Crystal was on duty behind the bar, and Jack liked talking to her … teasing her about her current boyfriend. Maybe he was drinking too much, but it was a helluva lot better than coming home to an empty house.

Jack turned his head so he could see the family photo sitting on the end table beside him. Taken back when his boys were in their teens and his wife was healthy, the picture was his favorite link with the past. The photographer had come to the house and after several shots taken with them seated on the couch and then standing in front of the fireplace, he'd suggested they go outside in the back yard. There they gathered in front of the hedge, a slight breeze ruffling Barbara's hair and the sun giving her skin a rosy glow. John was half-turned toward the garage, and Jack could almost hear his oldest son grumbling about having to get to a softball game. Richard, on the other hand, stood almost at attention. They should have known even then that Richard would be a career Marine.

When the proofs were delivered, Barbara picked the picture where they were all standing in front of the fireplace and had a twelve by fifteen made of that one. It now hung in their bedroom. Jack had preferred this one. For him it captured his family best: Barbara's natural beauty, John's energy, and Richard's natural leadership. Jack even liked the way he looked back then: happy.

How quickly the years had passed since that photo was taken. With Barbara gone, it all seemed like a dream. He wished he'd spent more time with his family and less on the job. Now all he had was the job and even that would be ending soon. Two more years and he would retire. Then what?

He sighed, put out his cigarette and lit another.

John wanted him to move to Virginia. But if he did, who would look after Barbara's father? The old man rarely recognized him anymore, but with Barbara's mother gone and no other living relatives around, Jack felt it his duty to drive to Kalamazoo and visit the nursing home at least twice a month. And what about his own parents? His sisters were always nagging that he didn't visit their mother and father often enough. He knew he should, that they, too, would be gone soon, but the drive to Chicago always seemed so far, and brought back so many memories: the first time he saw Barbara, their wedding, the birth of their sons, and the death of his partner.

He had enough memories.

Most of the time what he wanted to do was forget.

He took a long drag on his cigarette and slowly let out the smoke. He was getting maudlin, that's what he was doing. Well, if he was going to cry in his beer, he might as well have another one. Or maybe it was time to switch to Scotch. A couple of shots should help him sleep.

He stubbed out his cigarette and pushed himself up from the couch. He was halfway to the cabinet where he kept his liquor when the telephone rang. A glance at the clock on the television confirmed it was nearly ten o'clock.

Calls after nine o'clock always worried him.

Had his father-in-law passed on? Was something wrong with one of his parents? With John? Richard?

Jack worried about his younger son's safety. As a general, Richard shouldn't be in the fighting, but nowadays no one was safe. Those terrorists would love to take out a command headquarters.

Jack changed direction and stumbled toward the kitchen. Damn, maybe the chief was right, maybe he was drinking too much. His hand shook as he raised the receiver to his ear. 'Rossini speaking.'

The racing of his heart slowed as he listened to the voice on the other end, his breathing taking on a more natural rhythm. Finally he spoke. 'How old an old lady?'

CHAPTER NINE

SATURDAY MORNING, MARY didn't make it down to the kitchen until nine o'clock. She wasn't sure if it was arthritis or muscles still stiff from Thursday night's activities, but it had taken her a long time to get moving, and she'd barely had time to prepare a cup of coffee before Ella called. 'Oh good, you're OK,' Ella said as soon as Mary answered.

'Why wouldn't I be?' Mary asked, easing herself onto the stool.

'Didn't you hear about the attack last night?'

'No. What happened?'

'A gang of boys attacked an elderly woman and stole her purse,' Ella said, a quaver in her voice. 'It happened just three blocks from here. Over at the Mini-Mart. It was on the news this morning. They didn't give the victim's name, and I was worried it might be you.'

Wrong night, Mary thought. 'I'm fine. What about the woman? Is she all right?'

'They said she has non-life-threatening injuries, whatever that means.' Ella gave a deep sigh. 'First those two boys, now this. What's this neighborhood coming to?'

Mary hoped the two incidents weren't connected, but she had a feeling they were.

Again Ella sighed. 'Remember when we first moved here? This was the nicest neighborhood in Rivershore. Great schools, well-kept yards. Nowadays I'm afraid to go out of the house. What would you do if they came after you?'

Mary knew what she *had* done, but she couldn't tell Ella that. Finally, she said, 'I'm not sure.'

'Maybe your son's right. Maybe we should move into a retirement home.'

'I'm not quite ready for that.' Mary stared out the kitchen window. Big, fluffy snowflakes silently dropped to the ground. November first might not be winter, but someone had forgotten to tell the weatherman.

Ella made a grunting sound. 'Couldn't afford it, anyway. I don't

know about you, but I'd have to sell this house before I moved anywhere. Should have sold it when Bud died. Back then I could have
gotten a decent price for this place, but now? Who's going to buy a
house in this neighborhood? It was bad enough before these attacks.
Now no one's going to want to move here.'

'Well, I'm not selling, and I'm not moving, not unless I have to.'
Mary wasn't about to abandon a house that held so many wonderful
memories, certainly not so she could move into a retirement home.

'You know what we need,' Ella said. 'We need a Neighborhood
Watch. We need to band together and get rid of these damn
hoodlums.'

'What are you planning on doing, shooting them?'

'Not shoot, but … but …' Ella hesitated. 'I don't know. Just get
rid of them.'

Mary heard and understood the frustration, and she knew how
satisfying it felt when one of the bad guys was eliminated. She also
knew the feelings of guilt and remorse when the wrong person was
killed.

Closing her eyes, she turned away from the window. She hadn't
thought of that for a long, long time. Hadn't wanted to think of it.

'So, are you with me on this?' Ella asked.

'With you on what?' Mary blinked her eyes back open, yet
the memory of one woman's face and the sound of a child's voice
remained.

'On starting a Neighborhood Watch.'

'Oh, sure.'

Mary shook off the memory of the mother and boy. One thing
she'd learned growing up was not to dwell on the things that went
wrong. If you couldn't change it, then forget it, and move on. Harry
hadn't understood what she meant when she told him that, so she'd
never repeated the mantra to him, just to herself.

'What we need to do,' Ella went on, 'is keep a lookout for
anything out of the ordinary. Groups of teenagers. Strange cars.
People—'

'That reminds me,' Mary interrupted. 'Did you happen to notice
a black car last night? Shannon said it drove by the house several
times.'

'What kind of car?'

'I'm not completely sure. It was getting dark when she pointed it out, and I didn't see it again after that, but it had four doors and the windows were tinted, so you couldn't see who was inside.'

'Could have been a parent's car,' Ella said.

'Could have been,' Mary repeated, but she didn't think it was. Call it intuition, or maybe paranoia, but she had a feeling the driver of the car had been looking for her. Even Shannon had been nervous about the car.

'Shannon was at your place last night?'

'She helped me give out candy.'

'I'm surprised she wasn't at a party or something. She's such a pretty girl. Doesn't she have a boyfriend?'

Mary chuckled, remembering her granddaughter's comments on that subject. 'She does, but he's in the doghouse this weekend. Seems he forgot there was a party, and he and his dad went up north to prepare their cabin for deer camp. Shannon wasn't exactly happy.'

'Her boyfriend's a hunter?' Ella's tone clearly indicated her feelings about that. 'Well, I wouldn't be happy either. Can you imagine shooting something?'

Easily, Mary thought, remembering the hours she'd spent practicing at the shooting range and the times she'd put that practice to work. In her youth her vision had been 20/20, her hand steady. Now she wondered if she could hit the side of a barn. Not that she owned a gun or planned on doing any shooting.

'The hunting doesn't seem to bother Shannon, but having him promise he'd take her to a party and then back out on that promise had her upset.'

'So she came and spent the evening with you. She is a sweet girl.'

Mary wouldn't disagree, but she knew the real reason behind Shannon's generosity. 'She's trying to talk me into going to Europe with her next summer.'

'So are you going to?'

'No.' That was one thing she knew for certain.

Jack didn't need to stop by Mary Harrington's house that afternoon. He wasn't on the clock, and she wasn't a person of interest in any

50

investigation. There were no outstanding warrants under her name, and her car was no longer parked on Archer Street. Nevertheless, at two o'clock Saturday afternoon he walked toward her front door.

Although the two-storey house had to be at least seventy-five years old – or maybe even older – it had weathered the years well. At some time or another white vinyl siding and green vinyl shutters had replaced what were probably originally wood, and Jack doubted the double-pane plate-glass window facing the street was an original part of the house. The yard looked equally well cared for, the ever-green shrubs growing under the front window and along the edge of the property nicely trimmed and shaped. Even the lawn, dotted with thin patches of snow from that morning's flurries, was thick and manicured.

He could hear music coming from inside the house. Loud music. Not the kind his wife used to play. Barbara loved opera and songs from Italy. The clamor extending through the wooden front door reminded him of what his boys played in their teens. Barbara had hated listening to the twangy guitars and screeching voices. Most of all she'd hated rap.

This wasn't rap.

Contemporary, his last partner had called it. One step above easy listening and several steps below R&B. Jack wondered if Mary would be able to hear the doorbell over the music. Just to be sure, he rang it twice – then again.

'Don't wear it out,' she grumbled the moment she cracked open the door. 'I heard it the first time. Oh, it's you.'

'I have a few questions,' he shouted. 'Can I come in?'

She said nothing for a moment, but he noticed her eyes narrowed slightly, and then she nodded and closed the door.

He heard the chain rattle before the door opened again. Wide this time. Without waiting for him to step inside, she turned her back on him and started for the kitchen. 'Close the door behind you,' she called over her shoulder. 'I'll turn down the music. And it's *may* not *can*. Since you managed to make it to my front door, I assume you *can* walk into a house.'

He did as told, closed the door, and followed her into the kitchen. Damn if she didn't sound like the nuns he'd had as teachers. '*May I* not *Can I, Jackson,*' Sister Margaret always said. Mary Harrington even walked like his old English teacher, a slight hitch in her gait.

'How's your leg today?' he asked, her black sweatpants, long-sleeved black sweatshirt, and sneakers covering her bruises.

'A little better.' She tapped a button on the stereo sitting near her coffee maker, silencing the music, then turned to him. 'Tea? Coffee?'

'Nothing.' He was caffeined out. 'Did you hear about the woman who was mugged last night? It happened in front of that little grocery store just three blocks from here.'

'I heard.' She eased herself onto a chair at the table and gestured to one on the other side. 'My friend Ella called me this morning and told me about the incident. Is the woman all right?'

'They beat her up pretty badly. She has a broken arm and a concussion.' He settled onto the indicated chair, all the while watching her face for a reaction. He wasn't sure why, but he felt Mary Harrington was in some way involved with this other woman's case. However, giving a description of the woman's injuries didn't seem to have any effect.

'The victim doesn't remember a lot, but she said the boys had tattoos and wore blue headbands. The store clerk confirmed the description. Sounds to me like they were from the same gang as those two boys the other night. The two you *didn't* see.'

He stressed the word and hoped describing the similar attire would prompt her to admit she did see those boys Thursday night and somehow or other had managed to turn the tables on them.

She shook her head. 'As Ella says, "What's this neighborhood coming to?"'

That wasn't the response he'd wanted, and her avoidance of what he knew had to be true irritated him. 'You know there wouldn't be a problem if you and your neighbors would step forward and identify these kids.'

'What about the woman last night? You said she identified them.'

'Last night, yes. This morning she's saying she doesn't remember what they looked like.'

'The store clerk?'

Jack shook his head. 'He's also developed amnesia. I think they got to him.'

Mary Harrington nodded. 'That happens.'

She said it with confidence, and he wondered if that explained her reticence. 'Did it happen to you?'

'I don't understand?'

'Did those two the other night, or someone from their gang, tell you to keep your mouth shut?'

'Why would I have to keep my mouth shut?' She stood and turned away from him. 'As I said, I didn't see anything the other night. I think I will have some tea. Sure you won't have something? Water? A soda?'

'No, nothing.' Her glib response irked him. 'The woman who was attacked looked something like you,' he said. 'She's about the same height. Gray, almost white hair. Slender build.'

Mary Harrington placed a mug under the spout of the single-cup machine and pressed a button. As hot water filled the mug she faced him again. 'Detective, a lot of women my age look like me, especially to anyone under the age of twenty.'

'If they're looking for revenge, others may be in danger.'

The machine sputtered and groaned as it spat out the last of the hot water. Her expression stayed neutral. 'Revenge for what?'

'You know.'

She shook her head, took a moment to drop a tea bag into the mug, and sat down again. 'Detective, I have no idea what you're talking about.'

He doubted that but decided to change the subject. 'I understand you owned a bookstore in town.'

'Years and years ago.'

'So did you work in a bookstore before opening one of your own?' If so, it might give him a clue to her past.

'No, but I've always been a reader … and a lover of books.' She gestured toward her living room. 'Just look at all the books in there, and now I'm even downloading them onto my e-reader.'

He saw the bookshelf on the far wall of the living room, crammed with books, but her reading habits weren't the purpose of his question. 'If you didn't work in a bookstore before you opened yours, what did you do before moving to Rivershore?'

'Traveled. I spent a lot of time in Europe during my twenties.'

Which meant there should be a passport, but he hadn't found a record of one. 'Did you travel as Mary A. Smith?'

She cocked her head to the side. 'Have you been checking up on me, Detective Rossini?'

'I was curious.'

'Is it common for the police to investigate law-abiding citizens?'

'Only if they have a few suspicions.'

'Suspicions of what?' She leaned toward him, a sparkle in her blue eyes that he hadn't noticed before. 'Just what are you suspicious of?'

He had a feeling she was enjoying this game of cat and mouse. 'Of how you got those bruises.'

Still smiling, she sat back in her chair and motioned toward the stairway that led to the second floor. 'As I said, I fell down. Just wait until you're my age. You'll find your balance isn't quite as good as it once was.'

'Yet you've said tai chi is good for your balance. I even stopped by the gym this morning and spoke to your instructor. He said he was sorry you'd fallen and hurt yourself, that he'd wondered why you weren't in class. He also said you're in exceptionally good shape for someone your age. Exceptionally well balanced.'

'We all have our off days.'

Jack shook his head. She had an answer for everything, but those answers didn't fit the facts. Two boys in their late teens – gang members – didn't simply fall down and sustain the injuries those two had from Thursday night. Even if Mary Harrington didn't cause the injuries, she had to have seen the boys that night, had to have been there when they were attacked. The neighbor woman he'd talked to that night might have been drunk, but he believed she did see an old lady hurrying away from the boys. She didn't mention anyone else, no other gang members, no irritated neighbor who might have taken it upon himself to stop a possible mugging. All the drunk had said was she saw an old lady. Even the boys that night had identified their assailant as an old lady.

It had to be Mary Harrington. He was sure of it.

He tried another approach. 'Do you have any suggestions where I might go for some martial arts classes.'

'Martial arts? No, not really. But why don't you sign up for the tai chi class?'

He watched her take a sip of her tea, and wondered if he'd misunderstood her the day before when she said she hadn't studied any martial arts. 'Are you saying you can learn how to defend yourself by taking that class?'

'Oh, I don't think I'd want to try to defend myself with any of the moves we've learned, but I have heard it called a soft style of martial arts. Mostly we learn how to relax. It calms the mind.' She looked him in the eyes and smiled. 'It might help you relax.'

'Mrs Harrington, what would help me relax is if you'd tell me the truth.' He could tell he sounded irritable, but dammit all, he knew she was lying.

Still smiling, she pushed her chair back from the table. 'OK. The truth is, I don't know of any martial arts classes being taught around here. Now, is there anything else you wanted to ask me?'

There were a lot of things he wanted to ask, but he knew he wouldn't get the answers he wanted. 'Not at the moment.'

'In that case, I've got things to do.'

She walked with him to the front door, moving stiffly but leading the way. As he stepped outside, she said, 'I'm sorry for that woman who was hurt last night. I wish I could help.'

'You could.' He paused and faced her. 'Explain what happened Thursday night.'

'I already have.'

He shook his head. 'No, you're hiding something. And now I'm wondering what it is, and why I can't find anything about you past forty-four years ago.'

For the first time since they'd met, her expression turned steely cold. 'If I were you,' she said sharply, 'I'd forget about my past.'

And then she shut the door in his face.

CHAPTER TEN

As soon as Mary was certain Rossini was gone, she limped into the living room, and slumped into Harry's chair. Even after two years the scent of him remained, comforting her. Eyes closed, she forced herself to breathe slowly and deep, to center herself as they taught in yoga. Breathe in, pause ... breathe out.

She kept trying, but she couldn't slow the panicky thoughts racing through her head. She'd screwed up. Royally.

Damn that detective. Why was he looking into her past?

Carl had told her she must never reveal what she'd done or anything about the agency. Her future – her life – depended on that. 'Keep a low profile,' he'd said. 'Become a new person.'

The day she moved to Rivershore, she became the woman she'd always wanted to be. Wealthy, but not ostentatiously rich, respectable, and respected. She'd chosen a bookstore for her business, figuring any slips she made she could always pass off as something she'd read in a book. The store also gave her a chance to get to know the people in the community and for them to get to know her. She hadn't expected it to lead to romance and marriage.

The first time Harry came into the store she hadn't been overly impressed with his looks. She had been glad to learn he was a dentist. She'd needed one. Over time an acquaintance became friendship and then grew into love. He bought into her story of wealthy but unloving parents who spent more time making money than caring for her, parents who then died in a car crash, leaving her financially independent. He said he understood why she'd spent her childhood reading, and he admired her tales of how she traveled alone in her twenties. It didn't seem to bother Harry that she rarely spoke of her parents, didn't have any pictures of them, and didn't mention other relatives. He'd accepted her as she was, no questions asked.

Every year of their marriage, she'd blessed the powers above that had led her to him – or maybe him to her. Theirs had been a wonderful marriage. Maybe not ideal and certainly not without problems, but one filled with love and laughter.

For the first time since his death, she was glad he was gone.

She sighed and looked upward. 'Do you know?' she asked aloud. 'Now that you're dead, Harry, do you know the truth about me?'

Mary wasn't sure if she believed in Heaven. There was a time in her other lives when she was sure God didn't exist. How could he? How could a Being who was supposed to be all knowing and all-powerful allow a fourteen-year-old to be raped by her mother's boyfriend? How could a loving, all caring God allow a dope addict to even have a child, much less raise her in filth and poverty?

There were times after ADEC took over her life that *she'd* felt like a god. She was the one who lured the victims into a false sense of security, learned their secrets, and finally pulled the trigger or administered the poison.

For thirteen years, Pandora Coye had had a mission. Eliminate the evil in the world.

And then, forty-four years ago, that all changed.

'We messed up,' Carl had admitted, 'and I know you want out, but if you ever reveal that you were once Pandora Coye, or tell anyone the true purpose of this agency, someone – maybe me – will find you and kill you.'

He paused, his expression completely serious. 'Do you understand?'

She did, and for forty-four years she'd made sure no one knew she'd once been Pandora Coye. Not once had she mentioned – to anyone – that she'd been an agent for ADEC, or what she'd done during those thirteen years of her life.

It wasn't as if many in Rivershore knew of ADEC's existence. Few people anywhere had ever heard of the American Department of Environmental Control, or knew its purpose, and ADEC liked it that way.

The agency had been created years before she was recruited. Supposedly the president and a handful of high-ranking offi-cials knew the agency's true purpose, and since it received federal funding every year, Congress must have sanctioned it, at one time or another. Nevertheless, Mary doubted any of the senators and representatives back then – or today – knew 'Environmental Control' meant removing unwanted dictators, gunrunners, human traffickers, and drug pushers from the earth.

She remembered how happy Carl and the other ADEC administrators always were when conspiracy theorists blamed the FBI or CIA for the sudden death or disappearance of a despot ruler. Absolutely no one in the agency wanted Congress asking questions about their operations, and all of ADEC's agents were warned about what would happen to a whistleblower.

Mary was sure she never would have been allowed to leave ADEC if the agency itself hadn't made the mistake. That mistake gave her a new life, but her ticket to freedom had cost a life ... *the wrong life.*

CHAPTER ELEVEN

JACK STOPPED AT the station before heading home. On his desk he discovered a manila envelope, just his name on the front indicating it had been hand-delivered not mailed. He took time to hang his overcoat on the hook at the end of his cubicle and grab a bottle of water before he sat down and opened the envelope. The moment he saw its contents, he smiled. As promised, Dr Schell had followed up on their conversation from the day before. On the doctor's note-paper was the name of another physician – Dr J.R. Barnes – along with Mary Harrington's name and seven words: *Says he saw her two years ago.*

Schell also had enclosed copies of a couple of articles, one from a newspaper, another from the *Journal of American Medicine.* Both articles had to do with the role of exercise and aging. Jack wasn't sure if they related to his questions about Mary Harrington or if Schell meant them as personal encouragement. The JAMA report included too many scientific terms and chemical formulas to be considered easy reading, but Jack plowed through it. The second article dealt with satellite cells and how endurance exercise improved muscle stem cells and levels of spontaneous locomotion.

Although Jack found the information interesting, as far as he could tell, all of the experiments had been done on rats. Mary Harrington definitely wasn't a rat, and Jack wasn't convinced that feeling as if one could get up and dance equaled taking out two teenaged boys. With the ratio two-to-one, even if she initiated the attack, she had to have acted before the boys knew what was happening. And since the boys never mentioned being hit by a baseball bat or any sort of an object, and no weapon was ever found at the scene, Jack figured it was hand-to-hand combat. Which meant their attacker had to have had some knowledge of the most vulnerable areas to strike. The sort of training one received in the military, the police academy, Quantico ... or through martial arts training.

Real martial arts training. Not tai chi.

So when and where did Mary Harrington get her training? And why couldn't he find anything about her prior to her arrival in Rivershore?

He knew one person who could help him with an answer.

Jack waited until he arrived home before he made the call. A child's voice answered the phone. Jack smiled as he asked, 'How's my favorite granddaughter?'

'Your *only* granddaughter,' six-year-old Laurie answered, giggling. 'Did you know I'm going to have a brother?'

'That's what I've heard. How's your mother doing?'

'She's getting fat.'

'I wouldn't tell her that,' Jack said, remembering how sensitive Barbara was about her weight when she was pregnant.

'That's what Daddy says,' Laurie answered, again giggling.

'Is your daddy home?'

'He's in the garage. Mama says the car has the hiccups.'

Hiccups. Jack could imagine his son's response to that automotive diagnostic. He smiled and leaned back in his easy chair. 'Could you get him, please?'

'Okey dokey.'

As he waited for his granddaughter to get her father, Jack considered how to make his request. Since Mary Harrington wasn't wanted for any crime, he couldn't make this official police business, but if she was the one who'd attacked those boys, she might be a future victim. The attack the night before on the other elderly woman had him worried. If that was a case of mistaken identity, Mary Harrington was in danger. Gang members didn't take losing face lightly. She would have to be taught a lesson.

'Hi, Dad, what's up?' a breathless John Rossini asked, ending Jack's musings.

'I have a favor to ask,' Jack said. 'If you don't want to do it, just say so, but I have a case that I need some help with.'

'Your captain would have to make an official request,' John said. 'I can't—'

Jack stopped him. 'No, this is nothing official. What I need is information about a woman's past.'

His son cleared his throat. 'Wow, Dad. Does this mean you've met someone?'

'No.' Jack grinned, imagining what his son was thinking. 'This is a woman who may or may not have been involved in a battery case. She's seventy-four years old, and has lived here in Rivershore for forty-four of those years. Thing is, I can't find anything about her prior to when she moved here.'

'May or may not have been involved?' John Rossini sounded confused. 'Is she unconscious or something? Did they beat her up so badly that she can't remember her past?'

'Well ...' Jack chuckled aloud. 'That's the thing. She's the one who administered the beating. At least, I think she did.'

For the next few minutes, Jack summarized the case for his son. 'I'm thinking the FBI would have the resources to dig into her past. She says she's never taken a course in martial arts, other than tai chi, but I'm convinced that she must have had some training. And when I mentioned that I'd been checking into her past, she got upset. Now I want to know why.'

'Interesting,' John said. 'Give me a minute to grab a pencil and paper.'

Once he'd relayed all of the information he'd gathered, Jack changed the subject. 'So, how's Angie doing?'

'Getting big.'

'That's what Laurie said. She also said it's going to be a boy. You're sure?'

'Yep, the Rossini name will live on. So when are you going to quit that job and move to Virginia?'

Jack knew the answer. 'I plan on retiring in two years, but I won't be moving, at least not while your grandfather's still alive. Someone has to make sure he's being taken care of.'

'He doesn't even know you when you go see him, does he?'

'Most of the time no.' Rarely if ever, if Jack were honest. 'But I know him. Your mother would want me to look after her father. You know that.'

'Yeah, I know, Dad, but we'd sure like to have you close by.'

'What, so you could look after me?' Jack asked. 'I'm not ready for the rocking chair. Not yet.'

'Dad, you know that's not what I meant. I'd just like to have you a little closer. Both Angie and I would. Laurie still talks about the time we visited you. Think of all the things you could do with your granddaughter ... and soon-to-be grandson.'

'One of these days,' Jack promised. 'One of these days.'

He hung up after that, and leaned back in his chair. Some days he wished he did live close to his son, days like today when being alone with just his memories made him wonder if life without Barbara was worth living.

CHAPTER TWELVE

ON SUNDAY MORNINGS Mary normally attended a yoga class. The hour of stretching complemented the reps she did on the weight machines during the week. But she wasn't going this morning. Her bruises were too noticeable, and she didn't want to explain to the instructor or others in the class what had happened, especially since she'd told the detective one thing and her son another. At ADEC they'd taught her to keep a lie simple. Change your story too many times and it will trip you up.

The wind rattled Mary's bedroom windows, and she was tempted to proclaim this Sunday a sick day and simply lie in bed. After all, for several nights now she hadn't slept well. Conflicting thoughts kept tumbling around in her head, questions she couldn't easily answer. Should she have killed the two boys who attacked her? If she had, an innocent old lady wouldn't now be suffering with a broken arm and concussion. Wouldn't be afraid to describe her assailants.

Pandora Coye was taught to leave no witnesses. Dead people didn't talk. But Pandora Coye no longer existed.

Or did she?

Could a person really change?

Forty-four years ago she'd left a child alive and her life had changed for the better, but leaving those two gang members alive was not turning out well. She needed to do something to stop others from being hurt.

But what?

Lying in bed was not the answer, she finally decided, and with a sigh she forced herself up. Once on her feet, she did a few sun salutations and basic stretches. Just enough to loosen sore muscles and get the blood flowing. It bothered her that two full days and three nights had passed since her confrontation with the boys and her body still ached. There'd been a time when she could have had that tussle on one night and been ready to take on another pair the following night. Back in her teens and twenties, she'd felt indestructible. Now...?

She hated to admit she was getting old, but the pictures on her bureau showed the progression of years. In their wedding picture, Harry and she had made a striking couple. It was one of the few times after arriving in Rivershore when she'd used her knowledge of makeup, had her hair done, and wore a dress that truly complemented her figure. The pictures of her with Robby recorded his growth and her aging. She knew, compared to some women, she still looked young for her age, but there was no denying the sagging skin and wrinkles. The camera did not lie. At least, the ones Harry bought didn't.

'Oh well,' she sighed as she eased herself down the stairs, holding onto the railing. 'Time marches on.'

She knew there would come a day when the house would be too much for her to take care of and a retirement home might be an option. She certainly wasn't going to go live with her son. As much as she loved Robby and Shannon, there was no way she could be around her daughter-in-law 24/7.

Clare Worthington Harrington, in Mary's opinion, was a stuck-up snob who valued money and position above all else. Because she was Robby's wife, Mary kept her mouth shut, tried to be a good mother-in-law, tried not to criticize or offer advice, and tried to help out when she could, and step back when her help wasn't wanted.

Nevertheless, a part of her always wondered how Clare Worthington Harrington would react if she knew her mother-in-law's past. Her real past.

Once downstairs, Mary headed for the kitchen, her mind on those first few years after moving to Rivershore. Initially she told everyone she met that she'd always wanted to live in a rural area, and when she was a child, it had sounded like paradise. In reality, however, she quickly discovered the change from city life wasn't easy. For most of her twenties she'd mingled with the rich and influential. Very few in Rivershore fit those categories. The town didn't offer fancy restaurants, plays, and concerts. Oh, she could have driven to Kalamazoo or Grand Rapids for those amenities, but it wasn't the same as being in D.C., Paris, or London. And in Rivershore the most important topics of conversation were about the crops, the kids, and soap operas.

She opened a bookstore because Rivershore didn't have one, and she felt reading was the gateway to expanding one's horizons. For a while she carried copies of the *Wall Street Journal* and the *New York Times*, but she sold so few copies, she finally dropped those orders. Mary sometimes wondered how long she would have stayed if she hadn't met Harry.

Dear Harry, who did read the *Wall Street Journal* and liked to talk politics. Harry, who laughed when she told him she'd used a dartboard to pick Rivershore over the hundreds of other small towns she might have moved to. Of course, she never did tell him it was also Rivershore's low crime rate that appealed to her. He didn't need to know she never again wanted to be in a position where she physically had to protect herself or others.

Not that she let herself go physically.

Harry supported her devotion to exercise. Even before the new, state-of-the-art gym was built, he encouraged her to stay in shape by running, playing tennis, and biking. And, in turn, Mary had encouraged both her son and husband to play sports and shun the golf carts.

Forty-four years later, it was her belief in the benefits of exercise that prompted her to agree to that newspaper article. And, she supposed, being in good physical shape had allowed her to overcome those two boys on Halloween Eve.

But at what cost?

If they wanted revenge, how long before they zeroed in on her? Or maybe they already had. She couldn't dismiss the thought that the black car Shannon pointed out was on Maple Street looking for her. After all, a parent watching a child trick-or-treat wouldn't drive around with the car's windows rolled up.

What if those gang members had come to her house Friday night when Shannon was with her? Hand-to-hand combat with two unsuspecting teenagers was one thing; defending herself and her granddaughter would have been a different situation.

Always be prepared for the worst, Carl had taught her.

Be prepared.

Mary closed her eyes for a moment, her mentor's voice as clear in her mind as it had been years before during her training sessions.

Think ahead, he'd lectured.

Doing so had saved her life more than once in the past, and to pretend everything was normal now, that nothing had changed, was foolish. That nosy, irritating police detective had warned her she was in danger. He was sure he could help her.

Amazing how the police always thought they could protect civilians.

According to Rossini, all she had to do was admit those boys had attacked her and that their injuries were sustained when she fought back. He seemed sure the legal system would take care of the problem.

She didn't believe that for a moment.

Even if the boys were arrested, tried, and convicted, others in the gang would be looking for revenge. The only difference between what would happen then and what was going on now was the gang would know exactly who she was and where she lived. Innocent old ladies wouldn't be attacked.

But she would be vulnerable.

And until the gang or a member of the gang acted, the police wouldn't be able to do a damn thing.

The men who created ADEC understood the weakness in laws that gave criminals the advantage. They shared the public's frustration when those responsible for so much evil not only profited but lived in luxury. Unlike the public, ADEC did something about it.

For thirteen years she'd shared their beliefs, followed their orders, and thought she was doing the world a service. And then they made that one mistake.

'So is this my punishment?' she asked aloud, the words swallowed up by the empty house. Would some punk kid eliminate her as she'd eliminated that mother so many years ago?

How ironic would that be?

She gave a sigh and sat at her kitchen table.

The snow from the day before was completely gone, but the sky remained a bleak gray. Through the window Mary watched the wind whip the branches of the two maple trees in her neighbor's front yard. One by one the leaves were torn from their moorings to wildly swirl and dance from his lawn to hers.

Her thoughts swirled in similar eddies, guilt entangled with anger. For forty-four years she'd lived a good life, hurt no one. She didn't deserve what was happening now. Or did she? Should she act or remain passive?

Damn those pot-headed kids.

Damn that nosy detective.

The doorbell rang.

Jerked from her thoughts, she glanced down at her faded cotton pajama bottoms and Harry's old T-shirt.

Were they here? Had the driver of that black car told the others in the gang where she lived? Had they now come to avenge their injured members?

It would serve her right for not getting dressed before she came downstairs. Well, at least she wouldn't have a bullet hole or blood on one of her nice outfits.

Prepared for her demise, Mary limped to the front door, chin held high, spine straight, and shoulders back. She didn't even bother to look through the peephole, simply removed the guard chain, and opened the door.

And laughed.

'What's so funny?' Clare Worthington Harrington demanded and frowned.

'You're not whom I expected,' Mary said, tension draining from her body as she stared at her daughter-in-law.

Tall and slender, wearing a dark-blue jacket and matching knee-length skirt, the color contrasted by a pale-yellow silk blouse, Clare Worthington Harrington could have stepped out of a fashion magazine. Three-inch heels gave Clare a definite height advantage, forcing Mary to look up. In addition to her diamond-encrusted wedding rings, Clare wore pearl studs and a single strand of pearls. Simple but elegant.

Clare Worthington Harrington did not buy costume jewelry.

'I don't have much time,' Clare said, her no-nonsense tone emphasizing her words. 'I'm on my way to church, but I felt this couldn't wait.'

'Come on in, out of the wind.' Mary stepped back and motioned for Clare to enter. Her daughter-in-law didn't budge, even though a stray strand of her salon-dyed blonde hair kept whipping across her face. Finally, Mary asked, 'What's up?'

'It's Shannon.' Clare brushed the hair back out of her eyes. 'You've got to stop telling her about your adventures in Europe. Maybe your parents didn't care what you did, but I do. Robert and I do.'

Mary smiled. It was always *Robert* with Clare, never *Robby*.

'I'm serious,' Clare said, her words clipped and her posture rigid. 'Shannon needs to go to college next year.'

'I fully agree.' Shannon was the one with other plans. 'Clare, it's not me who's enticing her to go to Europe. Are you aware that her boyfriend will be in Paris next summer?'

Clare's nostrils flared slightly, and she raised her chin. 'It's you she talks about.'

Which pleased Mary, but not if Shannon had lied to her mother.

'She asked me to go with her. I refused.'

'She's sure you'll change your mind.'

Mary shook her head. 'I won't.'

Clare Worthington Harrington said nothing for a moment, her eyes focused on Mary's face, then she gave a deep sigh. 'Well, I hope not. Robert said you fell or something. Are you all right?'

'Getting better every day.'

'Good.' Clare gave a slight nod.

Mary knew that would be the extent of Clare's concern, and sure enough, Clare changed the topic.

'I was tracing our family tree the other day,' she said. 'I found a lot of information about Father Harry's relatives, but I couldn't find anything about yours. Of course I'm not really surprised, Smith is such a *common* name. I mean, I did find a Carl and Joan Smith who lived in Washington D.C. They would be around the right age for your parents, but it didn't show them having a daughter, just two sons. And they didn't die in a car crash. Perhaps you could give me a bit more information.'

'Perhaps,' Mary said, inwardly groaning. Now she not only had that damned detective poking around in her past, but also her daughter-in-law. Using Carl's and his wife's names for her imaginary parents had been a mistake. She should have made up names, should have used Jones for her last name.

'Perhaps?' Clare looked down at her. 'I would think you'd want to provide that information; after all, it is *your* family.'

Mary caught the derision in Clare's tone. It would serve the woman right to discover just exactly what kind of a family tree she'd married into. Instead, Mary bluffed. 'I'll see what I can find. By the way, did you happen to notice if Carl Smith was still alive?'

Clare's look was suspicious. 'No. Why?'

'Just wondered.'

Clare glanced at her wristwatch. 'I need to be on my way.' She took a step back. 'I'll check with you later this week about your parents' information.'

'You do that.' *And if I'm still alive, I'll see what I can come up with*, Mary thought, then waved as her daughter-in-law headed for her car. 'Have a nice day.'

Standing in the open doorway, Mary glanced down the street, then sucked in a breath. Halfway down the block, on the opposite side of the road, sat a black sedan.

CHAPTER THIRTEEN

MONDAY, JACK TOOK time to clear some of the paperwork on his desk and checked his emails. Most were follow-up responses to emails he'd sent to other precincts, one was from his son Richard, who, as usual, simply said he was fine and little more, and one was a request for information about a business in Rivershore that, as far as Jack knew, didn't exist. Later that afternoon, Jack did another interview with Friday night's mugging victim. Mrs Irene Baker, aged sixty-eight, white-haired and slender. She looked older than her age; older than Mary Harrington. A widow, Mrs Baker normally lived alone, but now she was staying with a daughter, Gwen Pedrors, who lived close to the hospital. As Jack questioned Mrs Baker, the daughter hovered nearby, standing in the kitchen doorway. The younger woman was obviously worried about her mother.

Irene Baker looked a bit better than the last time he'd seen her, but Jack could tell she was still in a lot of pain. The side of her face had taken on a variety of colors, ranging from a muddied brownish-purple to yellow, and she carried the cast on her arm like a badge of honor. She sighed with every movement she made.

'I'm sorry to keep bothering you,' Jack said, knowing the daughter didn't want her mother disturbed. 'I'm just trying to get a better image of what the boys who attacked you looked like.'

Irene Baker's voice quavered. 'I told you Saturday, I don't remember. All I know is they were Mexicans.'

'And how do you know that?'

'Because they spoke Mexican.'

He was tempted to say 'Mexican' wasn't actually a language, but he didn't, and considering the way she said the word, he had a feeling Mrs Baker didn't care if her attackers were from Mexico,

Central, or South America. From his earlier interviews, he'd gathered she lumped all Hispanics together, good or bad.

'What about height? Tall? Short?'

She seemed to cringe a little. 'Tall. Taller than me, that is.'

Which would put them anywhere from five-four up. 'How about tattoos? Friday night you said they had tattoos.' A feature she had conveniently forgotten when he talked to her the next day. 'Do you remember now what those tattoos looked like?'

She looked at her daughter. A pleading look that said *Make him go away.*

He wasn't about to. Not yet. 'Any letters? Numbers?' he persisted.

She looked back at him and shook her head, her lips squeezed together as if blocking an answer, and her eyes taking on a watery film.

'Did someone threaten you?' Jack asked, leaning toward her, sure she had been threatened and that was why she'd changed her story. 'You don't need to be scared. We'll protect you.'

'No! Now stop! Leave my mother alone,' the daughter demanded, coming into the living room to stand by her mother's side. 'She's had a traumatic experience.'

He sat back and faced the daughter. 'Don't you want the boys stopped who did this to her?'

She shook her head. 'And what do you plan on doing to protect her? Are you going to give her a bodyguard? Have someone walk with her when she goes out?'

They both knew that wasn't possible. 'If we have a good description, we can pick the boys up. Arrest them and put them in jail.'

She snorted. 'And what about the others in the gang? You'd need my mother to testify in court. Do you really think they wouldn't stop her from doing that? I've read the papers. You people are letting gangs take over this town. Pretty soon it's going to be every man – or woman – for themselves.'

You people. Internally he cringed, knowing a part of what she said was true. Nationally gang violence was on the decline, but in smaller communities it was growing. Perhaps it was Rivershore's proximity to Grand Rapids, where gang violence had exploded over the last few years, or maybe it was the budget cuts that kept diminishing the number of officers they could hire. Either way they had a problem.

'I hope you're not considering playing vigilante, Mrs Pedrors,' he said. 'That would only get you in trouble.'

'I'm a nurse,' she said, resting a comforting hand on her mother's shoulder. 'My job is to help people get better. But maybe we do need to start standing up for ourselves. Maybe we need to be like that old lady who beat up the two gang members the night before this happened to my mother.'

Jack perked up. 'Where did you hear that?'

'At the hospital.' She smiled. 'Nurses do talk to each other, you know.'

'And what did you hear?'

'That an old lady – that's what they called her – caused their injuries. They swore it was…. That is, until their buddies showed up and told them to shut up. After that they said it was a guy dressed in black, and then they changed their minds again and swore they tripped and fell.' She laughed. 'Maybe one of them could have dislocated his knee and broken his nose when he fell, but both of them falling and getting those kinds of injuries?' She shook her head. 'I don't think so.'

'You hear if they said anything else?'

Again Gwen Pedrors shook her head. 'One of the nurses said she wouldn't want to be that old lady, that she'd bet those gang members wouldn't let her get away with beating up two of their members.'

She stopped talking and looked at her mother.

Jack knew she'd made the connection.

'What did that woman look like?' she asked.

'A lot like your mother.'

'So they thought…?'

'What?' Irene Baker asked, looking up at her daughter. 'What are you two talking about?'

'That maybe those boys went after you, Mom, because you looked like someone else.' Gwen Pedrors looked back at Jack. 'You've got to stop them, Detective. Next time they might kill someone.'

Which was exactly what he was thinking.

CHAPTER FOURTEEN

MONDAY, MARY KNEW she couldn't skip going to the gym, no matter how she looked or felt. She'd worked too hard to achieve the muscle strength she'd acquired to allow a few bruises, aches, and pains to erase those gains. She'd experienced the danger of relaxing her training schedule when Harry started getting sicker, the cancer spreading through his body. She'd stayed home with him back then, read to him, talked with him. She did everything she could to ease his suffering.

Then there was the funeral and the days that followed, days when simply getting out of bed took all of her energy. The day she returned to the gym, she almost quit. Twenty minutes on the treadmill had her panting. Weights she'd lifted with ease became impossible obstacles. It took her months to regain the vigor and strength she now possessed, and even that was only a fraction of what she'd had in her twenties.

Back then, she could take down a man twice her size before he knew what hit him.

She smiled as she stepped out of her car and started for the gym. It was good to know she hadn't lost all of her fighting abilities, that she could still defend herself. And defend herself she would, she'd decided.

She'd spent most of Sunday considering what to do and came to one conclusion. Thursday night's incident had nothing to do with what had happened in her past. Those boys would have attacked anyone they perceived as helpless, just as they'd attacked the woman Friday night. They were in the wrong, and dammit all, they needed to be stopped.

Near the gym door, she paused and looked back at her car. She'd picked it up that morning. Ella had driven her to the repair shop, chattering on and on about the meeting she was organizing for a Neighborhood Watch. 'I've talked to the Van Dykes and the Hoffmans,' she'd said. 'They're interested. And you'll come, won't you?'

'I'll be there,' Mary promised, although her plans for ridding the neighborhood of gangs didn't include involving the entire neighborhood.

Ella was gung-ho on the idea. 'I'll try to contact the others on our block this week, and I'll call the police. I'm sure they have guidelines for something like this.'

Mary doubted their guidelines would include her methods.

'If we don't do something, it's not going to be safe for any of us to go out of the house.'

That was one thing they agreed on.

'Also I need to find a meeting place.'

Ella looked at Mary, and Mary had a feeling her friend was waiting for suggestions ... or maybe for her to volunteer her house.

'I'd have it at my house,' Ella went on, 'but you know ... the cats.'

Mary did know. Too many cats. The smell was disgusting. She couldn't imagine holding a meeting there. 'Maybe the elementary school,' she suggested. 'Or a church.' They had several churches within a five-block radius and one elementary school.

'I'll look into it,' Ella said with a nod before letting Mary off at the auto shop. 'Do you want me to wait?'

'No, I'll be fine.' She'd thanked her friend as she grabbed her gym bag. 'They said it's ready.'

And it was.

She'd left the auto shop and headed for the gym, but before she'd gone a block, she saw a black sedan directly behind her. Not sure if it was the same black sedan she'd seen near her house, Mary purposefully changed directions, turning off the main road and taking several side streets. The car didn't follow her.

At least, she didn't think it did.

Except now, in a fast-food parking lot across the street from the entrance to the gym, sat a black sedan.

She stared at it, trying to figure out the make. Was it the same as the one following her earlier ... the same as the one she'd seen Sunday and Friday night? Back in the days when knowing if she was being followed or not was important, she would have known. Back then she could identify all makes of cars. Doing so had helped her avoid mistakes. Kept her alive.

Two teenagers came out of the restaurant, their jeans low on their hips and hoodies covering their heads and torsos. One walked with a limp. The other held his arm by his side.

The two from Thursday night?

She wasn't sure. Her eyes weren't as sharp as they used to be.

They were talking to each other, walking slowly toward the black car. Mary stepped closer to the gym door, triggering the automatic opener. Without looking away from the boys, she stepped inside, and then stopped. A girl came out of the restaurant behind the boys, half-running until she caught up with them. The boy who'd been holding his arm by his side handed her something – using that arm – and she pulled his hood off his head, rose up on her toes, and kissed him.

He had blond hair.

Not the boy from Thursday night. The three didn't even stop when they reached the black sedan, simply kept walking.

With a shake of her head, Mary turned and headed for her locker. She was getting paranoid in her old age. Gang members wouldn't be driving a sedan. Not one as new-looking as she'd been seeing. They'd be driving an SUV, or a truck … or a beater.

And how could a car following her – one she was sure she'd lost – know where she was going?

Think things through, Carl used to tell her. *Don't let your emotions rule your head.*

Of course, if she'd listened to her emotions on her last assignment, a young mother would still be alive.

And so would Pandora Coye.

Mary considered that as she spun the dial on her lock. If she hadn't killed the wrong woman, if the agency hadn't agreed to allow her out, where would she be today?

Probably dead, she decided.

Back when she turned thirty, she'd already become disillusioned with the agency, and had started questioning her assignments. She should have questioned her last assignment, done her own research. Never again would she allow someone else to control her actions.

Jack stared at the report Police Chief Tom Wallace, known by all as Wally, had just dropped on his desk. With their limited number of officers, the Rivershore Police Department wasn't large enough to have special units devoted to homicide, drug enforcement, vice, or gangs. Jack handled the majority of those cases, which up until a few years ago hadn't been an overwhelming assignment.

Not that Rivershore didn't have problems before the economy went bad, but those cases were usually confined to misdemeanors. Now, along with the increase in robberies, there'd been a spike in drug arrests. The meth labs were his biggest concern. He'd seen too many of Rivershore's citizens wasted on the drug. He worried about the impact on the families, especially the young children. Marijuana busts had also increased. He found it amazing how many farmers swore they had no idea how marijuana plants had popped up in their back yards or cornfields.

They'd rarely made an arrest for cocaine or heroin until Jose Rodriguez moved into town. Jose had been twenty-two when he decided to take up residence in Rivershore, Michigan. With him he brought a prison record and an attitude. In the two years since his arrival, gang violence among the Mexicans had increased, along with the drug problem.

Jose's parole officer swore Jose wasn't involved, that the man had turned over a new leaf. Neither Jack nor Wally believed that was true, but so far they hadn't been able to prove otherwise.

Jack put down the report he'd been given and looked up at Wally. 'Is this Pedro Rodriguez any relation to our boy Jose?'

'That's for you to find out,' Wally said. 'The guy had a kilo of cocaine in his car when Stewart stopped him. Stu says he couldn't believe it.'

'How'd he find it?' Jack asked. 'Did he get a tip?'

'Nope.' Wally pointed at the report. 'Started as a routine stop. Car was going so slow, Stewart thought there might be a problem. First thing he noticed was how nervous Rodriguez was acting, and when asked where he was going, the kid didn't seem to know. Stu could smell marijuana, so he asked Rodriguez to step out of the car. There weren't any obvious signs of drugs in the interior, so Stu asked Rodriguez to open the trunk. That's when the kid got really nervous, and at first he refused, but when Stu threatened to bring in a drug-sniffing dog, Rodriguez complied.'

Wally chuckled. 'Blew Stu's mind when he saw what the guy had under a blanket. Just under a blanket, mind you. Not even well hidden.'

Jack glanced over at the two holding cells. Both doors were open. 'Where's Rodriguez now?'

'In the Van Buren County Jail. They've got the car over there, too. Although Rodriguez was picked up within our city limits, I'm letting the county boys handle this. They've got the manpower and equipment to take that car apart and see if there might be more drugs hidden in its frame. But I told them I wanted you to talk to the kid. I'm hoping you can find out where he was headed. And while you're there, see if they found anything on the boy's cellphone that connects him to Jose. Maybe this is our break, our chance to send Jose back where he belongs.'

'Oh, now Wally, you know Jose doesn't need to go back to prison. He's turned over a new leaf. Just ask his parole officer.'

'Yeah, right.'

Jack stood, ready to grab his overcoat and head for the County Jail in Paw Paw. Wally stopped him. 'Oh, also, Allison took a call just a while ago. Some woman over on the west side of town wants to start a Neighborhood Watch. Seems those two assaults last week have her all riled up. What do you think? Should I have Carlson cover that?'

Since Rivershore didn't have a police officer specifically assigned as a community resource officer, or CRO, the chief usually rotated the assignments. Phil Carlson had lived in Rivershore for almost twenty years and knew many of the citizens personally, either because of multiple arrests or because their children had attended school with his. 'Yeah, he'll do a good job. The woman who called in.... Did she give her name?'

The chief glanced down at the phone message in his hand. 'Ella Williams. She lives on Maple.' He looked back up at Jack. 'Why?'

'Just curious.' Especially considering this woman lived on the same street as Mary Harrington. He thought about it for a moment, then decided. 'Tell Phil when he meets with them. I'd like to tag along.'

The chief nodded and sighed. 'Jack, what is it with all these gangs? We've never had problems like this before.'

'We've had problems, Wally, just never this serious. Our kids – your boy and my two – were in gangs. It's something kids do, especially teenagers. They form packs. It gives them identity. They're breaking away from parental control and forming their own families.'

'Yeah, but our boys weren't out beating up people or shooting at other kids.'

'Because we kept track of them, took action when we saw them getting into trouble. Most of the punks I've come in contact with lately either have parents who are too busy trying to eke out a living or too strung out on drugs to care.'

'You think this Neighborhood Watch will help?'

'Can't hurt.'

'So why isn't someone on the east side of town starting one?'

Jack didn't have an answer for that, and he said nothing as Wally walked away, grumbling under his breath.

It took Jack a moment before he remembered what he needed to do. Again he reached for his coat, and again he was stopped ... this time by the ring of his telephone. For a second he considered letting it ring – the caller could leave a message – then he changed his mind and picked up. 'Sergeant Rossini here.'

'Dad, what's going on?'

Jack sank back onto his chair. John rarely called him, much less at work. 'What do you mean, "What's going on?"'

'That woman you asked me to check on. I had a few moments this morning and thought I'd look into it.'

Jack heard his son take in a deep breath. That he'd paused bothered Jack. 'And?'

'And her file's restricted. In fact, ten minutes after I tried to access it, I was called into the SEO's office and questioned as to why I was looking into the name.'

Bingo. It had to be Witness Protection. 'So what did you say?'

'I had no choice. I told him you were investigating her and had run into a dead end.'

'And what did your SEO say?'

'He asked me why you were investigating her. I told him I wasn't sure. Then he asked me what police department you worked for. Dad, I'd be prepared for a call.'

'OK. Thanks for the heads-up. Hope I didn't get you in trouble.'

'No, but the way the assistant director acted was really strange. I don't know who called him, but it made him nervous. He kept telling me to forget this Mary Smith, forget I'd ever heard about her.'

CHAPTER FIFTEEN

MARY SNAPPED ON the light, and then held onto the handrail as she walked down the stairs to her basement. From the day the realtor first took them through the house, the basement had made Mary nervous. She blamed it on her training. One thing the agency had stressed was never put yourself in a position where you couldn't escape.

Both the realtor and Harry had pointed out the egress window, assuring her that she could get out through it if ever that became a necessity. And back then she could have escaped with ease. Today, after spending two hours at the gym, she wasn't sure she could haul herself up on the bookcase under the window, much less crawl through the window. The bruises on her wrist and ankle were still tender and her legs felt rubbery, making her wonder if she should even chance climbing on top of the stepstool they kept down in the basement.

Well, she needed to if she wanted to reach the box she'd squirreled away on top of the metal shelving units that lined one wall. Even when she'd been younger, getting that box up there had been a task, one she'd accomplished on her own while Harry was at work.

The day she left her apartment in Washington D.C. and became Mary Smith, she'd taken a bare minimum of clothing and personal items. She'd doubted she'd have any need for slinky, skin-revealing evening dresses or designer shoes while living in Rivershore. And she certainly wasn't going to use the cosmetics that had turned her looks from attractive to stunning, not if she wanted to blend in and become invisible. Her suitcases had been filled with quality clothes, in keeping with the story she'd be telling about having had rich parents, but nothing that would stand out and cause her to be noticed.

During the thirteen years she worked as an agent, she often used her looks and natural endowments to her advantage. When a man's eyes were locked on her bustline and his thoughts revolved around ways to get her into bed, he didn't consider his vulnerability. She still remembered her first decoy assignment. She'd used her sex appeal that night by pleading with the guard on duty at the gate for help with her car. How could he turn down a stranded female wearing four-inch heels and a dress so tight it was obvious she didn't have anything on under it?

She didn't have to hurt him, and she was glad. He'd seemed like a nice old man, a grandfatherly type. Not once did he hit on her. He simply walked with her back to her car, poked around under the hood, and reattached a loose wire. She'd actually been afraid he would return to the gate before her partner was out, but once she mentioned grandchildren, the guard was hers. He had seven and showed her pictures of each.

She doubted the guard ever realized what really transpired behind the wrought-iron fencing of that exclusive estate while he was helping her. The news reports she heard, along with the articles she read in the newspapers, all claimed the owner of the shipping company died in his sleep, a case of carbon monoxide poisoning caused by a defective portable propane heater. He was found the next day by his wife, who thankfully, the reporters said, had been away for the weekend with their children.

There never was a mention of the papers missing from the man's wall safe, or of the money that disappeared from an offshore account, but for a short time the shipment of arms to North Korea was disrupted.

Mary stood at the base of the stairway and looked around. The basement looked and smelled pretty good now, much better than when Harry was alive. Her husband had been a hoarder. Not the

78

terrible kind who filled every inch of his house and car with things he couldn't throw away, but bad enough, in her opinion. He'd confined his collections to the basement and garage, which was one reason why she'd rarely gone down into the basement and why the Chevy had spent most of its life parked in front of the garage, not in it. She used to call the garage 'Harry's above-ground landfill.'

After his father's death, Robby had offered to help her get rid of the junk. He knew she didn't like going down in the basement, and she almost took him up on his offer ... until she remembered the box she'd placed on the top shelf so many years before. 'I can take care of the basement,' she'd told him. 'After all, most of the boxes down there are full of books from my old bookstore. How would you know what I'd want kept and what I'd want tossed? You deal with the garage, OK?'

Which he did, taking the few tools he wanted, giving what was usable to the Salvation Army, and hauling the rest of Harry's 'treasures' to the dump. The garage now actually had room for the Chevy, and as soon as Robby fixed the garage door, she'd start parking her car in there.

As soon as.

Mary grinned. How long had it been now? Her son was great with numbers and figuring out what stocks to buy or sell, but he sucked at anything mechanical. If she wanted that garage door fixed, she was obviously going to have to call someone.

Or do it herself.

For the last two years, she'd been doing a lot of things on her own: paying bills, mowing the lawn, fixing leaky faucets. Every fall she had a furnace man come and check the furnace; it now rumbled with a pleasant familiarity, keeping the basement and upstairs rooms a comfortable temperature. It used to be she didn't mind the cold. When Robby was young, she used to go outside with him and play in the snow. Now she dreaded the idea of going out when the temperature dropped below thirty, and she wasn't comfortable unless she kept the thermostat set at seventy-two.

Mary stepped away from the staircase and over to the wall near the furnace. A folded-up stepstool hung on a hook, next to the few tools she'd decided to keep down here – a hammer, a crowbar, and a small handsaw. She eased the stepstool off the hook and carried it over to the metal shelving that lined the opposite wall.

Only half of the area under the house was what she would call actual basement. That area had a concrete floor and poured concrete walls. The other half was simply a dirt-based crawl space accessed through a removable wooden board. She'd never gone in there and didn't intend to. As far as she knew, that wooden board was the only way in or out.

A hot-water heater and a water softener, that had stopped working years ago, were near the furnace. The egress window and the small bookcase below it were on the wall in front of the staircase, and an eight-foot-high metal shelving unit lined the wall to the right of the stairway. Boxes of Christmas decorations, old photo albums, and several crates of books filled almost every inch of shelving. She focused her gaze on the top metal shelf where a heavily taped box resided between two cartons of books. For over thirty years, the box had sat there, undisturbed. Its placement implied it contained more books or memorabilia from the bookstore. Only she knew its true contents.

Mary opened the stepstool to its locked position, and using its arched metal handle to help keep her balance, she carefully started up. Only when she stood on the stool's top step was she able to reach for the box. Her wrist bumped against the metal edge of the top shelf, and she flinched but ignored the pain. Holding her breath, she grasped the narrow end of the box and carefully pulled it toward her.

If Harry had ever tried to move the box, he might have questioned its weight, and he might have wondered what was inside that could clink when the box was tilted to the side. The sound made Mary realize she should have used more stuffing.

Back on level ground, she blew the accumulated dust off the top of the box, and looked around. Although there was little chance anyone might walk past the back of her house and look into her basement through the egress window, Mary didn't want to take that chance. She didn't want anyone to see what she had and start asking questions. With the box firmly held close to her body, she climbed back upstairs.

She paused at the doorway at the top of the stairs, listening to make sure no one had entered the house while she'd been in the basement. It had been years since she'd been this edgy, and she was surprised by how fast her heart was beating. Slowly she stepped into the living room and looked around. Only when she was sure she was alone did she hurry into the kitchen.

The box went on her kitchen table, and she pulled the blinds closed before reaching for a knife. The tape had melded into the box over the years, but a sharp blade along the seams released the tape's hold. Within seconds she put the knife down and lifted the lid to view the few treasures she'd retained from her years with ADEC.

Lying on top of the packing material were two kubotans, one the agency had given her and one she'd made herself. Both were the length of a dollar bill and approximately an inch in diameter. First she lifted the kubotan the agency had given her out of the box – the black metal cool to the touch – and then she removed the one she'd fashioned out of wood. The smooth, metal kubotan had a flat striking surface and rounded ends, but she'd given the one she made grooves, making it easier to hold. She'd also chiseled the end to a point. 'All the better to inflict pain,' she'd told her instructor the day she brought it to class.

Thursday night she'd used her cellphone pressed against one boy's ear and the other's nose to inflict pain, but either one of these kubotans would have been more effective, and most people wouldn't recognize them as fighting weapons. All she needed to do was drill a hole in the broad end of the one she'd made, attach it to her keychain, and tell people it made it easier for her to find her keys.

She put the metal kubotan back into the box, but left the wooden one out. If she remembered correctly, Robby had left the electric drill in the garage for when he fixed the garage door. It shouldn't take her long to drill a hole.

Mary pushed the packing material in the box aside to reveal her nunchuck. Simply looking at the two wooden rods and the short chain that connected them brought back memories, both exhilarating and painful. It had taken long hours of working with a foam model before she learned to control the Okinawan weapon, but once she proved she could handle the nunchuck without breaking her own arm or neck, she was given a wooden one. She used that one for six years, continuing to practice and improve her skills, and it had served her well. But the day she visited the martial arts weapons store and saw the one now lying in the box, its wooden handles ornately carved with two matching dragons, she knew she had to buy it.

Carl had been proud of her skill with the nunchuck, and whenever a new recruit was brought into the agency, he would ask her to demonstrate the weapon's potential. Thinking back to those days, Mary marveled at the trust he'd had in her. At the end of each demonstration, he would hold a board in his hand, away from his body, and she would break it in two with a downward strike. She certainly wouldn't want to try that today. A few inches off and the nunchuck could as easily shatter a hand or arm as break a board.

Mary lifted the nunchuck out of the box, letting the tips of her fingers slide over the dragon carvings. It was still as beautiful as she remembered. She released one handle, letting gravity pull it and the chain connecting the two handles down toward the floor. Grasping the remaining handle with her thumb and forefinger at the upper area near the chain, she stepped back from the table and held her arm away from her body.

Slowly she began to rotate her wrist, then faster and faster until the chain and second handle twirled like a helicopter blade. She smiled, remembered sensations running up her arm. A change in her grip and the two sticks appeared to be one long stick. She tried a diagonal stroke, then a horizontal strike. A forehand. A backhand.

Mary recognized her movements weren't as smooth as they'd been years before, and she knew she wasn't good enough to enter a freestyle contest, but she was pleased that she hadn't forgotten everything she'd been taught.

That was, until she attempted to catch the second handle in her hand.

The moving staff hit her thigh with a sharp blow, and she yelped in pain. Her hand reflexively opened, and the two wooden rods with their attached chain fell to the floor with a clatter.

Sucking in a breath and blinking back tears, Mary pressed her hands against the point of impact. She would now have one more bruise to add to the collection.

She picked up the fallen nunchuck, and put it on the table. As far as she knew, nunchucks weren't illegal in Michigan, but if she wanted to use it, she was going to have to practice and hope she didn't break any bones in the process.

Digging through the packing material in the box, she found six metal throwing stars and two fighting fans, one made of bamboo and one of aluminum. She'd kept the fans for their beauty and the throwing stars because they easily fit in the box, but she didn't think it was worth unpacking them. She couldn't imagine using the fans this time of the year. With the temperature barely reaching fifty during the day – if that high – and the sun rarely making an appearance, people would really think she was crazy if she walked around with a fan. As for the throwing stars?

Her doorbell rang just as Mary reached for one of the metal stars, and for a moment she didn't move.

Had someone seen her with the nunchuck? Heard her yell?

The doorbell rang again.

Quickly Mary grabbed the nunchuck, dropped it back into the box, and closed the lid.

Again the doorbell.

Whoever was at the door was persistent. Mary opened the cupboard under her coffee maker, and shoved the box in on top of a pile of placemats. Quickly she closed the cupboard door, and started for the door … then stopped.

She couldn't leave the wooden kubotan on her kitchen table.

The doorbell rang again.

'I'm coming,' she yelled and grabbed the wooden stick, dropping it into her sweater pocket.

CHAPTER SIXTEEN

JACK COULD UNDERSTAND why Wally had turned Pedro Rodriguez's case over to the Van Buren Sheriff's Department. One of the many things Rivershore's police department didn't have was a well-equipped crime scene investigation lab. For forensic evidence they depended on the county or state labs. Yet it bothered him that they – the Rivershore Police Department – had made a big bust and another agency would get the credit for a conviction.

However, during the twenty-minute drive from Rivershore to Paw Paw, it wasn't the Rodriguez case that held his attention but his son's phone call. Mary Smith Harrington, or whatever her real name was, had to be someone important if simply researching her name resulted in such a quick and strongly negative response. He hoped his request hadn't gotten his son in serious trouble. Evidently his own recent searches hadn't triggered any alarms, but Jack could understand that. How far could a lowly sergeant from a small mid-western town take an investigation? Clearly not as far as an FBI agent.

'Be prepared for a phone call,' his son had said.

From whom? Jack wondered.

The United States Marshals handled the Witness Protection Program, and Jack knew the marshals were supposed to contact the local police department if a criminal was relocated to the area. If the Rivershore Police Department was notified forty-four years ago, he'd never heard anything. Of course Mary Smith would have arrived twenty years before he moved to Rivershore and joined the force. Back then, he wouldn't have been in the 'need to know' loop, and since then, from what he'd discovered, Mary Smith Harrington hadn't been involved in any crimes.

Although witnesses nowadays might be foreigners who could testify against foreign terrorists, back when the program was first established they were primarily involved with the Mafia. Mary Smith Harrington was clearly not Italian.

So what did she know that had made her so valuable she'd been given a new identity?

'Who are you, Mrs Harrington?' he muttered as he passed Maple Lake and entered the village of Paw Paw.

At the Van Buren County Jail on South Kalamazoo Street, Jack forced himself to forget Mary Harrington. He'd been sent to interrogate a prisoner. He had to keep his mind on that. Most cases were won or lost during an interrogation rather than in court. He didn't want to make any slip-ups that might allow a drug runner the chance to go free, and if they could connect this guy to Jose Rodriguez, he wouldn't care who got the credit.

During the time it took Jack to present his credentials and go through security, announce his intentions, and wait for Pedro Rodriguez to be delivered to a secure and private interrogation room, he prepared himself mentally and emotionally. He stood and smiled when Rodriguez arrived, and as soon as the handcuffs had been removed from Rodriguez's wrists, Jack offered his hand. 'Good morning, Mr Rodriguez, I'm Sergeant Jack Rossini, from the Rivershore Police Department.'

Rodriguez didn't shake his hand and didn't speak. He was a good foot shorter than Jack, dark-skinned with shaggy black hair, black eyes, and a tattoo of an eagle holding a snake on his forearm. The man now wore the county's issued orange jumpsuit, but according to the arrest report, at the time of his traffic stop Rodriguez had been wearing faded blue-jeans, a stained white T-shirt, a hooded gray sweatshirt, work boots, and a blue bandana tied around his wrist.

'Sit down,' Jack said and pointed at the chair on the opposite side of the table. 'Would you like to be called Mr Rodriguez or Pedro?'

Again, Rodriguez didn't say anything, and when he didn't move, Jack wasn't sure if the man understood English. Then Rodriguez slowly walked around to the opposite side of the table and sat.

'Because you were arrested, I have to advise you of your rights.' Jack placed a copy of the Miranda rights in front of Rodriguez and read, line by line, from his copy. When he finished reading, he asked, 'Do you understand your rights, Mr Rodriguez?'

Rodriguez nodded, his expression sullen.

'You need to answer out loud,' Jack said, knowing the video tape of the interrogation would show Rodriguez's nod, but it was better for a jury to hear the man say he understood.

'I understand,' Rodriguez grumbled.

Jack suppressed a sigh of relief. At least Rodriguez understood and spoke English. If he hadn't, they would have had to get an interpreter in the room, which would lessen the intimacy Jack wanted to establish.

'Could you please initial each line and sign that paper, indicating you understand your rights?'

Jack handed Rodriguez a pen, and Rodriguez initialed and signed the paper. As soon as Jack had the signed paper and his pen back, he began his questioning. 'How old are you, Mr Rodriguez?'

'Twenty.' Rodriguez looked around the room, probably searching for the hidden video camera and microphone. When he faced Jack again, he added, 'You call me Pedro, OK? And I call you Jack.'

'That's fine with me, Pedro. So where do you live?'

'I stay in Detroit, Jack.' He said it boldly and proudly.

Pleased that Rodriguez was finally talking, Jack pulled out his notebook. 'Where in Detroit? What is your address?'

Once Jack had that information written down, he went on. 'You live alone, Pedro, or with someone else?'

Pedro gave a glib smile. 'I'm a good boy. I live with *mi madre*.'

As much as Jack wanted to comment on the 'good boy' bit, he kept his question neutral. 'Anyone else live with you and your mother?'

Pedro shook his head, then evidently remembered Jack's order that he speak aloud. 'No. No one.'

'Does the car you were driving belong to your mother?' Jack already knew from the report he'd been given that the car was registered to an Andy Gomez.

'It belong to *mi madre's* boyfriend.'

Jack feigned surprise. 'Oh. So does this boyfriend also live with you and your mother?'

'Sometimes, *sí*. Sometimes no.'

'Did this boyfriend ask you to drive his car over here?'

Pedro looked away and stared at a spot on the bare wall.

After a long moment of silence, Jack revised his question. 'Does your mother's boyfriend know you have his car?'

Again Jack waited. Finally Pedro shook his head, and then looked back at Jack. 'No. But he say I can use it any time I want.'

'So last night you took him up on that offer,' Jack said, concerned that a defense attorney might use that information to indicate Pedro had no idea the cocaine was in the trunk.

His job, Jack knew, was to somehow prove Pedro was delivering the cocaine to Jose Rodriguez. He decided to try a more gentle tone. 'You're a long way from Detroit. What brought you over on this side of the state?'

'I dunno,' Pedro mumbled, keeping his gaze averted.

'Do you have friends in Rivershore?'

'Maybe.'

'Explain to me. Who are these friends?'

'Maybe a cousin.'

'Maybe?' Jack repeated and smiled. 'Is Jose Rodriguez your cousin?'

Pedro nodded.

'You have to speak up,' Jack reminded him. 'Tell me how you're related to Jose.'

This time Pedro looked at him. 'He my father's brother's son.'

This was information Jack wanted. 'So you're first cousins. Do you come over here often to see Jose?'

'Sometimes.' Again he shrugged. 'I come when I can.'

'Did Jose ask you to bring him something? Maybe something from his father. Or maybe from your mother's boyfriend?'

Pedro started fussing with a spot on his arm, rubbing it with his other hand. Jack couldn't see anything on the arm and knew Pedro was simply stalling, trying to come up with an answer.

'Did Jose ask you to bring him the cocaine we found in the car you were driving?'

'No.' Pedro finally answered. 'I didn't know there was cocaine in the car. I was just driving around. Just driving.'

Not the answer Jack wanted, but he went on. 'So you were surprised when Officer VanDerwell found the cocaine?'

'Si. I surprised.'

Jack wasn't sure if he believed him. 'Are we going to find more cocaine in the car?'

'No.'

'How about anything else? Will we find anything else in the car?'

'Like what?'

'You tell me.' Pedro's expression alone told Jack they would find something.

'Maybe some marijuana.'

Jack already knew about the marijuana. Stu had found a bag of it shoved under the driver's seat. 'Anything else besides the marijuana?'

Pedro didn't answer, and Jack waited, hoping the silence would become uncomfortable, and Pedro would talk. But when a couple of minutes went by with Pedro saying nothing, Jack tried again.

'You know if I can tell the DA you were cooperative, I'm sure he'll go easier on you.'

Pedro sighed and licked his lips, then shrugged. 'Maybe, if you look under the spare tire, you might find a few rocks.'

Bingo. Jack knew these wouldn't be rocks like the ones in a field and alongside a road. These 'rocks' would be crusted, brownish lumps of cooked cocaine. Crack cocaine. And if Pedro knew about them, he would have known about the cocaine under the blanket.

'You planning on selling those rocks?'

'Me? No, I no sell anything like that,' Pedro insisted.

Right, Jack thought and smiled. Selling a kilo of cocaine on the street would be difficult, but the cost of a rock was reasonable: five to ten dollars a hit. 'If you weren't going to sell it, who were you delivering the cocaine and rocks to?'

'No one, man.'

'Oh, come on,' Jack said. 'You expect me to believe that? Where were you headed? To Jose's?'

Pedro shook his head, but beads of sweat were starting to form on the boy's forehead.

Jack leaned toward him. 'You know, I appreciate how cooperative you've been, but you're not cooperating now. If I don't get some answers, we could just turn this over to the feds. You get convicted, and you'd be spending a lot more time in a little cell.'

Jack saw a flicker of fear in Pedro's eyes, and played on it. 'Like

I said before, what you tell me today, Pedro, can make things go easier. Where were you headed when Officer VanDerwell stopped you?'

'I was just driving,' Pedro said, running his fingers through his thick, black hair. 'Just driving.'

'I see.' Jack sat back and watched Pedro nervously rearrange a lock of hair. 'So you drove from Detroit to Rivershore, about 170 miles give or take a few. You did this with a kilo of cocaine in your trunk and who knows how many rocks … just for fun?'

'Sure.' Pedro nodded. 'I like to drive.'

Jack shook his head. 'I don't believe you, Pedro. And no judge or jury will believe you. If you weren't delivering that load to anyone, then you must be the dealer. That means you'll be an old man before you're out of that prison cell.'

Pedro looked down at his lap, but Jack could see a tear slide down the boy's cheek. The kid probably was a mule, an expendable in the world of drug pushers. 'Who were you delivering the cocaine and rocks to?' Jack repeated, his voice softer this time, more consoling.

'I …' Pedro sniffed. 'I talk to you, they'll kill me.'

'We'll protect you,' Jack said, though he wasn't sure if they really could.

The boy must have had the same thought. He raised his head, and looked Jack in the eyes. 'I think I don't want to say anything more. I want a lawyer.'

'You're sure?' Jack waited, hoping the boy would change his mind.

'I'm sure. I want a lawyer.'

'Then we're through.' Jack closed his notebook and put away his pen. As he rose to his feet, he smiled at Pedro. 'Why do you think you were stopped last night?' he asked, dropping his voice slightly, as if letting Pedro in on a secret. 'I mean, you weren't doing anything wrong. You hadn't broken any laws. Didn't you wonder why you'd been stopped?'

'I wonder,' Pedro said, his expression suspicious.

'We knew.' Jack said with what he hoped appeared to be an all-knowing nod. 'Your cousin Jose may think he has loyal followers, but one of his gang is talking.'

'Impossible,' Pedro insisted, shaking his head. 'No one crosses Jose.'

'Impossible?' Jack chuckled and stepped away from the table. 'When you see him, tell him he'd better watch his back.'

CHAPTER SEVENTEEN

THE TENSION MARY had felt when she heard the doorbell disappeared the moment she looked through the peephole and saw just the top of a head, the white hair peeking out from under a purple bandana short and curly. Ella Williams might be considered a nosy neighbor, but she certainly wasn't a gang member out for revenge.

'Ella,' Mary said, smiling as she opened her front door. 'What brings you out in the cold?'

'I've been talking to neighbors,' Ella said, a shiver in her voice as she pulled at the sides of her red wool coat in an effort to cover her rounded hips and stomach. 'About the Neighborhood Watch.' She glanced past Mary. 'May I come in? I thought you'd want to hear what's up.'

'Of course.' Mary knew, whether she wanted to or not, she was going to hear what Ella had been doing. 'Come on in.'

She closed the door and waited as Ella removed her scarf and gloves, stuffed them into a pocket, and finally shrugged out of her coat. 'I can't believe how cold it is,' Ella said, rubbing her hands together.

'A cup of tea should help,' Mary offered, placing Ella's coat on a peg next to her own black windbreaker, before leading the way to the kitchen.

A few minutes later, they were both seated at the table with mugs of hot tea and slices of a pound cake that Mary had bought on the way home from the gym. 'I called the police department this morning,' Ella said after a bite of the pound cake. 'They're supposed to have one of the officers contact me.'

'You're serious about this, aren't you?'

'Aren't *you*?' Ella frowned. 'Sometimes, Mary, I just don't understand you. Here we are, two widows living by ourselves. It could have been one of us attacked the other night.'

'And you think a Neighborhood Watch would have stopped what happened?'

'Maybe. Maybe we've all been too complacent. Didn't you say you saw a strange car hanging around on Halloween?'

'Which may have belonged to a parent.' Not that Mary truly believed that.

'Fine. Maybe it did, but if we knew our neighbors and what cars they drove, we'd know for sure, wouldn't we?'

'OK, maybe you're right.' Mary studied her friend. In the thirty-five years she'd known Ella, she'd never seen the woman so enthusiastic about anything ... other than her cats. 'But are you sure you don't simply want to know what our neighbors are up to?'

The moment the words were out of her mouth, Mary knew she'd said the wrong thing.

'I am not a nosy gossip,' Ella said, sitting back in her chair, her double chin lifted and her mouth puckered. 'No matter what George Figer says.'

Mary didn't think it wise to mention that Ella seemed to know a lot about everyone in the neighborhood and didn't hesitate to pass the information on to anyone who would listen. 'I take it George wasn't receptive to the Neighborhood Watch idea.'

'Said he wasn't spying on his neighbors, not like some people he knew.' Ella snorted. 'Looked right at me when he said that.'

'I wouldn't let him bother you,' Mary said, feeling a little sorry for Ella. 'He's always been the neighborhood grouch. So how many people have you talked to?'

'Everyone up and down our street.' Ella relaxed her shoulders and took a sip of tea before going on. 'I didn't try anywhere else today. I'm a little afraid about going over onto Archer Street after what happened to those boys last week. Maybe if you went with me...?'

Mary heard the implied question and shook her head. She was not going anywhere near Archer Street, not as long as there was the possibility someone might remember seeing her there the night the boys were attacked.

'Why not?' Ella asked. 'Some of those people might recognize you from that newspaper article, might be more willing to talk to you than they would me.'

'Ella, I'm not going around talking to people. I'm sorry I even talked to that reporter.'

'I don't see why,' Ella said. 'It was a good article. It's about time people realize we're not all sitting around in our rocking chairs, knitting, and watching games and talk shows.' She chuckled. 'Well, maybe I do, but you don't. That was a good picture of you.'

Which was the worst part of the article, in Mary's opinion. She'd agreed when the reporter asked if they could take a picture of her on the treadmill. Mary had even suggested they take the picture from a distance, to show the variety of exercise machines available to seniors. Then, as the photographer took his pictures, she kept her head turned slightly, so her face wasn't clearly visible. Which may have been why they didn't use any of those shots. Instead they used a picture Mary hadn't known they'd taken. One that clearly showed her face as she lifted barbells. All she could hope was her white hair, sagging chin, and wrinkles would keep anyone from her past from recognizing her.

'I'm not going around talking to people,' Mary repeated.

'OK, OK.'

Head down, Ella took another bite of her pound cake. Mary said nothing, simply waited for Ella's next request. She didn't have to wait long.

'Do you still have that fancy printer Harry bought before he died?'

'I still have it.' Even though Robby had longingly eyed the printer/scanner/copier after his father's death, Mary had decided to keep it, along with Harry's PC.

'Would you be willing to make some copies of fliers I could pass out?' Ella asked. 'I mean, I'd pass them out. You'd just have to make the copies.'

'Sure.' Mary couldn't see any harm in that.

'We'll need them to let people know when our first meeting will be ... and where.' She looked toward Mary's living room. 'I guess we should meet somewhere other than a house. I mean, if we have a lot of people come, we wouldn't have enough room in someone's house.'

'Have you checked with any of the churches?'

'Not yet.' Ella finished her last bite of cake and took one more sip of tea before she pushed herself back from the table and stood. 'I guess I'd better do that next.'

Mary walked with Ella to the door. As she waited for her friend to put on her coat, scarf, and gloves, she let her fingers play over the grooves on the kubotan in her pocket. She didn't think about what she was doing until Ella asked, 'What's that you have in your pocket?'

'My pocket?' Mary jerked her hand out of her pocket. 'Nothing.'

Ella's eyebrows rose suspiciously.

'It's just a stick.' Mary knew Ella's curiosity would be worse than showing her the kubotan, so she pulled it out. 'It's just something I picked up. I liked the shape.' She smiled, hoping her voice sounded natural. 'I've been using it like one of those worry stones. It makes me feel a little safer.'

Ella glanced at the wooden stick, then back at Mary. 'See, even *you* worry about your safety. We really do need this Neighborhood Watch.'

CHAPTER EIGHTEEN

'DID YOU GET anything helpful?' Wally asked.

Jack looked up, shrugged, and closed the Rodriguez file. 'He said he's Jose's cousin, but he wasn't about to admit he was on his way to see Jose.'

'Anything in the car to connect the two?'

'Nothing obvious. Our boy Pedro had some fast-food wrappers and a throwaway phone, but that was it. The Sheriff's Department had already gotten a warrant for the phone, but the only number

Pedro had called that immediately checked out was to his mother. They're working on the others.'

'Any to this area?'

'One, but it must have been to another throwaway.' Which didn't surprise Jack.

'Any chance this cousin might turn?'

'Would surprise me if he did.' Jack remembered the look on Pedro's face. 'Guy's scared.'

'Probably just a mule. Like the phone, a throwaway.' Wally shook his head. 'Sometimes I feel sorry for these guys. They don't realize the risk they're taking. Some don't even know they're transporting drugs.'

'Oh, he knew he had drugs. He fessed up to the crack cocaine they found in the car. The spare-tire section had been modified, and the rocks were hidden under it.'

'Why hide those and not the kilo?'

'No idea.'

'Was this guy an illegal?'

'Looks like it. Driver's license was fake. But I wouldn't feel sorry for him. He spoke good English, and he told me exactly where to find the rocks.'

'Damn.' Wally started to walk away, then turned and came back. 'Jack, we have got to find something on Rodriguez. Anything that would give us a reason to raid his place. In all the years I've been here, we've never had drug and gang problems like we've had since that bastard arrived.'

'I'll keep on it,' Jack promised, then remembered something else that had been on his mind. 'You've been here a lot of years, Wally.' Thirty-five years, as far as Jack knew. 'You ever hear anything about a woman being put here under the Witness Protection Program?'

'Witness Protection?' Wally shook his head. 'No, not that I've heard of.'

'Would have been back about forty-four years ago.'

'Way before my time.'

'And mine,' Jack admitted. 'But wouldn't you have been given something when they made you chief? Some kind of file that would include information like that?'

The way Wally scrunched up his forehead, Jack knew he was thinking, but then Wally shook his head. 'Hell, it's been more than ten years since I was promoted to chief. If there was any such file, I sure don't remember where it might be. Why? Do you think we have someone under that program here in Rivershore?'

'It's sure looking like a possibility.' He quickly summarized his request to his son and John's call to him that morning. 'I checked my messages when I got back here, and I didn't have anything, but from what my son said, it sounds like you or I will hear from someone. The only possibility I can think of is Mary Smith Harrington is under that program.'

'I'll look through the old files, see if I can find anything.' Wally gave a grunt. 'Think we've been harboring someone famous all these years?'

'Maybe infamous.' Though Jack couldn't quite imagine Mary Harrington fitting that category.

Eleven days after having been attacked by the two gang members, Mary wished she still had the resources that had been available to her when she worked for ADEC. Although computers were barely coming into being when she left, she was sure the agency would now have the latest tech available. The computer she had was three years old and already outdated, but up until now it had been all she needed.

It wasn't as though she used the computer a lot. Although she had an email address – Harry had talked her into getting one – and belonged to Facebook – Shannon had begged her to be a 'friend' – Mary had kept the amount of personal information available about her to an absolute minimum. No pictures, no accurate date of birth, nothing that would have linked her to her past. She had gone on the Internet occasionally for a new recipe or to look up a word for a crossword puzzle, but up until two weeks ago she hadn't done a lot of research, not like she'd done lately.

Day after day, she'd been learning about gangs, about tattoos, about the wearing of colors, and gang hierarchy. She'd even started asking complete strangers what they knew about gangs: the librarian, the grocery store clerk, and anyone at the gym who looked young enough to know about gangs or who might have children who would know. By the end of the week, her head was full of facts but nothing concrete.

Growing up in San Francisco, she'd known gangs. There were the Italians who visited the neighborhood and hired her mother as a 'hostess'. For the most part they treated her nice, called her a cute *ragazza*, and said they were just borrowing her mother for a little while and to be good while she was gone. Her mother liked the Italians, said they paid her well, but there were times when her mother came home with cuts and bruises and swore she would never do business with one of those wops again. And she might not have if she hadn't been hooked on the drugs they could provide.

The gang wars in high school were the Negros against the Chicanos, as the Latinos were called back then. It was important to know who 'owned' a street, whose turf she was on. For her, hooking up with Raphael after her mother died was for protection as well as a way to make money. If she hadn't gone with Carl after Raphael died, she would have been vulnerable.

She hadn't thought about gangs when she moved to Rivershore. Oh, there'd been groups of kids that formed what might have been called gangs, but for the most part they came and went with the seasons. When Robby was young, there were very few blacks living in Rivershore – there simply wasn't enough work to bring a large number of them to the area – and most of the Mexicans who worked in the fields were migrants, here when the crops ripened and gone after the harvest. She did, however, remember one year when Robby was in high school that he complained about a group of black kids that had harassed one of his friends.

When Robby called Wednesday night – her son's usual phone call to see how she was doing – she asked him about that incident.

'You mean Ethan?' Robby said in response to her question. 'Yeah, he had a lot of trouble with those black kids, and all because he turned a girl … one of their girlfriends … in for cheating on a test.'

'So what did he do about it?'

'He moved,' Robby said, matter-of-factly. 'Don't you remember, Mom, how upset I was? He was one of my best friends.'

'Why didn't he stay and fight back?'

Robby scoffed. 'What, and get himself killed? I never told you *everything* they did to him, but it was scary.'

'Like what did they do?' Robby was right. He'd never told her any of this.

'Slashed the tires on his mom's car and threatened Ethan's little sister. I think it was when Ethan's dad found a dead cat on their doorstep that he decided to ask for a transfer and took that job in Ohio. Ethan felt so guilty.'

'Why didn't you ever tell us this?'

'And what would you and Dad have done? Told them to go to the police? They did, and the police did nothing.'

Mary could hear the disappointment in her son's voice and knew he was right, Harry would have suggested Ethan's family go to the police. She also knew the problem with law enforcement was they had to enforce laws, which meant they had to have proof of a crime. If the gangs in Rivershore were anything like the Mafia, they either scared witnesses so much no one would testify against them or they left no witnesses.

'I might have been able to help,' she said, even though she knew that wasn't true. She wasn't like the super heroes in comic books. She couldn't fight crime in a costume and be viewed as a typical housewife and mother in her day-to-day clothes.

'It turned out all right, I guess,' Robby finally said. 'Ethan did well at his new school, got into Harvard, and now works for Google.'

'What about Shannon? Has she ever been bothered by gangs?'

'Not that I've heard about.' Robby snorted. 'You'll have to ask her. Lately she barely talks to her mother, and with me it's always, "Everything's fine, Dad."'

'I will ask her,' Mary said, hearing her son's frustration. 'It will get better, Rob. She's just trying to figure out what she wants to do with her life.'

'Go to college, that's what she's to do,' he said firmly, and Mary understood why Shannon rarely talked to her father.

CHAPTER NINETEEN

THE FOLLOWING WEEKEND, Mary took Robby up on his suggestion and asked Shannon if she'd like to go shopping in Grand Rapids and then have dinner. With Christmas less than six weeks away, Shannon readily agreed, and Mary picked her up at two o'clock. On the drive to Grand Rapids they talked about school; or rather, Shannon talked. 'It's so boring, Grandma. All the teachers talk about is "When you go to college." Even my friends talk about it. Their parents have them filling out applications, writing essays.'

'What about your boyfriend?' Mary said. 'Aren't his parents pushing for him to go to college?'

'No. He's got the neatest parents.' Shannon practically bounced when she turned in her seat toward Mary. 'They told him they think he should take a year or two to find himself, decide what he wants to do for the rest of his life. They want him to experience what it's like to live in another country, learn other languages and cultures.'

On the surface it made sense to Mary. 'Does he have a plan on how he's going to accomplish this?'

'Sort of. I mean, like I told you, he'll be on that bicycle trip this summer. And then, after we get together in Paris, we're going to get a place to live and learn the language. And then we'll travel to other countries. Germany. Italy. Africa. Like everywhere. You know.'

Mary knew. She knew it sounded fun and romantic. She also knew Shannon's plan had flaws. 'And how do you plan on paying for a place to live and for all of these trips?'

'We've been saving our money. Aiden has almost a thousand now. And I, well ...'

'I believe you said you had around five hundred.'

Shannon sighed. 'Maybe more like four hundred. I sort of had to buy some new shoes.'

Mary chuckled. 'I don't think four hundred dollars will last very long.'

'Yeah, but ...' Shannon hesitated, and Mary glanced her way. The girl licked her lips, and gave Mary a longing look. 'I kinda hoped, you know, like maybe you could loan me a little. Just enough until Aiden and I find jobs.'

'Oh, Shannon.' Mary shook her head and kept her eyes on the road. 'Your mom and dad would kill me if I gave you any money for a trip like that.'

'But don't you agree it would be a wonderful experience for me?'

'Yes, but not the way you have it planned.'

'Then how?' Shannon asked and sighed. 'How can I get Mom to even consider the idea?'

'You're going to have to come up with a proposal that shows her why a year of travel would better prepare you for college. You're going to have to figure out a way to pay for that year.' She paused and glanced at her granddaughter. 'A way that doesn't include me.'

'But how?'

'There are programs you could apply for, overseas jobs. Get on the Internet. See what is out there.'

Shannon leaned back in her seat. 'I never thought of that. Yeah, if Aiden and I had jobs lined up before we even got over there, we'd be set.'

Mary laughed. 'Shannon, if you want to go on this trip, I definitely wouldn't tell your mom and dad that you're planning on living with your boyfriend, not unless you plan on wearing a chastity belt while you're there.'

'A chastity belt?' Shannon screwed up her nose. 'What's that?'

'It's …' Mary glanced at Shannon, then shook her head. 'Never mind, just don't say anything to your mom and dad about living with Aiden.'

It started raining as they neared Grand Rapids, a downpour that demanded Mary's full attention, so she decided to hold off questioning Shannon about gang activities until they'd finished shopping and were having dinner.

Mary's favorite restaurant in Grand Rapids was Charlie's Crab, and Shannon didn't object when Mary suggested they have dinner there. Nestled just off Fulton Avenue with a view of the Grand River, the restaurant was known for its seafood, and both Mary and Shannon ordered crab. 'I have a question,' Mary said, after the waitress had taken their orders. 'Lately I've been hearing a lot about gangs. In fact, my friend and neighbor, Mrs Williams, is so worried about gangs, she wants to start a Neighborhood Watch. What do you know about gangs, Shannon? Do we have them in Rivershore?'

'Do we?' Shannon rolled her eyes. 'They're terrible. I think Mrs Williams is right, Grandma. You old people should have some sort of way to watch out for each other.'

Mary wasn't sure she liked the way Shannon said 'you old people', but that was beside the point. 'Have you or any of your friends ever been bothered by gang members?'

'I think they bothered Aiden. He won't say anything about it, but one day last spring he came to school with a black eye, and he told me I shouldn't go out alone at night.'

'What about you? Have they ever bothered you?'

'Yeah. Sort of.' She looked away, not meeting Mary's gaze.

'What happened?'

Shannon looked back. 'A couple girls stopped me after school.'

'And...?'

'They wanted me to give them some money.'

'And then what?'

Shannon looked down at the table. 'I told them I didn't have any, but they said I'd better find some or something bad would happen to me.'

'So what did you do then?'

Her granddaughter lowered her head even more and whispered her answer. 'I took some from Mom's purse and gave it to them.'

'Oh, Shannon.' It took Mary a moment before she could think of what to say. 'You've got to tell your mom what's going on ... and your dad. This has got to stop.'

'But how? What...?' Shannon stopped talking when the waitress brought their salads, then went on, almost at a whisper, once the waitress left. 'There's this guy. Jose something or other. They say he's really mean, that he's already been in prison. They say if they don't bring him money, he'll kill them. That he'll kill me.'

'Jose.' She had what she wanted. A name – a person – to focus on. 'Find out this Jose's last name. Then tell me, and I'll take care of the problem.'

Shannon's look expressed her disbelief. 'You will?'

Mary realized she'd said too much. 'In a way, I will,' she faked. 'I've got a friend in the police department. He needs to know about this Jose guy.'

Jack hadn't seen or talked to Mary Harrington for over two weeks. He also hadn't been called by anyone about his search into her background, and neither had the chief. That surprised Jack, but he was willing to let sleeping dogs lie.

He had other matters on his mind, had thought Pedro Rodriguez might be a way to get to Jose Rodriguez. But once Pedro had a lawyer, he stopped talking, and as soon as he was arraigned and his bail posted, he disappeared. He was supposed to check in with the Detroit Police Department, but he never did, and when Jack followed up on the address Pedro had given him, '*mi madre's*' house turned out to be an abandoned warehouse.

Big surprise. The guy had lied to him.

Jack doubted they would ever see Pedro again, unless as a corpse.

Gangs and drugs weren't the only activities keeping Jack busy. Two African-Americans had robbed the downtown bank. It took Jack two days before he had their names. One turned himself in after Jack talked to the man's sister. The other one offered no resistance when Jack and Officer Carlson visited his home.

Paperwork also took up a good part of Jack's time, along with a court appearance on a rape case he'd handled a year earlier. He was glad when the verdict came in as guilty. The man had been a minister, had preached on Sundays and raped underaged girls during the week. Jack had been afraid the jury might have been swayed by the minister's age and looks. He could have passed as Santa's double, but his victims said he was anything but a sweet old elf.

Some people wondered why so many cops had drinking problems. Jack figured if those people met as many scumbags as he did, they'd also have drinking problems. That Monday night he really wanted to stop in at the Shores after work and have a couple of beers, but he'd told Carlson he'd be at Ella Williams' Neighborhood Watch meeting, and Jack figured it probably wouldn't look good if he came in smelling like a drunk.

Phil would be in charge of the meeting, but Jack was curious to see what these people were thinking. He also wanted to see if Mary Harrington would be there, and if she did attend, what she would say.

Would she confess to the group that she'd had an encounter with two gang members? Tell them how she defended herself?

No matter what she and the boys said, Jack was sure she was the one.

In truth, he doubted she'd say anything. If she was in the Witness Protection Program, she'd already learned what happened when you testified against a gang. Being a good citizen could make you move, force you to leave your family and friends, and require you to take on a new identity.

He wondered what she would say if he told her someone was still protecting her past.

Several cars were already parked in the lot beside the Rivershore Elementary School. Jack parked back near the far edge of the building, got out of his car, and locked it. The night air was cold and crisp, causing his nose hairs to tingle, but it hadn't snowed since the day after Halloween, and the sky was clear, a three-quarter moon already high above the school. He lit a cigarette and took a long drag. He hoped this meeting didn't last too long. Not that he had anywhere to go, he just wasn't looking forward to a long-drawn-out discussion about how bad things had gotten and how the police weren't doing enough.

He watched more cars pull into the lot and park. Singles, couples, even a family of four exited the vehicles and headed for the main entrance. Before he finished his cigarette, Jack stubbed it out on a metal post, made sure it was fully extinguished, and dropped it into the outside pocket of his overcoat. Taking his time, he ambled toward the entrance.

A teepee straw bundle, tied with binding twine, was propped up next to the entrance door, three large pumpkins at its base, while pictures of hands colored to look like turkeys covered the door's glass panes. A sign had been taped on the outside of the door, covering several of the 'turkeys' and directing those attending the Neighborhood Watch meeting to go to the student cafeteria. Even without the sign, Jack could have found the location by following

102

the sound of voices. Neighbors were greeting neighbors, women giving hugs, men shaking hands, children gathering in groups. Jack eased himself into the room and took a chair at the back.

Phil Carlson, in full uniform, stood at the front of the cafeteria talking to a short, pudgy, white-haired woman who could have been anywhere from sixty to eighty. It took Jack a moment to find Mary Harrington. He'd just started thinking she hadn't come to the meeting when he spotted her talking to an overweight, elderly man who practically hid her from view. For the first time since Jack had met her, she wasn't wearing sweatpants, and the tailored black pantsuit and light-purple blouse she had on accentuated her slender form. He had a feeling she'd been quite a knockout in her younger years. The way the man talking to her was smiling, Jack knew he wasn't the only one who found Mary Harrington attractive.

Jack could tell the moment she spotted him. Her smile turned to a frown, and she gave a slight shake of her head. He might have gotten up and gone over to talk to her, except a middle-aged woman wearing the typical Rivershore Hospital's nursing uniform of a pink top, white slacks, and white shoes picked that moment to sit next to him. 'Hi,' she said. 'I'm Dolores. Dolores Tredwell. You look familiar. Have we met before?'

'Perhaps,' he said and offered his hand. 'I'm Sergeant Jack Rossini. You've probably seen me at the hospital.' He nodded toward the front of the room. 'I'm just here to give Officer Carlson a hand, if he needs it.'

'Oh, of course.' She laughed and shook his hand. 'For a moment I thought we had a new neighbor. I mean, you're not in uniform so I thought, that is ...' Again she laughed, almost a giggle. 'I don't know what I thought. You'll have to excuse me. I just finished a fourteen-hour shift, and I'm not thinking straight.'

'You're forgiven.' Jack glanced around the room. 'Does everyone here live on Maple Street?'

'Quite a few of us do, but I think Ella also talked to people on Oak and Archer. They've had trouble on Archer, you know.' Dolores laughed again. 'Of course you know. You're the police. Were you there that night? I saw those boys when they came in, babbling that some old lady had attacked them. I didn't see the tox report, but they had to be high on something. Those two were no wimps. I wouldn't have wanted to run into them at night.'

'But they were saying an old woman attacked them.' Jack looked over at Mary Harrington.

'That was what they said at first, then their friends showed up, and the boys changed their story, claimed someone dressed in black attacked them. Later I heard they changed their story again, said they simply tripped and fell.' She shook her head in disbelief.

'And what do you think?'

'Don't know, don't care,' she said, and faced forward at the sound of a gavel pounding on a table.

CHAPTER TWENTY

'WILL EVERYONE PLEASE sit down,' Ella ordered, her voice cracking on the word 'sit'.

Mary glanced toward the door. Coming to this meeting had been a mistake. She'd tried to back out when on the way over Ella had told her she'd invited homeowners from Archer Street, along with those on Oak and Maple. So far, thank goodness, none of the Archer Street people had shown any indication of recognizing her from the night before Halloween, but with Sergeant Rossini here, who knew what might happen, especially if he brought up the incident with the two boys. People might remember she was wearing this same black pantsuit and black jacket that night.

All she had to do was slip by Ella and out the door. Although Ella had picked her up and brought her to the meeting, it wasn't that far back to Maple Street, and it wasn't that cold out. Mary figured she could leave a note on Ella's car saying she'd walked home.

'Come sit by me,' Fred Strong said, and snagged her hand before she could move.

'I need to …' Mary started, but Fred wasn't listening, and she found herself being pulled toward two of the dozens of folding chairs that had been set up in the cafeteria.

Fred had been one of Harry's closest friends, and for the last twenty minutes – ever since she'd arrived with Ella – Fred had been talking to her about Harry and the many fishing trips the two of them had taken when they were younger. She'd enjoyed sharing those memories. That was, until she saw Sergeant Jack Rossini enter the cafeteria.

She doubted if many others in the room knew Rossini was with the Police Department. Unlike the uniformed officer standing next to Ella, Rossini was dressed like most of the men in attendance, his brown-tweed sports jacket, white shirt, multicolored tie, and brown slacks gave no indication he wasn't a homeowner. He'd had on a tan overcoat when he first entered the cafeteria, but he'd immediately taken it off and draped it over the back of the chair next to him.

He looked tired, and she mentally cast a thought in his direction. *Go home. Get some sleep.*

He didn't leave; instead he looked directly at her, and for a moment she thought he might get up and come over to where she and Fred were standing.

She'd scooted to the left, using Fred's bulk to block her from view.

The next time she chanced a glance Rossini's way, he was talking to Dolores Tredwell. Mary hoped the nurse was telling him he looked tired and to go home and get some rest, but from Rossini's expression, Mary knew that wasn't the case. He nodded and said something.

Damn, what were they talking about?

Her?

Stop being so self-centered, she chided herself. After all, Rossini was a good-looking man, and Dolores was divorced. Mary had no idea if Rossini was married, divorced, or a widower. Could be Dolores and he were simply getting to know each other, making plans to meet later.

Go now, Mary willed the two. *Take off. Go get a drink somewhere. Make wild passionate love.*

They didn't leave, and now it seemed she couldn't leave either, not until the meeting was over.

'I've been meaning to call you,' Fred said as he sat beside her, the folding chair giving a creak that made her wonder if it would hold his weight. 'With your Harry gone and my Silvia having passed on last year, bless her soul, I was thinking you and I should get together for dinner and a movie sometime.'

No way, Mary thought and smiled his way. 'That sounds like a nice idea, Fred. Give me a call sometime.'

And I'll make sure I'm busy.

She didn't need another man in her life, not when she had a task to accomplish.

Mary barely listened as Ella introduced Officer Phillip Carlson of the Rivershore Police Department and thanked everyone for coming. The thoughts running through Mary's mind weren't about starting a Neighborhood Watch, but how to eliminate a gang without reverting back to the person she was before moving to Rivershore.

That gang members had bothered Shannon, upset Mary. If anything happened to her granddaughter ...

'And now,' Ella said, interrupting Mary's thoughts, 'Officer Carlson will tell us what we must do to make our neighborhood safe.'

Want to make the neighborhood safe? As far as Mary knew, there was only one way. *Eliminate the gang leaders. Attack before being attacked.*

But did she want to become a killer ... again?

She wasn't ashamed of the jobs she did for the agency. She and others, working together and alone, had eliminated dictators, cartel bosses, slave traders, gunrunners, and other malfeasants. Over the years, since leaving the agency, every time she heard or read about an untouchable being killed in a car accident, a plane crash, or committing suicide, she wondered if it was truly an accident or suicide or if the deceased might have had a bit of help.

Would they even need a Neighborhood Watch if a certain gang leader had an accident?

Mary quickly dismissed that thought. There would be no accident. Pandora no longer existed.

Or did she?

'You, all of you here tonight,' Officer Carlson said, pointing at his audience, 'along with all of your neighbors, are our best resource. Get to know each other. Know what cars you drive, what your normal schedules are: when you go to work, to school, and come home. Talk to each other. Going to be gone? Tell your neighbors. Ask them to keep an eye on your house. Then, if you see something out of the ordinary, call us. Call the police.'

Mary watched the officer stroll across the front of the room, his gaze scanning the crowd. 'If you see someone breaking into a house, or a group of kids or people hanging around, call us.' He stopped and faced one woman seated in the front row. 'Don't confront them, that's our job. See someone being attacked, like that woman was the other night, call us.'

And what good will that do? From what Mary had heard, the police were called and the attackers were still on the loose.

'And those boys,' one woman from the second row called out. 'They were attacked on my street.'

'Did you see the attack?' Officer Carlson asked, stepping closer to where the woman sat.

Mary cringed, her gaze locked on the back of the woman's head. Had this woman seen her? Could she identify her?

'No,' the woman admitted, shaking her head. 'But I heard all about it, and one of my neighbors saw what happened. She told the police what she saw, but no one believed her.'

'We're following up on that report,' a deep male voice said from the back of the room, and Mary knew it was Rossini speaking ... and how he was following up on that report.

'I'd like to introduce Sergeant Jack Rossini, head of our Criminal Investigations Unit,' Officer Carlson said and pointed at the back of the room.

Mary saw Fred turn to look that direction. She didn't. She held her breath, hoping Rossini wouldn't say anything about interviewing her or about his suspicions.

'We follow up on all reports,' Rossini said, and Officer Carlson nodded.

'And here's the information we need in a report,' Carlson said, once again taking control of the meeting. 'We need the time of the day when the incident occurred, where it happened, and what you witnessed. We want as many details as you can supply. A description of who was involved, whether it was a man or a woman, how tall, their build, hair color, skin color, and age. Was there a car involved? What was the license plate number?'

'What if it's dark out and you can't see the license plate?' another woman in the audience asked.

'Then tell us as much as you can about the car. Was it a sedan or an SUV? What color? Was it noisy? Music noisy or muffler noise? Could you see how many were in the car? Tell us anything you can about them. The more information you give us, the faster we can find these people and stop what's going on.'

'I've seen a black car driving up and down Maple Street,' one woman said. 'I don't think it belongs to any of my neighbors.'

So she wasn't the only one who'd noticed the car. Mary wasn't sure if that made her happy or not.

'Then after this meeting, tell me what you remember about this car,' Carlson said, and looked around the room. 'Folks, that's what we need to know. Maybe there's nothing wrong with this car being on that street, but you need to be aware of its presence and call us if it keeps hanging around. Some of you have young children. We don't want anything happening to them.'

Mary nodded. She hadn't thought of a pedophile in connection with the car, but it certainly was a possibility, especially since she and Shannon had seen it hanging around on Halloween.

'What is being done about these gangs?' a man seated somewhere near the back of the room asked. 'All I'm hearing lately are stories about fights and shootings. This used to be a quiet, peaceful town. What is going on?'

Others in the audience sounded their concerns, and Mary hoped Carlson or Rossini would give some specifics, like the names of the gang leaders or where they usually hung out. If she was going to eliminate the threat of these gangs harming others, those details would certainly make her job easier.

But neither man supplied that information.

Typical of the Police Department, Carlson spoke in generalities. The police were working on the problem. It wasn't as bad as the media made it sound. Having a Neighborhood Watch would help.

She had a feeling that meant they didn't know how to stop the violence, that the gang leaders, like so many leaders in the criminal world, used subordinates to do their dirty work, leaving no evidence that they were connected. Nothing to incriminate them.

How she missed ADEC's research department. They were the ones who gathered the information, filtered out the extraneous, and zeroed in on the real behind-the-scenes culprits. Once the target was identified, her role, along with the other agents, was to get close to that person and quietly and efficiently remove the problem, leaving no evidence that ADEC or any law enforcement agency was involved.

As far as Mary knew, only once had the research department made a mistake.

Her luck the mark was hers.

By the end of the Neighborhood Watch meeting, Mary didn't feel she'd accomplished anything by coming. There'd been talk about drugs, robberies, gangs, and abandoned houses, but nothing that gave her what she wanted.

As people rose from their seats, some going up front to talk to Officer Carlson and Ella, others gathering in groups to talk to each other, and some leaving, Mary once again considered leaving and walking home by herself. She changed her mind when Fred Strong took a firm hold of her wrist and said, 'I know you came with Ella, but let me give you a ride home. It would give us a chance to get to know each other better.'

'I can't,' she lied, not liking the way he was possessively holding onto her arm. She was beginning to suspect his idea of getting to 'know each other better' might involve more than talk. 'I promised Ella I'd help her finish up here.'

Fred glanced around the room. 'She doesn't need your help. Come on, let's go.'

She didn't react until his fingers tightened around her wrist, and he took a step forward, pulling her toward the door. He didn't react until she stepped back and twisted her wrist down and toward her body, freeing her wrist from his grasp. He stopped and faced her, his expression going from surprise to a frown.

Mary knew her own expression was rapidly changing. Someone had put an arm around her shoulders, stopping her escape.

CHAPTER TWENTY-ONE

'WANT TO HELP me put up these chairs?' Jack asked, smiling at the shocked look Mary Harrington gave him the moment he stopped her backward motion.

'Yes.… Of course,' she said, after a slight hesitation. Then she smiled at the man who had been holding her wrist. 'Thanks for the offer, Fred, but my mama taught me you always go home with the one that brung you.'

'I was just …'

The man didn't finish his excuse, and Jack said nothing. Silence, he'd learned, was often more effective than words.

'I'll … I'll call you …' Fred said, looking at Mary as he took a step back. 'Sometime.'

She also didn't respond, and Jack had a feeling if Fred did call, she either wouldn't answer the phone or would tell the guy to get lost. He also had a feeling, considering how rigid her shoulders felt under his arm, that she'd also like him to get lost. He lowered his arm.

'Thank you,' she said, keeping her gaze on the other man's retreating figure.

'You're welcome. That was a nice escape.'

She glanced up at him, then away, her expression guarded.

He grinned. 'If these people want protection, they should hire you to patrol the streets.'

'Is there something you wanted, Detective?' she asked, half-turning toward him.

'Just to say hello.' He chuckled. 'I take it you don't like being pushed around.'

'It's not one of my strong suits.'

'And I'm not a detective,' he said. 'Just a sergeant.'

110

She gave a nod. 'I'll remember that, Sergeant Rossini.'

'A Neighborhood Watch only works if people report trouble. Pretending it didn't happen, even if you do best your attackers, doesn't put the criminals behind bars.'

'After tonight, I'm sure you'll be getting calls if anyone in this neighborhood sees trouble.'

'You know what I mean.'

She gave him a sweet, grandmotherly smile. 'In fact, I would like to report that my granddaughter and I also saw that dark-colored sedan. According to my granddaughter, it went by the house several times on Halloween night. I only saw it once that night, but I did see it again, a few days later.'

That wasn't the report he'd had in mind, and she knew it. 'This isn't funny, Mrs Harrington. I could arrest you for hindering a gang-related investigation. For all I know, you were on Archer Street that Thursday night trying to buy drugs from those two ... or maybe you were there to sell drugs.'

'Please,' she said, shaking her head. 'I was on that street because my car stopped running. I'm sorry I can't help you, but I've told you all I can.'

Told you all I can, she said. *Not all she knew.* Jack stared at her, wishing he knew how to get her to talk, how to persuade her to tell him the mystery of her past. She hadn't even blinked when he'd said he could arrest her. The woman was absolutely frustrating.

Finally he gave up. 'All right, you said you and your granddaughter saw a dark-colored car Halloween night. Can you be more specific?'

'Not really.' She actually sounded regretful. 'My granddaughter was giving out candy for me that night, and it was getting dark by the time she mentioned the car and I saw it. I'm not even sure if that car and the one I saw a few days later were the same. Both had four doors. The one I saw in the daytime was definitely black, and I'd say it was a fairly new model, but I couldn't tell you if it was a Ford or a Chevy or one of those foreign cars.'

'Did you see the license number?'

'No.' She shook her head and looked to her right, as if trying to remember what she did see that night. 'I should have called, especially now that I've heard that someone else in the neighbor-hood was worried about the car.'

He snorted. 'That makes two things you should have reported.'

'If you say so.' She extended her hand. 'It's been nice talking to you, Sergeant. And again, thanks for earlier. Now I really should see if Ella needs any help.'

He shook her hand, her grip firm. She hadn't truly needed his assistance earlier, and they both knew it. They both also knew there was more he wanted to know about her. 'Don't try to be a crime-fighter on your own, Mrs Harrington. I will arrest you if you interfere in police matters.'

'I'm sure you would.' She slid her hand free from his. 'Have a good night, Sergeant.'

Jack watched her walk to the front of the room. She stopped and said something to Ella Williams, then something to Phil Carlson. He wondered what they were talking about, but that thought was interrupted by a young boy.

'Are you carrying a gun, mister?' the boy asked.

He looked to be around eight or nine: a redhead with freck-les. The woman standing close by also had red hair and freckles, and Jack assumed she was the boy's mother. She stepped closer, smiling. 'I'm sorry to bother you, but my son said he heard police officers always carry a gun, even when they're not in uniform.' She looked down at her child. 'He thinks he wants to be a policeman when he grows up.'

'Good for you, son. And yes, I am carrying a gun.' Jack unbut-toned his jacket and pulled the right side away from his belt, revealing his Glock. 'A policeman always has his gun with him when he's on duty. As you can see, I've been wearing this one so long it's worn a hole in the lining of my jacket. I either need to buy a new jacket or sew a patch there.'

The boy looked at the Glock, then at Jack's jacket. Finally he looked up at Jack. 'I think you should buy a new jacket.'

Jack laughed. 'Looks that bad?'

'It's pretty old, mister ... Officer ... Uh ...'

'Sergeant,' Jack supplied. 'And you're right. This jacket is old, so I'll take your advice under consideration.' As he again buttoned his jacket, he looked at the boy's mother. 'Which street do you live on?'

'Oak. Why?'

'We're still following up on that incident on Archer Street. Have you noticed any gang activity on your street?'

She shrugged. 'Not exactly gang activity, but there have been some cars that go by our house that worry me. These are old cars, with real loud music playing. And the kids driving them have tattoos on their arms and make obscene gestures if I'm outside. I've stopped letting Kenny play out front.'

'Call us the next time you see one of those cars.'

'I will,' she said, and took her son's hand. 'Come on, Kenny. Time for us to go home.'

It was time for him to go home, too, Jack decided.

Ella talked constantly during the short drive from the school back to Mary's house. 'Did you see how many people showed up?' she said. 'Way more than I expected. I think Officer Carlson was surprised.'

So was I, Mary thought.

'And he gave us some really good information. I mean, we should, shouldn't we, be letting the police know if strange cars are in the neighborhood? Did you know they found drugs in a car they stopped just last week? Or maybe it was two weeks ago. Anyway, he said they figured it was a drug run to one of the gangs here in Rivershore.'

Mary perked up. 'Did he say which gang?'

'Not exactly, but I got the feeling it was one of those Mexican gangs. I keep telling you, things aren't the same as they were when we first moved into this neighborhood. Remember how we let our boys play outside until dark? We didn't worry about gangs back then, or drugs.'

Mary remembered. Robby had played with Ella's son, had been best friends with him until Robby went away to college and Ella's boy joined the army, never to come back alive. She also knew, now, that back then they should have worried about gangs, that according to Robby gangs did exist, and not everything was as sweet and peaceful as Ella remembered.

'Officer Carlson did say they thought those two boys that were beat up on Archer Street were part of a gang. He said they really didn't have a problem with the Mexicans until some guy got out of prison and moved here. I told him I thought they should make him leave, but he said they didn't have enough evidence against him to do that, and that's why what I'm doing – what we're doing – is good.'

'What *you're* doing,' Mary said. 'This has been your idea from the start.'

'But you're helping.' Ella pulled up in front of Mary's house. 'Has Robby been working on your garage door?'

'My garage door?' Mary turned in her seat to get a better look at her garage. The door, instead of being flush with the apron, was now up at least two feet.

For a second, Mary stared at her garage, her mind racing. Robby hadn't said anything about coming over and working on the garage door. In fact, if she remembered correctly, when she'd told him she was going to a meeting tonight, he'd mentioned he also would be at one. But why was the garage door open?

She knew from past experience that once that door was up it was a chore to get back down. It couldn't be done from the outside, only from the inside. Even if you pushed it down and thought it latched, it would slowly creep back up to about the level it was at now. Robby knew that. He knew the only way to keep it down was to use the latch inside the garage ... and that was why she never parked her car in the garage, even now that there was room for it. If she did use the garage, after backing her car out, she would have to go back into the garage, close the garage from in there, and then go through her house and out the front door to get to her car.

Way too much work.

'How long has it been since you were able to park inside?' Ella asked, as if reading her mind.

'I don't even remember,' Mary answered, still staring at her garage. *Who*, she wondered, *tampered with the door?*

'Harry did like to collect things. I still think you should have put those old records on eBay. I'm sure you could have sold them.'

'Robby had a friend who collects them, and I didn't need the money.'

114

'Must be nice,' Ella said, but Mary wasn't really paying attention.

Did they get inside the house? She remembered locking the inside door to the garage after using the drill to put a hole in the end of her kubotan, but she didn't remember turning the deadbolt.

Her gaze switched to the front window. The drapes were drawn, but she could tell it was dark inside. *Did I leave a light on or not?* She usually did when she left at night, but did she this time?

Damn the memory. It wasn't what it used to be.

Only one way to find out, she decided, and looked back at Ella. 'Thanks for the ride.'

'I was going, I mean, of course I was going ... so I just thought, I mean, why should we both drive?'

'I appreciated it.' Mary opened her door and slid out. 'Drive carefully now,' she said and grinned.

Mary waited on the sidewalk as Ella continued down the street, past the next two houses, and then turned into her own driveway. Ella's garage door went up smoothly, and Ella's car slowly disappeared from view. As the door slid shut again, Mary glanced up and down the street. No black car. No traffic at all. Those neighbors who'd attended the meeting had either already returned home or gone elsewhere afterwards.

No one around to hear me cry for help.

Muscles tense and nerves on edge, she pulled her keys out of her purse, taking the kubotan she'd attached to the key chain in her hand. A dog barked somewhere in the distance, disturbing the stillness of the night, and a gust of wind cut through her pant legs, sending a shiver up her spine. She took in a deep breath and let it out slowly, trying to calm her mind and ready herself. She had two choices. Stay where she was and call the police or go inside and see if anyone was there.

If she called the police, they'd want to go inside her house, and before leaving for the meeting, she'd been looking through her box of weapons. She should have put it away before walking out the door, but time had slipped by faster than she'd realized, and she'd hurried to grab her purse and get outside when Ella honked.

She'd figured, with the doors and windows locked and the window coverings drawn, no one from the outside would see that box and its contents.

But if someone was inside ...

It was too late to worry about what someone inside might have seen, but she certainly didn't want the police noticing her weapons and asking questions.

That left one option. She alone would have to go inside and face her intruder – or intruders.

She unlocked her front door as quietly as she could and pushed it open. She didn't enter right away, simply stood on the threshold, looked, and listened. There were times when she wished she still owned a dog. They'd had three over the years they'd lived in the house, mutts rescued from the Humane Society. The last one had had to be put down the year before Harry died, and Mary had decided no more. Not at her age.

A dog might have given her an idea if someone was in the house, might have alerted her to a stranger's location. A dog might have deterred someone from entering.

But she didn't have a dog.

Mary cautiously stepped inside and snapped on a light. She left the door open behind her, and took a few more steps in so she could look into the living room and kitchen.

She saw nothing unusual.

No one.

Slowly she walked through each of the downstairs rooms, snapping on the lights as she went, looking behind doors, in closets, and under the bed. She locked the door that led down to the basement. If anyone was hiding down there, they'd have to use the egress window to get out. Only when she was certain there was no one hiding on the main floor did she go up the stairs to the second floor.

Kubotan in hand, ready to use, she tried to make a silent ascent, her legs heavy and reluctant. The third step from the top creaked, setting her heart racing. She paused. Listened.

All she heard was the thumping of her heart.

Again she took in a deep breath and slowly exhaled. And then again. Two more steps and she reached the landing.

She looked up and down the hallway, then slowly made her way to the nearest upstairs bedroom, the one usually reserved for guests.

She heard a car go by outside, but by the time she looked out the window, all she saw were tail lights. She waited for a while, looking out the window and wondering if the car would return. Listening for any unusual noises. Listening for the sound of breathing, the rustle of material, or the scrape of a shoe.

She heard nothing.

Leaving the guest bedroom, she checked Robby's old bedroom, looked in the closet, and under the bed. She wished her son still lived in this house. Wished her husband were still alive.

Reluctantly, she left Robby's room and moved on to the upstairs bathroom. Only when she was certain there was no one upstairs did she again descend to the main floor and close her front door, making sure it was locked and the chain was in place.

As far as she could tell, nothing had been taken. She would have to look closer to be sure, but her television, computer, and printer were still in their proper places, as well as her coffee maker and radio. She was heading for her bedroom to check her jewelry case when the telephone rang. She hurried to answer it, wondering if it might be Ella, if maybe her neighbor's house had also been broken into.

'Yes,' she said, far more breathless than she'd expected.

'Are you missing something?' a muffled voice asked.

'What?'

'I have it.'

'Who is this?' Mary asked, the muscles in her stomach tightening.

All she heard was the click of a phone being disconnected.

It was then she noticed her box of weapons had been moved. It no longer sat in front of her chair, but now resided at the end of the table, facing away from where she'd been when Ella honked her horn.

Muscles tensed, Mary walked over to the table and lifted the lid.

For a moment she thought everything was there, her array of throwing stars, the metal kubotan, and her two beautiful fighting fans. And then she realized one item was missing … the nunchuck.

CHAPTER TWENTY-TWO

'You're shittin' me.' Jack looked up from the report Wally had handed him. 'She was robbed last night? While we were at that meeting?'

'The house was broken into, at least the garage was. She said nothing was taken. This is the woman you've been investigating, isn't it? The one you said we might get a call about?'

'She's the one.' Jack could feel Wally's questioning gaze and looked up. 'She's all right?'

'She's fine. Both Jennifer and Steward said she's a very interesting person. Spry for her age. Alert and intelligent.'

'Did they feel she was holding anything back? Not telling them everything?'

Wally smiled. 'Jennifer said she was almost too calm. That most women who lived alone and had their house broken into would be all nervous and anxious. Mrs Harrington, according to Jennifer, didn't seem all that rattled, told them what she'd noticed when her neighbor dropped her off and what she did.'

'Which was?'

'Went inside and checked all the rooms.'

'She shouldn't have gone inside. She should have called us.'

'Correct, and both Jennifer and Stewart told her that. Jennifer wonders if she would have called at all if she hadn't been afraid to go down into the basement.' Wally chuckled. 'She'd locked the basement door. Told Stewart if anyone was down there when she arrived home, they either climbed out the window or were still there.'

'I take it no one was down there.'

'No one ... and the egress window was closed and locked from the inside. Same with the front and back doors of the house,' Wally said. 'The person who broke in evidently did so through the garage.'

'Any of the neighbors see anything?'

'I sent Carlson over this morning to question them, but I don't think he'll learn much. Mrs Harrington indicated that most of her neighbors were at the meeting last night.'

'And this intruder took nothing?' That didn't make sense, unless the break-in had some connection to the incident on Archer Street ... which he'd bet it did.

'Nothing according to her, and Jennifer said the usual booty was untouched – TV, computer, jewelry.'

'Guns?' Jack had never seen one in her house, and he hadn't found any record of a gun purchase, either by Mary Harrington or her late husband, but that didn't mean she didn't have one.

'There were none, according to her.'

'Any signs of drugs?'

'Stewart found some prescription drugs in the medicine cabinet, all made out to her late husband and out of date. As far as he could tell, the pills in the containers were what they were supposed to be. She said she didn't take anything except an occasional aspirin and some vitamins.'

'Quite the amazing lady.' Jack thought of his mother and the pills she took each morning for high blood pressure and arthritis. His mother-in-law had been worse, her day regulated by when she needed to take her pills, and the nurses at the retirement home were constantly giving his father-in-law pills.

Mary Smith Harrington, on the other hand, was a workout junkie. Strong, as he'd discovered. Quick, as demonstrated by her escape the night before from that one pesky gentleman. And a liar. Jack had no idea what was true or false about her.

'I might drop over and talk to her later today,' he said.

Wally grinned. 'I had a feeling you might. Meanwhile, how'd the meeting go last night? Phil said he was surprised by how many people showed up.'

'There was a nice crowd, mostly people who live on Maple and Oak, just a handful from Archer Street.'

'Doesn't surprise me,' Wally said and took back the report he'd given Jack to read. 'I'm going to talk to the village council. They've gotta do something about those empty houses on Archer. They're constantly being broken into, stuff taken. Maybe it's the same ones that broke into her house.' He waved Mary Harrington's file between them.

'Except nothing was taken from her house,' Jack reminded the chief.

'Talk to her,' Wally said and started for his office. 'See if that's really true.'

It was afternoon before Jack had a chance to drive over to Maple Street. He noticed two things as he neared Mary Harrington's house: her car wasn't parked in front of her garage, and a white Impala was parked two houses down from hers. Her garage door was closed, down flush with the driveway, which could mean her car was in the garage. On that assumption, he parked and walked up to her front door.

At the same time Jack pressed the doorbell, he also heard a car door open and close. A glance back told him a man had gotten out of the Impala and was walking toward Mary Harrington's house. Jack watched the man as he neared and noted several things. The guy walked with an air of self-assurance, looked to be in his fifties or sixties, and had a touch of gray in his brown hair. Although the temperature had to be in the mid-thirties, the man wasn't wearing an overcoat, and his suit looked tailor-made. Jack could also tell the guy was carrying. The gun barely made an impression beneath the black jacket, but years of experience had taught Jack the signs of a concealed weapon – the way a jacket hung and moved as it brushed over the holster.

Jack automatically moved his arm to his side, ready to reach for his weapon.

The man walking toward him smiled and moved his arms away from his sides in a passive gesture, but Jack didn't relax. 'Afternoon, Sergeant,' the man said as he neared. 'She's not home. At least she's not answering the door.'

'Have we met before?' Jack asked, wondering how the man knew his rank.

'Not that I'm aware of. I'm Agent Burrows. Department of Special Forces.' He stopped a comfortable distance away.

Jack watched as Burrows removed a folder from his inside pocket and flipped it open, showing a badge and ID card. He handed it to Jack, who took a moment to read the information.

The Presidential Seal looked official, the photo a decent picture of the man standing in front of him, and the name – David Jerome Burrows – followed by the word 'Agent'. Jack handed the folder back. 'And you know me because…?'

Again Burrows smiled. 'I looked you up, Sergeant. Jack Rossini, Criminal Investigator for the Rivershore Police Department. Age fifty-eight. Widower. Two sons, one working for the FBI. You shouldn't use your son to do your investigating, Sergeant.'

There'd been a hint of warning in that last statement. When his son said he'd be contacted, Jack hadn't expected it to be a personal meeting. 'I believe in being thorough,' he said, unwilling to make excuses for asking John's help.

'Has Mrs Harrington been involved in a crime?'

That was the rub. 'Not officially.'

'So this is personal?' Agent Burrows gave him a quizzical look. 'Isn't she a bit old for you?'

It took Jack a moment before he understood and laughed. 'It's nothing romantic.'

'Then what is it?'

Jack didn't like being questioned, didn't like feeling threatened. Although he hadn't seen Burrows move, the man seemed closer than before. Jack had to look up to see his face. 'I think she was attacked a couple weeks ago.'

'Is she all right?'

Jack heard the concern in Burrows' voice, saw it in his eyes. 'She's fine.' His turn to smile. 'I can't say the same for the two boys who attacked her.'

Burrows nodded. 'What did she say about the attack?'

'That's the problem, she denies she was attacked, says she wasn't there.'

'But you're sure she was.'

If he hadn't been before, he was now. Agent Burrows' presence was telling more than the agent probably intended. 'Who was she before she moved here?'

'No one you need to worry about.'

He wished that were true. 'The two boys that jumped her were part of a gang. I'm pretty sure they're looking for revenge. Her place was broken into last night.'

'And...?' Burrows frowned. 'What did she do?'

'She was at a meeting when the break-in occurred. She called us when she realized someone had been in the house.'

'Anything taken?'

'She said no.' But Jack knew she'd lied before. Why not this time, too? 'Is there something they could have taken that she wouldn't want the police to know about?'

'I have no idea,' Burrows said, again smiling.

The guy's smug attitude irked Jack 'I can't say I've ever heard of the Department of Special Forces.'

'We try to keep a low profile.'

'When she was younger, was Mrs Harrington a member?'

'No.'

That was all Burrows said. A flat 'no' that Jack interpreted to mean 'End of conversation'. But he wasn't ready to end it. 'I know she's had martial arts training. I couldn't find any record of her being in the military. FBI? CIA?'

'It's time you drop the investigation, Sergeant.'

'And if I don't?'

'Your actions could have consequences.'

'Is that a threat?' Jack had never responded well to threats.

Once again Burrows gave Jack a smug smile. If the man was going to say anything more, he didn't have a chance. The sound of a car caught their attention, and both Burrows and Jack looked up the street. Jack recognized the gray Chevy as the one parked on Archer Street the night before Halloween and registered to Harry Harrington, now deceased.

CHAPTER TWENTY-THREE

MARY SLOWED HER car as she neared her house. She recognized Sergeant Jack Rossini, but she wasn't quite sure about the other man standing by her front door. He looked vaguely familiar. *A memory from her past?* She knew they'd seen her, that Rossini must have recognized the car. For a brief moment she considered driving by, but just as quickly, she realized that wouldn't solve anything.

Besides, she was curious about the other man.

Where did she know him from?

Damn old age. The memory was definitely going. She hated it when she couldn't remember a word or a name. It was there, on the tip of her tongue, but not there. It would come to her later, sometimes hours later.

Absolutely frustrating.

She pulled onto her driveway and parked. She'd nailed the garage door shut last night, after the police left. If someone was going to break in through the garage, it wouldn't be as easy this time. Not with all the nails she'd used.

She left the groceries she'd purchased in the car. She wanted her hands free when she talked to the two men. Not that she thought Rossini would try anything, but something about the way the other man stood made her wary. He made her think of a leopard, poised to attack, his eyes riveted on her, slightly narrowed and piercing.

It came to her then ... who he was. David Burrows had been twenty-one when he joined ADEC. He was six years her junior, fresh out of college, smart, and ambitious. Even back then he'd narrowed his eyes the same way when concentrating. In his twenties, he'd been tall and lanky. He was still tall, but over the years his shoulders had broadened, and she noticed his suit didn't completely conceal the weight he'd gained around his middle. He'd also acquired crow's feet near his eyes, a set of worry lines near his mouth, and quite a bit of gray in his sideburns. Not that any of those changes made him less attractive than back when they worked together. What a pair they'd made. While she seduced the men, David's looks had captured the women's attention. She'd liked him back then, maybe too much, but they'd kept their relationship professional, and when she left the agency, she'd told him he'd go far. He'd said he hoped so.

'Is it really you?' she asked, looking at David as she neared the two men, but afraid to use his name in case he was using another.

'David Burrows in the flesh,' he said, giving her a wink before he looked over at Rossini. 'The sergeant here was telling me your house was broken into last night. How dreadful.'

'It was upsetting,' Mary said, not quite sure why either man was at her house. 'Sergeant Rossini, what brings you here? I thought I told those two officers everything they needed to know last night.'

'Just doing a little follow-up.' Rossini glanced at the man standing near him. 'Agent Burrows here has been filling me in on your past.'

Mary doubted that, and she saw the slight shake of David's head. The message was there. *Tread carefully.* 'It's been a long time since David and I have seen each other. A very long time.' She smiled and looked at David. 'You're an agent now?'

'With the Department of Special Forces.'

'We met when I was traveling in Europe,' she told Rossini, sticking to the story she'd been given when leaving the agency and hoping David hadn't said anything to the contrary. She looked at David. 'How did you know where I lived?'

'I saw your picture in an article about physical fitness. I was surprised. You were always one to avoid publicity.'

His message was subtle but there: she shouldn't have given the interview.

'That article was a mistake on my part,' she said, willing to admit her mistake.

'It's on the Internet now, you know.'

She hadn't known. 'Big mistake,' she repeated.

'I thought it was a good article,' Rossini said, watching her a bit too closely for her comfort.

She shrugged. 'As David said, I don't really like publicity.'

Rossini kept looking at her. 'So I've noticed.'

'The sergeant said you've been having some problems with a local gang.'

'He seems to think so.'

'Come on, now,' Rossini said. 'Are you going to tell me you don't think they broke into your place last night?'

He sounded irritated. She didn't care. 'I have no idea who broke into my house.' And that was the truth. 'Anyone could have. Ella advertised that meeting all over the neighborhood. I'm surprised other houses weren't broken into with all of us at the school.' It would seem logical. 'Were other houses broken into?'

'None that we're aware of.'

'Well, they didn't take anything, so maybe we all came home before they had a chance to do more than break into my place. Now, is there anything else?' She wanted Rossini gone so she could talk to David, see what he'd said to Rossini, and if that damn article had compromised her situation ... turned her into a termination.

Rossini looked at David, then at her. 'I suppose I could come back later.'

'Good. My friend and I have some catching-up to do.'

Again he looked at the two of them. 'I'll bet you do. I'll see you later, Mrs Harrington.'

She watched him go to his car. David said nothing, but she was aware of his presence, the way he was looking at her. Only after Rossini drove away did she face her former partner. 'Well, I won't say it's good to see you, not under the circumstances. Should I bother getting the groceries out of my car, or figure I'm not going to be around long enough to worry about anything spoiling?'

He smiled. 'It's good to see you, Pan. And I'll help you with those groceries.'

'I'm Mary, now,' she said as David walked with her back to her car. 'Mary Harrington. But, of course, you already know, don't you?' He would have seen her name in that article. 'It's not the article and picture that has him nosing around.' She handed him the heaviest of the two bags of food. 'It's because I was attacked by a couple of punks.'

'The sergeant said you came out the better in that confrontation, but won't admit it.'

'Came out the better?' She laughed and pushed the car door shut. 'I nearly had a heart attack. Had bruises and sore muscles for a week.' She led the way to her front door. 'I thought I was in decent physical shape. Well, let me tell you, I'm not. This getting old is the pits.'

He chuckled. 'You're telling me. I worked out with one of the younger agents last week and was stiff and sore for days. I've had a desk job for too long.'

'You're looking good.' She glanced his way before turning the key in the door. 'Damn good. You married?'

He shook his head. 'You know how it is in this job.'

'So is ADEC now called the Department of Special Forces?'

'It is this week. Today.' He followed her into the kitchen. 'The badge generally works, especially with these smaller police forces. Ever since 9/11 anything that sounds like national security works.'

'Congress still has no idea what the agency does?'

'Not so far, thank goodness.'

She picked up on his irritation and looked back at him. 'Not so far?'

'A couple of hotshot senators have decided to take a closer look at the budget. Gotta seem like they're trimming the deficit, you know. The assholes are questioning every expenditure. Asking questions about what we actually do.'

David had always had a negative opinion of politicians, so his attitude toward members of Congress didn't surprise her. 'You think they'll figure out ADEC isn't really worried about controlling the environment?'

He grunted. 'I told them the money is used to rid the environment of anything that will damage our way of life here in the United States. They don't need to know anything more.'

She sat her bag of groceries on the counter and turned to face him. 'And is that why you're here, David? To get rid of me before I damage the agency's way of life?'

'What do you think?'

She knew the answer. 'That you wouldn't tell me if you were. That if you are here to eliminate me, one of these days, maybe today, Sergeant Rossini will find me dead, and it will either appear that I died of natural causes or that I committed suicide. Or maybe it will look like that gang did it. No one will know who I was or what I did in the past. Mary Smith Harrington will be buried next to her husband. One more loose end tied up.'

'Rossini has been checking into your past, you know.'

'He's a nosy cop.'

'Someone else, too.'

'Someone else? Who?'

'Peter Dubois.'

126

'I don't know anyone by that name.'

'You killed his mother.'

'Oh.' She stared at him, remembering back in time. The boy coming in the back door, calling out, 'Mama.' The look on his face, seeing her with the gun in her hand, his mother on the floor. Bleeding. Dead.

In that instant, she'd raised the gun and pointed it at the boy, thoughts flying through her head. She could have shot him, made it look like Mendez killed both the mother and her son. But no one had told her there'd be a boy. Pandora Coye's assignment was to kill an international drug dealer's girlfriend using the dealer's own gun to commit the murder.

According to the file they gave her on the woman, her name was Isabella – Isabella da Bello – and she was not only Dario Mendez's girlfriend but also his partner. She was an Italian, in her mid-thirties, of medium height and build, with dark hair and brown eyes.

There was nothing in the file about children.

Maybe, if there'd been a decent picture of the woman, Pandora would have realized she'd been given the wrong address, was at the wrong house. But no, the only pictures she'd seen of Isabella da Bello were grainy, distant shots, and the woman who lived at the house Pandora entered fit Isabella's description. At least she sort of did.

Turned out Francine Dubois was French, not Italian, and Francine Dubois had a six-year-old son.

Kill the boy.

That day, almost forty-five years ago, those words had echoed in her head. She'd known she should kill the boy. Had to. If the boy lived, he would tell the police his mother wasn't murdered by Dario Mendez but by a woman. A woman the child could identify.

Kill the boy.

In his eyes, she'd seen the shock, the disbelief, and then the fear. Finger on the trigger, she'd fought an internal war. He was so young, was an innocent. Why didn't they tell her the woman had a son?

She knew that within the hour Dario Mendez would die in a car accident. That was David's assignment. The French police would probably find Mendez's car and his body in the ravine along the side of the road to his house after they found his girlfriend's body. They would assume the drug dealer shot his girlfriend, and then died on his way home. After all, the gun used to kill da Bello would be found in the car with his body. The police would write it off as fate, an evil man killed by his own recklessness.

At least that was how it was supposed to go.

But she'd never killed a child. Never.

Mary shook off the memory. 'This Peter Dubois,' she said. 'Is he still living in France?'

'His maternal grandparents adopted him. They brought him back to the United States and he grew up in Florida. From what we've discovered, he's worked at a series of dead-end jobs, was fired from several and quit others, but he's a whiz with computer stuff.'

She had a feeling she already knew the answer, but she asked anyway. 'Where is he now?'

'We don't know where for sure, but he's somewhere here in Michigan.'

CHAPTER TWENTY-FOUR

BACK AT THE police station, Jack ignored Allison when she said an Ella Williams had called twice and wanted to talk to Phil or him. He didn't go to his desk, didn't take off his windbreaker, and didn't pay attention to the blinking light on his phone. Without a word to anyone, he headed straight for the chief's closed door.

He rapped his fist against the wood harder than necessary, the tension in his body needing an outlet. All the way back to the station he'd strangled the steering wheel until his knuckles turned white. Over and over he'd cursed himself for letting the presence of a man – a complete stranger – intimidate him.

Not once in his twenty-four years with the Rivershore Police Department, or his ten years on the force in Chicago, had he actually felt his life was at risk simply by talking to another man. Even the day his partner was shot and killed, and he himself was dodging bullets, he hadn't felt the same sense of danger. Back then, the adrenaline had kept him going, had guided his reactions. Only after the shooter had been killed did Jack's legs start shaking and the realization of how close he'd come to being shot himself set in.

'Come in,' Wally called out from the other side of the door.

Jack stepped inside the office and closed the door behind him. For a moment he stood where he was, not quite sure what to say or do next. Then he headed for one of the two chairs in front of Wally's desk and sank down onto it.

'What happened?' Wally asked, frowning slightly as he studied Jack. 'You look ...' He paused, as though searching for the right word. 'Upset.'

'I am.' More than Jack liked to admit. 'I met someone today. A man. He identified himself as Agent David Burrows, of the Department of Special Forces. He ...' *How to explain?* 'I think he threatened me.'

'What did he say?'

Jack wasn't sure he could explain why he'd felt threatened. More than the words, it was the tone of Burrows' voice, his posture ... the look in his eyes. 'He told me to stop checking into Mary Harrington's background. Said if I didn't, my actions could have consequences.'

'Hmm.'

Jack could tell Wally didn't understand. 'It was more than what he said. He ...' Jack groped for a way to describe his fear. 'I had the feeling ...' His legs were shaking now, and he didn't like it. 'I had the feeling he wouldn't think twice about killing me.'

'Hey, come on now, Jack. You've met guys like that before.'

'Not like this one.' He shook his head and gave an embarrassed laugh. 'I don't know. Maybe I am making this guy into something more than he was. I just can't describe the look in this guy's eyes or how he made me feel.'

'But he's one of the good guys, right?' Wally said. 'An agent from the Department of...?'

'Department of Special Forces.'

'Can't say I've heard of that one.'

'I said the same thing. He said they keep a low profile, and the badge and credentials he showed me did look official. I asked if Mrs

Harrington had been a member of that organization when she was younger. He said no, but it was after that he told me to back off my investigation.'

'Do you think this Burrows guy had anything to do with breaking into her house last night?'

'No. I got the feeling he just arrived in Rivershore today.' Jack remembered one thing. 'He said the article about her that appeared in the *Gazette* was now on the Internet, and that seemed to bother her.'

'Well, you already wondered if she was in the Witness Protection Program, so that makes sense. Maybe this Department of Special Forces is part of the US Marshals Service. I'll look into it, see what I can find out. OK?' He looked Jack straight in the eyes. 'You going to be all right?'

'Yeah, sure.' Jack stood. He did feel better. 'Guess I just don't like people threatening me.'

'Well, no matter what agency he's from, he'd better not break any laws around here, or he'll be suffering the consequences. Right, Jack?'

'Right,' Jack agreed and left the chief's office, deciding he, too, would learn what he could about the Department of Special Forces.

'I shouldn't have let the boy live,' Mary said. 'But I just couldn't ...'

Burrows nodded and glanced at her coffee maker. 'Fix me a coffee?'

'Sure.' She turned on the machine and grabbed a mug from the cupboard. 'You take anything in it?'

'No, black as usual. And yes ...' He pointed at her bags of groceries. 'You'd better put anything perishable away.'

As the water in the machine heated, Mary grabbed the milk and eggs she'd purchased and placed them in the refrigerator. David continued talking. 'You shouldn't have had to decide between letting the boy live or die. Research screwed up, you didn't. Dario Mendez's girlfriend had no children.'

'I know, and if I'd realized there was a child, I never would have killed that woman. But by the time the boy came into the house, it was too late.'

'I'll be honest,' David said as she placed a package of pork chops in the freezer, 'for a while I thought you did it on purpose, pretended you'd been given the wrong address. After all, you'd told me more than once that you wanted out but didn't think they'd ever let you out alive.'

Mary faced him. 'I did not kill that woman on purpose.'

He raised a hand in defense. 'I know, I know. I've checked the records. It was clearly a clerical error, not yours.'

'You're in administration now?' She grabbed the package of chicken thighs she'd purchased. She'd been going to divide the thighs up, freeze some and keep two out for her dinner. She placed the entire package in the refrigerator.

'I'm now the director.'

'Really?' Again she faced him. 'What about Carl?'

'He died ten years ago.'

She should have known that, she guessed. Ten years ago Carl would have been in his late eighties. Nevertheless, hearing her friend and mentor was no longer around saddened her. 'I owe my life to him, you know,' she said. 'Both the life I had at ADEC and my life here in Rivershore. Carl was the one who recruited me, and the one who convinced them to release me and give me a new identity.'

'We all knew you were his favorite. And I'll be honest, not everyone in the agency agreed with his decision to give you a new identity, which is probably why he was so secretive about where you went and what name you were using.' David glanced out her kitchen window. 'So, have you been happy here?'

She didn't hesitate to answer. 'Yes.'

'Really?' The lift of his eyebrow expressed his disbelief.

She smiled and went back to the coffee machine. 'It's the truth,' she said, and placed a new single cup in its holder before pressing a button to start the process.

'I've driven around this town, Pan. It's Nowheresville. How could you switch from the glamour of running with the jet set to here?'

'How?' She leaned back against the counter as the coffee maker did its thing. 'It was a little difficult at first. For a time I did miss going to fancy restaurants, wearing beautiful clothes, and meeting exciting people. I even missed the adventure of luring a victim into my web. But then I'd remember that gut-wrenching fear of getting caught and the sickening feelings I had after eliminating the target. It got so I didn't like being a weapon of destruction.'

'We destroy those who destroy others.'

'Now, that's a good motto.' She handed him his coffee. 'Have you used that with those senators?'

He chuckled. 'Those pompous asses would have a fit if they discovered how we go about "controlling the environment."' Yet I've never heard one of our law-abiding politicians complain when an autocratic tyrant meets an unexpected death.'

'Speaking of which, I actually thought ADEC had been disbanded when Bin Laden wasn't eliminated after 9/11.'

David groaned and shook his head. 'I can't tell you how many times we could have taken that man out, how the CIA could have eliminated him, even before 9/11. Blame it on the President. He's the one who interfered. And blame it on all the secret pacts we have with Saudi Arabia, Pakistan, and half the Middle East. We had agents who could have infiltrated Osama's inner circle. We could have saved the lives of those people in the Twin Towers, but no. The President wouldn't give the order, and the man who took over Carl's place was a wimp.'

'Now he's no longer director, you are. So what happened to him?'

'Accidental death,' David said and smiled.

Mary understood

'And if those Navy Seals hadn't taken Bin Laden out when they did, he would have also had an accidental death. We were that close.' David held his thumb and forefinger a millimeter apart. 'But back to you. All these years, you've never used your training?'

'I've never had to ... until those punks tried to take my purse.' She put another mug under the spout and activated the machine for hot water. 'It was when the taller one started to get pushy. I don't know. I just sort of went into automatic mode.'

'That's what they trained us to do. So what do we do with that detective?'

'I was hoping he'd get tired of trying to find out about my past, especially if nothing else occurred to make him want to know more. And he might have, but those gang members seem to be looking for revenge, which keeps bringing him back to me.' She sat across from her long-ago partner, and wondered how he would eliminate her.

'You know,' she finally said, 'I understand doing that interview was a mistake, and that I'm now a liability to the agency. I appreciate that you came personally, didn't send someone I didn't know, and I've been thinking ... probably the best way to kill me would be to push me down the stairs.'

Burrows started to interrupt, but she stopped him. 'No, I'm serious, David. When Rossini first interviewed me about those two gang members, I told him I fell down the stairs, and that's how I ended up with bruises on my arm and leg. If you make it look like an accident, he'll think I was telling the truth, and he'll drop his investigation into my past. He ...'

'Pandora, stop,' Burrows ordered. 'I am not going to push you down the stairs. Now, that detective said your house was broken into but nothing was taken. Is that true?'

'That's what I told the police, but something was. I didn't realize it at first, but soon after I arrived home, I received a phone call. I didn't recognize the voice, but it was male. He gave no name, simply said, "Are you missing anything?" And then he added, "I have it," and hung up.'

'You're sure you didn't recognize the voice?'

'No, it was muffled.'

'So what did he take?'

'My nunchuck. The one with the dragon carving. I'd been practicing with it while waiting for my neighbor to pick me up for a meeting. I lost track of the time, so when I heard her honk, I simply put it back in the box, put the cover on, and left it here, where I always sit.' She pointed to the placemat in front of her. 'After that phone call, I realized the box had been moved, and the nunchuck was missing.'

David leaned back in his chair. 'Dubois has had martial arts training.'

'You think he's here, then? Here in Rivershore?'

'It's certainly a possibility. Are you still as good as you used to be with the nunchuck?'

Mary chuckled. 'Not hardly.' She pulled up the right pant leg of her black trousers and showed him her bruises. 'I've hit myself twice now. I need one of those foam nunchucks.'

He smiled. 'You were always so cocky, so sure of yourself with that weapon.'

'Well, I wouldn't want to have to defend myself with one now.' An event that would never occur, since she no longer possessed a nunchuck. 'Why do you think he took it? Just to scare me? To let me know he's here, in Rivershore?'

'Maybe.'

'If he goes to the police ... tells them about me ...'

David nodded. 'It would be bad for both you and the agency, especially if any of what you've done in the past got back to that congressional committee.'

'I should have killed him.' Her past had caught up with her. 'So what do we do?'

CHAPTER TWENTY-FIVE

JACK IGNORED THE blinking message light on his phone and decided he would call Ella Williams later. While it was fresh on his mind, he wanted to learn what he could about the Department of Special Forces. He started by going on the Internet.

He found sites for Special Forces in the armed services, and there was a Department of Special Operations, formed after World War II, but that had morphed into the CIA, and Jack knew Agent David Burrows' ID and badge weren't CIA. Some metropolitan police departments had departments of special forces. Again, that wasn't what Burrows' ID or badge had indicated.

After checking several sites, Jack logged off. Either the DSF didn't exist or its existence was highly classified. He considered calling his son, and asking him if he knew anything about a Department of Special Forces, then decided not to. He'd gotten John into enough trouble by asking him to investigate Mary Harrington's past. No sense in jeopardizing his son's job. And maybe the chief would come up with something. Meanwhile, the Rivershore Police Department had other cases he should be working on, including following up on the break-in at Mary Harrington's house.

While Jack had been looking for information on the Internet, Phil Carlson had returned to the station. He was now at his desk, typing at his computer, and Jack went over to see him. 'You talked to Mrs Harrington's neighbors?'

Phil stopped typing and looked away from the monitor as Jack took the chair next to his desk. 'Just writing up my report now.'

'Anyone see anything?'

'No. Seems most of them were at the meeting last night. Talking to them this morning did give me a chance to reinforce the sort of information we need when they call in, but no one could tell me anything today. Not one noticed any unusual activity before leaving for the meeting or after returning home.... That is, up until Jennifer and Stewart responded to Mrs Harrington's 911 call.'

'Do you think there actually was a break-in?' Jack was sure Mary Harrington had lied about her involvement with the two teenagers, and he considered her extremely bright, but the woman was seventy-four, and maybe she wasn't as calm and collected as he'd thought. Maybe simply attending a Neighborhood Watch meeting had made her so nervous she thought someone had broken into her house.

'I don't know,' Phil said. 'When I stopped at her place, her first comment was, since nothing was taken, there was no sense in us wasting our time with her. Only after I convinced her that we had to follow up on the case did she take me into her garage. Seems, when I arrived, she was in the process of nailing the garage door shut. So I looked around, and there were marks on the bottom of the door that might have indicated a crowbar or tire iron was recently used to pry it open. However, I also saw other, similar marks on the door, not just the one set, and she admitted that she herself had pried the door open a few times. She said she rarely parks her car in the garage because the door is so hard to open and close.'

'No automatic door opener?'

'Broken, according to her. She said her son is supposed to fix it.' Phil chuckled. 'She seemed a little put out that he hasn't.'

'So this person or persons pried open the garage door and walked into her house? No lock on the inside door to her house?'

'She said she remembered locking that door, but she couldn't remember if she turned the deadbolt. If she didn't, a credit card could have sprung the door's lock.'

'How about fingerprints?' There should be some on the door-knob or the door jamb. Hers, at least.

Phil shook his head. 'Stewart dusted for fingerprints on both the garage door and inside door and didn't find any. Not one. Not even hers. And ...' Phil lifted a finger to make a point. 'She refused to have her fingerprints taken.'

'Darn.' Jack had been hoping they would get her fingerprints. A fingerprint might have given him a connection to her past. 'She say why?'

'I guess she told Stewart there was no need for him to have her prints since it was obvious that the person who entered her house either wore gloves or wiped the areas he touched clean. Jennifer's report stated that once they assured Mrs Harrington there was no one in the house, she wasn't all that cooperative. Talking to her this morning, I felt the same way. I have a feeling she wouldn't have made that 911 call if she hadn't been afraid to go down into the basement.'

'So she does have a weakness.' He'd begun to wonder if Mary Harrington was some sort of wonder woman, capable of beating up gang members, and escaping from unwanted suitors.

'Well, keep me posted.' Jack pushed himself up from the chair, then paused. 'You ever hear of a Department of Special Forces?'

'You mean like Special Ops?'

'No, something like the FBI or CIA. Some kind of government bureaucracy.'

'Can't say I have. Why?'

'I met someone today who said he worked for the Department of Special Forces, but I can't find any record of such a department.'

Phil grinned. 'Maybe it's like the NSA. No Such Agency.'

'I'm beginning to think so.'

'Call for you, Jack,' Allison yelled from the reception area. 'It's that Williams woman again. I'm switching it to your line.'

The phone on his desk began ringing, and Jack hurried over to pick up the receiver. 'Sergeant Rossini,' he said and eased down onto his chair.

'There's a car,' a woman whispered. 'Parked across the street.'

'Speak up, Mrs Williams. I can barely hear you.'

'There's a car,' she said just slightly louder. 'A white car. And earlier there was another car, one of those SUVs. I think it was blue. A dark blue. Or maybe black.'

'Yes.' Jack was beginning to get the picture. 'Is there someone in the house with you, Mrs Williams? Someone who you don't want hearing what you're saying?'

'No.' She paused. 'Just my cats.'

'Then you can speak in a normal voice, Mrs Williams. You don't need to whisper.'

'Oh,' she said, her voice rising. 'I just thought ... that is ... when I saw ...'

Jack wasn't sure she would ever finish a sentence and decided to interrupt. 'About this white car. Is there something you wanted to tell me?'

'Well, yes. You told us to call if there was anything suspicious. Well, this car is. Suspicious, that is. I mean, a man got out of it some time ago and met up with a man driving the other car ... the blue one ... or maybe it was black. And then Mary came home ... Mrs Harrington, that is. Mary—'

'Yes, I know. I was the other man,' Jack said, again interrupting her.

'You were?' Ella Williams was silent for a long pause before she went on. 'So you know about the car ... cars?'

'Yes, one was my car. I drive an unmarked blue Durango.'

'Oh. So you know about the white car ... and the man.'

'I know a little,' he said, wishing he knew more. 'What can you tell me? Is the car still there?'

'Yes. He went inside with Mary ... with Mrs Harrington when the other man ... that is, when you ... when you left, and ...' Again she paused and whispered, 'he's still inside with her.'

'And are you worried about her safety?' Jack hadn't sensed a threat to Mrs Harrington. To himself, yes, but not to Mrs Harrington. But maybe Mrs Williams knew more.

'Cleopatra, get down off the counter.'

Ella Williams yelled the command, and Jack jerked the phone away from his ear.

'Just a minute,' Mrs Williams said, and he heard the clunk of her phone being dropped or set down. In the distance, he could hear her scolding what he finally realized was a cat. A full minute went by before she again spoke into the phone. 'Now, where were we?'

Jack tried a different approach. 'What do you know about this man who's in the house with Mrs Harrington?'

'Why, nothing. Nothing at all. That's why I called you.'

'So you're simply reporting the car and that a man you usually don't see in the neighborhood has gone into Mrs Harrington's house. Is that right?'

'You told us to call if we saw anything unusual,' she reminded him. 'And last night her house was broken into.'

'You drove her home, didn't you? Did you see anything unusual when you dropped her off?'

'The door to her garage was up a little.'

'And it wasn't when you picked her up earlier?'

'Of course not, why would she leave it up? I know there's not much in her garage, not anymore. There used to be. Oh my, her husband came home with the craziest things, and he never threw anything away. But Harry's gone now, and her son cleaned everything out. I mean, I think she has a few tools in there.... Gardening tools. Mary has the nicest flower gardens every summer. They're all dead now ... the flowers, I mean. What the frost didn't get the snow the other day got. Even my—'

'Mrs Williams,' Jack interrupted, afraid she would go on and on. 'Did you go into the house with Mrs Harrington last night? Did you see signs that her house had been broken into?'

'No. When I dropped her off, we noticed the garage door was up a little, and I asked her if she wanted me come inside with her. She said that wouldn't be necessary. She said she probably didn't latch the door down tight enough and that's why it was up. It was only later when I saw the police car that I realized there was a problem.'

'Thank you. You've been very helpful.'

'I ... Of course ... Do you want me to call when that man leaves her house?'

'No. No, that won't be necessary. But do make a note of it,' he told Mrs. Williams. 'Just in case we need to know.'

'I will. Just let me know when you ... Cleopatra, what did I say!'

Jack hung up before she totally blew out his eardrum.

CHAPTER TWENTY-SIX

THE CHILLY AIR and darkness outside Mary's kitchen window were in sharp contrast to the warmth and festive atmosphere inside. For hours, David and she had been sharing stories from their pasts. Now the aroma of honey-glazed chicken thighs baking in the oven, along with red potatoes, and fresh green beans cooking on the stove, filled the entire house. David had removed his suit coat and placed it on the empty chair next to him, but he hadn't taken off his shoulder holster or removed the Glock it held.

Sometime around four o'clock, their mugs of coffee and tea had been replaced with glasses of wine. 'It's five o'clock somewhere,' Mary had said as she poured a Syrah for David and a Chardonnay for herself.

By six o'clock, both of their glasses had been refilled twice, and Mary knew she needed to eat soon or she'd be flat on her face. 'Remember the winery in Tuscany,' she said with a giggle, 'when I had to hide in that vat of grapes?'

David nodded and chuckled. 'And came out with grape stains on your hands and feet.'

'And clothes,' she reminded him. 'I never could get that dress clean. Had to toss it.'

'I also remember you almost fell on your keister when you kicked the gun out of Mario Bertoloni's hand.'

'Oh, yes, Mario. What an ass he was.' She laughed at the

memory. 'What a giant. I doubt I could get my foot that high again.'

Wondering if she could, Mary stood and moved over to the counter. Holding onto the edge, she kicked up her leg, karate style. The top edge of her shoe actually reached shoulder height before her loafer went flying off her foot and crashed onto the table, knocking over her wine glass and the Chardonnay she hadn't finished.

'Oops.' She laughed and did a one-shoe hobble over to grab a towel from next to the sink. 'Glad it was my wine and not the red that spilled.'

David had already straightened her glass, and Mary quickly sopped up the liquid on the table and floor.

'You're still pretty limber,' he said and refilled her glass from the bottle of Chardonnay.

'For an old lady, you mean?' She tossed the towel back onto the counter and retrieved her loafer.

'I read the report on those two boys you wiped out. You haven't lost it.'

Eyebrows raised, she looked at him. 'How'd you see that report?'

'We have our ways. Remember?'

'And reading that report you knew it was me?'

'Your Sergeant Rossini started checking into your background right after that incident. It didn't take much to make the connection.'

'That night I was surprised by how much I did remember. It's been a long time.'

'That article in the paper said you exercise regularly.'

'Yes, but I haven't taken any martial arts classes other than tai chi, since—' The sound of a key in her front door stopped Mary. Only two people had keys to her house: Ella and her son, Robby.

She wasn't surprised when the front door opened and a male voice called out, 'Mother?'

'In the kitchen, dear,' she called back. 'Come on in. I have company.'

David stood and quickly slipped his jacket back on, covering his shoulder holster and gun. By the time Robby entered the kitchen, David was standing beside her. Mary was proud of her son and his financial success, but she smiled at the contrast between the two men. David dwarfed her son, both in size and presence.

When she'd been younger, she'd wondered what it would be like to have David's child. He'd been twenty-two and she'd been twenty-eight when the agency paired them as a team. David had been pure masculine virility, and her biological clock had started ticking. But working together they'd decided it would be safer to avoid any romantic entanglements. So she'd forced herself to think of him as the younger brother she'd never had, and she supposed he saw her as the older sister.

'Robby, I'd like you to meet David Burrows, a friend from a long, long time ago,' she said, amused by the stunned look on her son's face. 'David, this is my son, Robert Harrington.'

David nodded and extended his hand. 'Do you go by Robby or Robert?'

'Mom calls me Robby,' her son said, hesitating a moment before shaking David's hand. 'My wife calls me Robert. So you knew my mother when?'

'Back when I was traveling in Europe,' Mary said, hoping David would let her lead the conversation.

David nodded. 'She became like my big sister. Told me where the best eating places were, cheapest pensions, and helped me figure out currency exchanges.' He looked at her. 'That's easier now with so many countries using the euro.'

'Every so often our paths would cross,' she said, which was the truth. Even though they'd only worked a few assignments together, she'd helped with his training, and their paths had crossed other times.

'And what brings you to Rivershore?' Robby asked, the question loaded with curiosity.

'Your mother, of course.' David winked at her. 'I saw her picture in the paper a few weeks ago, and when business took me to Chicago, I knew I had to drive over here and say hello.'

'So you're not staying long.'

It was a statement, not a question. Or maybe it was an order. Mary frowned at her son. 'Robby, that's none of your business.'

'It's …' He glared at David, then looked at her. 'If Dad were alive …'

'He'd be sharing a glass of wine with David and me, but since he's not …' She wasn't about to make excuses to her son. 'Was there a reason you stopped by? Would you like a glass of wine? Dinner?'

Robby looked at the two glasses and two nearly empty bottles of wine on the table, then back at her. 'Are you drunk, Mother?'

'No.' Though she had a feeling her cheeks were flushed, and she wished she could sit down again.

'I stopped by,' Robby said, watching her closely, 'because I heard the police were here last night.'

'Oh.' She smiled, hoping she looked like someone who didn't care. 'How did you hear that?'

'Ella called me today. She said you were robbed.' He glanced into the living room where her TV sat in its usual spot. 'What did they get?'

'Nothing,' she said. 'Nothing at all. But they did come in through the garage door. You know the one you keep saying you're going to fix. The one that won't open using the remote and won't latch properly even when it's pushed down.'

If he got her message, he ignored it. 'But you're all right?'

'I'm fine. I nailed the garage door shut today.'

'OK, OK. I'll fix it this weekend.' He glanced at the stairway and up to where his bedroom used to be. 'You're sure they took nothing?'

'Nothing as far as I can tell.' Or as far as she was going to tell. 'The police think the person or persons who broke in probably fled when they heard people coming back from the meeting last night.'

Robby shook his head. 'You should have called me, Mom.'

'And what would you have done? Told me to call the police. Right?'

'Yes, but …' He sighed in frustration. 'I keep telling you, Mom, you shouldn't be living here alone. Who knows what could happen to you.'

The way he looked directly at David, Mary was sure her son was including David in the possibility of something bad happening to her. 'I'm fine,' she insisted. 'And I'm not moving into a nursing home.'

'Shoreside isn't a nursing home. If you moved there …'

'I know, I know,' she interrupted. 'I'd have all the comforts of home, I'd be closer to you and Clare, and when I do become feeble, everything would be in place for them to plop me into their nursing facility.'

'You make it sound like a death sentence.'

'Isn't it?' To her it certainly sounded like one. She'd visited residents at Shoreside. Seen the old ladies sitting around with their blank stares and drool dribbling down their chins. A person had no privacy there. They ate in a community dining room. The rooms were right next to each other, and the walls were so thin you could hear your neighbor's TV.

'I'm not moving, and that's that.' She looked toward her front door. 'If you're not staying for dinner, you'd better head home. You know how Clare doesn't like you coming home late.'

Her son's nostrils flared, and Mary knew she'd hit a nerve. As she'd intended. In a way, he was in his own prison.

Robby didn't move. Instead he turned to David. 'It's been nice meeting you. I assume you're driving back to Chicago tonight. You'll probably want to leave soon. Traffic can be a bear.'

Mary tried not to smile when David said, 'Oh, I'm not leaving. Not tonight, at least. Your mother and I have a lot of catching-up to do.'

'Lots of great memories to share,' she said, and motioned toward the front door. 'Always good to see you, Robby. Thanks for your concern, and say hi to Clare and Shannon.'

Her son didn't move, his gaze switching from David to her and then back to David. 'But…?' He let the word hang in the air until he finally gave a deep sigh. 'If you're sure.'

'I'm sure,' she said, though she wasn't sure of what.

'Then I'll see you this weekend … when I fix the garage door.' He started for the front door, then paused and looked back. 'Don't be surprised if Shannon shows up. She's still sure she can talk you into a trip to Europe. At least now she's talking about simply going in the summer.'

'She's always welcome, and she can talk all she'd like, but I don't think I want to go back to Europe.' She glanced at David and grinned. 'Some things simply shouldn't be repeated. Right, David?'

CHAPTER TWENTY-SEVEN

JACK WAS ON his third beer when Officer Jennifer Mendoza came into the Shores. She paused for a moment, then smiled and headed his way, taking the stool next to him at the bar. 'Coffee,' she ordered, then turned to Jack. 'I thought I'd find you here.'

What could he say? He was predictable, if nothing else.

'I have a cousin,' she went on, not waiting for a response. 'Actually a second cousin. His mother has been ill, so my mother and I stopped by their place this afternoon with a casserole for their dinner. Carlos is seventeen, a senior at Rivershore High. He's told me he wants to go into law enforcement or maybe be a lawyer, so he's always asking me questions about my job. Today it was the other way around. While my mother talked to his mother, Carlos took me out back.

'He said he was in the school john the other day and overheard some Latinos talking about teaching an old lady a lesson. He said they didn't mention any names, but one said he knew where she lived. Carlos also heard them complaining about that drug bust Stewart made a couple weeks ago. I guess they'd been planning on using that cocaine to pay for some guns they've ordered.'

The bit about the guns interested Jack. 'Did your cousin say when they're getting these guns?'

'No. I asked, but he didn't know. He said he'd keep his ears open.'

'I hope you told him not to be too obvious.' Jack liked the idea that her cousin was interested in a career in law enforcement, but he didn't want the boy putting his life in danger.

'I told him.' She nodded a thank-you when the barkeeper delivered her coffee. 'Carlos is smart. He knows when to keep his mouth shut.'

Jack waited until Jennifer had her first sip of coffee. Although it had been years ago, he still remembered working the graveyard shift. He'd lived on coffee back then.

He glanced down at his beer.

Now it seemed he lived on beer and Scotch. If he wasn't careful, he'd turn into an alki.

He pushed his glass away.

'Another one?' the bartender asked.

Jack shook his head and turned to Jennifer. 'Tell me about that B and E call you answered on Maple last night.'

'What do you want to know?'

'Anything seem suspicious to you?'

She smiled. 'Like why wasn't anything taken? Yeah, I wondered what was up, especially since there were no signs of forced entry, other than with the garage door. The old lady ... Mrs Harrington ... she wasn't even that upset, other than she wouldn't go down into the basement. She said she'd once had a bad experience in a basement, and the way she was acting, I believed her.'

'I understand she refused to be fingerprinted.'

'Yeah, that was weird, too, but we really couldn't force her to, especially since we didn't find any fingerprints on the doorknobs.'

'None at all?'

'Not one.' She cocked her head toward Jack. 'So what do you think? Is the woman loco? Did she pry that door up herself?'

If last night's incident had been the first time Jack had heard about Mary Harrington, he might have said yes, but over the weeks, he'd seen too many facets of the woman to consider her daft. 'You want my opinion?' he said. 'I think that woman is sharper than either of us. Something went down last night, something she's not telling us.'

Something he wanted to know.

Jack pushed himself off his bar stool, grabbed his change from the counter – leaving a tip for the bartender – and gave Jennifer's shoulder a pat. 'I understand you're going solo tonight. Take care, and thanks for letting me know what your cousin overheard. Let me know if you hear anything more.'

He knew he should go home, but home was an empty, lonely place. Once in his car, Jack drove toward the west side of town. Slowly he cruised down Archer Street, paying particular attention to the area where the two boys were injured. As far as Jack could tell, the abandoned houses were empty and all was calm in the occupied homes. Of course, one never knew what went on behind closed doors. There could be a domestic fight occurring in one, incest in another, a robbery being planned in yet another.

From Archer Street, he traveled along Oak Street. Here there were fewer houses for sale and none that looked abandoned. Two teenaged boys were on the sidewalk in front of one house, talking. They turned and waved as he passed. He blinked his headlights and drove on.

He saw the white Impala the moment he turned onto Maple Street, still parked in the same place. He'd bet Ella Williams was watching it, waiting for the driver to leave so she could report the departure time to the police.

So Agent David Burrows was still with Mary Harrington. Jack glanced at the clock on his dash. 9.05. Was the man going to spend the night?

That's none of your business, he told himself. If Mary Harrington wanted to spend the night with Burrows, why should it matter to him? She was certainly an attractive woman for her age, and Burrows was good-looking. Younger than her, Jack figured, but not all that much younger. The guy dressed well. Drove one of the more expensive rental cars.

And is scary as hell, he silently added, still confused by his gut reaction to the man.

It was the guy's eyes – the look he'd given Jack – along with the guy's body language. Agent David Burrows reminded Jack of a cobra, poised and ready to strike. Coiled energy. Danger.

Jack gave himself a shake.

'You're an idiot,' he said aloud as he drove closer to Mary Harrington's house. Burrows was no cobra, Mrs Harrington obviously knew him, and there was no reason to suspect the man was a killer.

He stopped pondering his reaction as a sporty red Ford Fusion zipped past him, going at least ten miles over the speed limit. Jack considered going after the car and giving the driver a speeding ticket, then changed his mind when he saw the right-turn blinker come on and the car pull onto the driveway next to Mary Harrington's parked car.

He pulled his own car over to the curb and watched as a willowy blonde got out of the Fusion and headed for Mary Harrington's front door.

And then there were three, Jack thought and headed for home.

By nine o'clock, dinner had been eaten and the dishes stacked in the dishwasher or washed. David had rolled up his shirtsleeves and dried. Cups of coffee had once again appeared, replacing the glasses of wine. Mary chose decaf. 'Otherwise I'll be up all night,' she told David. 'Caffeine does that to me.'

'I should go get a room at the motel,' David said, but he made no move to put on his jacket or get up to leave.

'Why spend money on a motel room?' she said. 'Stay here.'

'Are you suggesting something?' he asked, a slight lift to his eyebrows.

Mary wasn't sure what she was suggesting. Because of Harry's cancer and death, she hadn't had sex for years, wasn't sure she could still please a man like David. Maybe she was in good physical condition, but her hours in the gym hadn't stopped the pull of gravity and the signs of age. No more pert breasts, tight butt, or flat stomach. Her skin was wrinkled and marred with age spots. 'I don't know, I ...'

The sound of the doorbell cut off her reply. She frowned when she looked at the clock on the wall. 'Now what?' she asked, and headed for the front door.

Although it was dark out, her living-room drapes were open, and the moon provided enough light for her to see Shannon's red Fusion parked next to her car. She glanced back into the kitchen. David had rolled down his shirtsleeves and was slipping on his jacket. She chuckled. Either she went without company for weeks, or everyone showed up.

'And to what do I owe this late-night visit?' she asked as soon as she'd opened the front door.

Shannon stepped inside and glanced around. 'Is he still here?' she whispered.

'If you mean my friend David, yes, he's still here.'

Shannon grimaced. 'Dad sent me,' she said, still whispering.

'Come on in. Let me introduce you.' Mary walked away from her granddaughter, leaving her to close the door. David stood by the table, and Mary stopped by his side. 'David, I'd like you to meet my favorite granddaughter, Shannon Harrington. Shannon, this is a friend of mine from years ago. David Burrows.'

'Your only granddaughter,' Shannon said, coming into the kitchen. She extended her hand. 'Mr Burrows.'

'Call me David,' he said and engulfed her small hand in his. 'You remind me of your grandmother. I always thought she was one of the most beautiful women alive.'

Shannon looked at her, and Mary knew her granddaughter was trying to visualize her as a younger woman with blonde – not white – hair, and smooth, non-wrinkled skin.

He went on. 'She's still beautiful, and so are you.'

'Yeah, uh well.' Shannon pulled her hand free from his grasp. 'Thank you.'

'Is that your pin she's wearing?' David asked, pointing at the pin on Shannon's coat.

Mary nodded. 'I gave it to her for her birthday. I hope you don't mind.'

'No, of course not,' he said, but his frown indicated otherwise.

'This is the man who gave you the pin?'

Shannon looked at David, and then at Mary, and Mary could imagine the thoughts running through her granddaughter's head. 'We were …' She hesitated. 'Good friends.'

David chuckled. 'You've heard about Pandora and her box of evil. Your grandmother was the wicked one.'

'I was not,' Mary said, searching for something to say that would get them off the subject of Pandora before one of them said too much.

It was Shannon who changed the subject. 'Grandma,' she said, clearing her throat. 'Can we talk?'

'Sure.' Mary wondered what her son wanted her to say to Shannon that she hadn't already told the girl.

'Privately.' Shannon's gaze shifted to a door off the living room. 'Maybe in your bedroom. There's ah, there's … there's something I need to discuss with you.'

'If it's about that trip to Europe ...'

'No.... No, something else.' She took Mary's hand and gave a tug.

'I'll be right back,' Mary told David as she allowed her grand-daughter to lead her to her bedroom.

As soon as they were in the room, Shannon closed the door. 'Grandma, are you sleeping with him?'

Not yet, Mary wanted to say, wondering if David and she would have ended up in bed if Shannon hadn't arrived. Or if they still might. What she managed was, 'I don't think that's any of your business.'

'Dad said he was good-looking. My god, Grandma, he's boss.'

'Boss?'

'Studly. I mean, he's old, but he's ...' Shannon grinned. 'Studly.'

Mary laughed, but the description did fit the man. 'So does that mean you approve?'

'No.' Shannon shook her head. 'I mean ...' She blew out a breath. 'Jeez, you're my grandmother.'

'Meaning I shouldn't be having sex.'

'We shouldn't even be talking about it.'

Mary agreed. 'Shannon, David and I are friends. I think what we do ... or don't do, should be between us.'

'Dad's worried about you.'

'I know.' Mary remembered her son's reaction.

'He thinks this guy is after your money.'

'Now, that's funny.' Or maybe it wasn't. Mary hated to think her son was afraid she'd be foolish enough to be taken in by a man. 'Honey, David is not after my money. He saw that article about me and thought it would be nice to reconnect, especially since a confer-ence he's attending in Chicago put him closer to Rivershore.'

'So he hasn't asked for any money?' Shannon didn't look con-vinced. 'Hasn't told you about an investment that will make you lots of money?'

'No, all he's told me is someone else I knew years ago, someone I really don't want to see again, is looking for me.'

'Eww.' Shannon frowned. 'That sounds bad.'

'Hopefully, it won't be.' Mary put her hand on the doorknob.

'Now, if I'm not mistaken, you have school tomorrow. So you need to head home.'

'And leave you two alone. Right?' Shannon didn't move. 'Promise me, if he asks for money, don't give him any.'

'I promise,' Mary said, remembering how much money she'd earned during her years with the agency. Unless David had made some bad investments, he wouldn't need to ask anyone for money, now or ever.

'Well then, I guess ...'

Mary opened the bedroom door, and Shannon started for the living room. From her position behind her granddaughter, Mary could see David seated at the kitchen table, turning his coffee mug around in his hands. She also could hear a vehicle coming down the street, its muffler so loud it sounded like a jet engine.

Later she would wonder what made her clamp a hand on Shannon's shoulder, stopping her granddaughter from stepping into the living room.

'What?' Shannon started to ask as the sound of squealing tires turned into the scraping crunch of metal on metal.

Two blinding bright lights poured into the living room, then moved away, and Mary caught her first glimpse of the truck outside her house. It had changed its collision course, but was on her lawn. She saw an arm snake out of the passenger-side window and throw something. The glow of a flame came toward the front window, and Mary pushed Shannon to the floor.

She used her own body to shield her granddaughter as a thunk against her plate-glass window was followed by the sound of a bottle breaking, then an explosive bang.

For a second she didn't move, and then Mary pushed herself back on her haunches and stared at the window. Flames leapt out of the bushes that bordered the front of the house.

She could hear the truck as it roared off into the night, but she didn't have a chance to move as another set of lights lit up the living room.

'Stay down,' David yelled from the kitchen.

Mary obeyed, again covering Shannon as she heard another thunk, followed by another explosion.

'What's happening?' Shannon cried out as Mary moved off her granddaughter's back.

'We're being attacked,' she said and crawled over to the phone by her bed. Quickly she punched in 911.

CHAPTER TWENTY-EIGHT

LESS THAN AN hour after driving away from Mary Harrington's house, Jack was back, standing on her front lawn, looking at the scorched bushes in front of the house and the tire tracks on the grass. Fire trucks and police cruisers, their flashing lights illuminating the night sky, filled the street, while an acrid, smoky stench filled the air. Neighbors had come out of their houses wearing hastily thrown-on clothes and robes, some simply gawking at the scene, others talking amongst themselves. All would have to be interviewed.

The blonde he'd seen get out of the red Fusion stood by the back of her car, staring at the crumpled fender and broken tail light. Mary Harrington stood beside the girl, her arm around the girl's shoulders. The blonde was obviously shaken, her face ashen. Mary was talking to her, her words too softly spoken for Jack to hear over the noises surrounding him.

'Since you were asking me about the break-in last night,' Officer Mendoza told Jack, 'I figured you'd want to know about this. According to Agent Burrows,' Jennifer indicated the man Jack had met earlier that day, 'there were two vehicles. First a truck, then a car. They came one right after the other, a Molotov cocktail being thrown out of each.'

'He was in the house at the time?' Jack hoped Ella had continued her watch of the car parked across the street from her house. If she had, she might be a good witness.

'He said he was in the kitchen, and the two women – Mrs Harrington and her granddaughter, Shannon – were just coming out of the bedroom when the first vehicle hit the granddaughter's car, came across the lawn, and the first bottle was thrown against the living-room window.'

'Good thing the window didn't break.' They would have been looking at a lot more damage if either of the bottles had gotten inside. He assumed they'd been filled with gasoline, an oil-soaked rag used as a wick. Once that bottle broke and the gasoline was released, the explosion would have spread the fire over everything in its path, possibly including the two women.

'Agent Burrows said the same thing. You'll want to talk to him.' Mendoza led Jack over to the man.

'We meet again,' Burrows said, extending his hand.

Jack accepted the handshake, noting the man seemed quite calm concerning what had recently happened. 'You were inside when this occurred?'

'In the kitchen. I heard a really loud muffler and had just gotten up from the table to see what was making so much noise. For a moment I thought the truck was going to run right into the living-room, but as you can see,' he pointed at the tire tracks that led toward the house and then veered away and back to the street, 'they turned just before they reached the bushes.'

'Did you see what kind of truck it was?'

Burrows shook his head. 'As I told Officers Mendoza and VanDerwell, all I can tell you about the truck is it was dark colored. Maybe black, dark blue, or green. The car that followed, however, was a Buick. Older model. Probably early 90s. It was white.'

'See who threw the bottles?'

'Not out of the truck. That took me by surprise. But the car had at least three people in it, all male as far as I could tell, and the one who tossed the bottle had some sort of tattoo on the back of his hand and up his wrist.'

Not a lot to go on, but a good start.

'Truck was black,' Mendoza said. 'We found some paint chips on the ground near the Fusion.' She grinned. 'Black with some red now on its front fender, I'd guess.'

That would help narrow the investigation.

'Also, one of the neighbors said she recognized the driver of the car. If she's right, he belongs to Jose's gang.'

'Jose?' Burrows said.

'He's ...' Jennifer started, but Jack interrupted her.

'Officer Mendoza, I believe you're wanted over there,' he said, pointing to where Officer VanDerwell stood by the crime-scene tape that had been installed, talking to one of the onlookers.

She got his message, nodded to Burrows, and headed for her fellow officer, leaving Jack alone with Burrows. 'And this Jose is?' Burrows asked again.

Jack shook his head. 'We'll take care of this, Mr Burrows.'

'Agent Burrows,' the man corrected.

'For an agency that doesn't seem to exist.' He watched Burrows for his reaction. What he got was a smile.

'I take it you tried looking up the Department of Special Forces.'

'And found nothing.'

'We don't advertise, but if you want to call the President, I'm sure you'll get a confirmation of our existence.' His smile widened. 'And probably a visit from Secret Service.'

'So I'm simply supposed to take your word that there is such an agency?' Jack wasn't that gullible.

'Yes.' Burrows looked over at Mary Harrington. 'She needs protection.'

'Because?' Jack hoped Agent Burrows would tell him something about Mary Harrington's past, about her connection to this non-existent agency.

Burrows frowned. 'Because her house was broken into last night and tonight they're trying to burn it down. Isn't that a good enough reason?'

'What connection does she have with this Department of Special Forces?'

'No connection.'

Burrows said it firmly, and Jack almost believed him. Almost. 'What about in the past?'

'Sergeant,' Burrows ground out the word, 'I'd suggest you focus on the present. Although I've had no contact with this woman for years, I consider her a friend, and I don't want to see anything happen to her. She needs protection.'

'OK.' He got the message. The man was not going to reveal any-thing about Mary's past. 'We'll increase patrols by her house. I'm pretty sure she pissed off one of our local gangs. We'll pull those gang members in and check their vehicles. It shouldn't take us long to find the two that were used tonight.'

'And then what? Put a couple kids in jail? You need to eliminate their leader.'

'We're working on it.'

'I'm glad to hear that. And this leader's name is...?'

Jack would admit the man was persistent. 'Forget it, Burrows. You're out of your jurisdiction ... whatever that might be. And if you mess up the investigation we have going, big-shot agent or not, you'll end up in prison right alongside him.'

Burrows merely smiled.

'And,' Jack pointed at Burrows' jacket, where he knew the agent's gun was strapped, 'I'd better not find any bullets in any of the gang members that match your weapon.'

'Trust me, Sergeant, that would never happen.'

'And you'd better tell your girlfriend to come clean with us.'

As if she knew they were talking about her, Mary Harrington came toward them. 'David, I'm going to drive Shannon home,' she said as she neared. 'And as long as this is a crime scene, I'm going to spend the night at my son's.' She held up a reusable shopping bag. 'Officer Mendoza let me go inside and get a few things. Will you be around tomorrow?'

Burrows nodded. 'I'll be around.'

Mary Harrington switched her attention to Jack. 'How long before I can reclaim my house?'

'Maybe you should stay somewhere else for a few days,' he suggested. 'Until we catch the people who did this.'

'No.' The set of her chin matched the firmness of her response. 'I'm not letting them scare me out of my home. How long do you expect this to take?' She indicated the scene in front of them.

'I don't know for sure.'

'Do you think I can come back tomorrow afternoon?'

'I suppose.' As far as Jack could tell, the evidence they needed was outside of her house, not inside.

'Good.' Again she looked at Agent Burrows. 'Stop by tomorrow afternoon.'

'Are you coming, Grandma?' the blonde called from the driveway.

'Coming.' Mary Harrington jiggled the set of keys she held. 'We're leaving her car here, taking mine. You won't need to take hers anywhere, will you, Sergeant? We'll want to get the insurance adjuster to look at it as soon as possible.'

'It will stay here,' Jack said, noticing Agent Burrows' smile as the man reached out and caught a blackened piece of wood dangling from Mrs. Harrington's key ring.

'This the kubotan you made?' Burrows asked.

'It is. I thought it might be handy to have around.'

Burrows nodded and released the wood. 'Take care of yourself, Pan. I'll see you tomorrow.'

Pan? Or did he say Pam? Jack smiled. *Like in Pamela?*

He had a clue.

CHAPTER TWENTY-NINE

SHANNON DIDN'T STOP talking during the drive from Mary's house to Robby's and Clare's, and Mary didn't try to stop her. Listening to her granddaughter, Mary remembered her reaction after her first assignment. The mixture of fear and adrenaline had her pacing the room as she told Carl exactly what had transpired. He'd calmly listened to her, just as she was with Shannon, until exhaustion finally took over.

The high in her case, however, lasted for days, maybe for years. Back then she'd loved the danger and excitement that went along with the job. It wasn't until she'd reached her late twenties that the tension began to wear on her, and she started questioning how long she wanted to work for ADEC ... or if she could ever quit. She'd come to a point in her life where taking someone else's life – justified or not – didn't seem right.

'Dad ... Mom ... You won't believe what happened,' Shannon yelled the moment she stepped into the four-bedroom three-bath ranch house that Robby had bought overlooking the eighteenth hole of the Rivershore Country Club's golf course.

Mary saw the confusion on her son's face when she entered the house behind her granddaughter, then his frown as he glanced out the front window and saw her old Chevy parked in the driveway, not Shannon's new Fusion. 'What happened to your car?' he demanded, his tone accusing.

'It's at Grandma's. A truck ran into it, and the police wanted it left there until they're finished with the crime scene.'

'Crime scene?' Clare repeated, coming down the hallway, her face covered with some sort of white cream. 'Oh ... Mother Harrington, you're here, too.'

Clare's gaze hopped from Shannon to Mary and then back to Shannon. 'You committed a crime?'

'Not Shannon,' Mary said, feeling she'd better speak up before either her son or daughter-in-law said something they'd regret. 'Her car was parked in my driveway when some teenagers drove across my lawn and hit the Fusion's rear bumper.'

'And threw a bomb at Grandma's house,' Shannon added. 'Two bombs. And Grandma was so cool. She didn't get all panicky at all. Just pulled me down on the floor and covered me with her body, and then we got back in the bedroom, and she called 911. And ...'

'Stop! Wait!' Robby looked directly at Mary. 'Someone threw a bomb into your house?'

'It wasn't exactly a bomb,' she said. 'Just one of those Molotov cocktails. And it didn't come into the house. They both bounced off the window and landed in the bushes out front.'

'A bomb,' Clare repeated, and simply stared at Mary.

'It was all so scary,' Shannon continued. 'The police came ... and the fire department. And David was so cool, he actually ...'

'David?' Robby said, once again frowning. 'You mean Mr Burrows?'

'Not Mr Burrows, Dad. Agent Burrows. Did you know he works for the government? I saw his badge. And he was carrying a gun. He pulled it out before he went outside.'

Mary was impressed by how much her granddaughter had observed and remembered. 'David works for some sort of defense agency,' she said, hoping that would satisfy her son's curiosity.

'And while he's visiting you, your house is bombed?' Robby didn't look satisfied.

'Purely a coincidence,' Mary said, but she was glad David had been there. At least he'd kept that police detective off her back.

'He put the fire out before the fire department even arrived,' Shannon said. 'And he kept all the neighbors off the lawn so the police could see the tire tracks, and … and …' She sighed, and Mary could tell the girl was running out of steam.

'You're probably exhausted,' she said, giving her granddaughter a hug. 'Why don't you go take a hot bath and get ready for bed. I'll explain everything. You've got school tomorrow. I don't have anything important to do.'

'You're going to see David tomorrow,' Shannon reminded her.

'Yes, I'm going to see David.' Mary looked at her son and daughter-in-law and knew she had a lot of explaining to do, and not just about the attack on her house. 'Clare, think I could have a cup of tea?'

Robby prepared the tea while Clare wiped the cream off of her face. Mary told him she'd wait in the living room, if he didn't mind, until his wife returned so she didn't have to repeat her story twice. She, too, could feel the after-effects of the adrenaline rush, and was glad to sink into the plush recliner that faced the couch. She was sipping her hot tea when Clare came back into the room and sat on the couch beside her husband.

'I gave Shannon a pill to help her sleep,' she said, looking at Mary. 'She'd better do well on her test tomorrow. If she doesn't keep her grades up, she's not going to get into a decent college.'

'I'm sorry she was at the house when all of this happened.' Mary kept her voice level and wondered if her daughter-in-law would realize Shannon wouldn't have been at the house if they hadn't sent her there.

'What is going on, Mom?' Robby asked. 'Why are people bombing your house? And who is this Burrows guy, really?'

Mary wondered how to explain without telling more than she wanted her son and daughter-in-law to know. 'He's a friend. A friend from before I moved to Michigan. Before I even met your father.' She looked at Clare. 'I don't know if Robby told you, but David saw that article about me, and since he was in Chicago on business, he decided to drop by and say hello.'

'He certainly stayed a long time,' Robby said. 'Was he going to spend the night?'

'I'd invited him to,' she said, knowing that was going to upset her son even more. 'But Shannon arrived before he had a chance to accept or decline.'

'Thank goodness,' Robby said, before he realized sending his daughter over there had also put her in jeopardy. 'I mean ... Mom, it's been years since you've seen this man. You know nothing about him. For all you know, he's the reason those cocktails, or whatever they're called, were thrown at your house.'

'Molotov cocktails,' she supplied. 'And I know David wasn't responsible for that. I'm just thankful he was there. As Shannon said, he had the fire out before the fire department even arrived. I've lost a few bushes and may have to have some siding replaced, but that's it.'

'So if it wasn't because of him, why did these people try to burn down your house?'

'I, ah ...' How to explain? 'I think there's a gang that's upset with me because I refused to give up my credit cards and keys to a couple of the gang's members.'

Clare frowned. 'Gang members? When did this happen?'

'Just before Halloween.' Mary hoped they wouldn't make the connection.

Robby did. 'Was it those boys who live a couple blocks from you?'

'I don't believe they live there,' she said. 'I think they were just hanging around one of the abandoned houses.'

'The ones who were beaten up so badly?'

She could see her son was remembering back and making the connection. She smiled. He was a smart kid. Always had been, which was why, she was sure, he was so successful as a financial advisor.

'Mom, those boys were severely injured that night. Do you

realize what might have happened to you? How lucky you were? What if the person who beat up those boys had been around then?'

She chuckled. Maybe he wasn't that smart. 'You're right,' she said. 'I was lucky. But, for some reason, they feel I'm responsible for what happened to them.'

'Oh, my.' Clare leaned slightly forward as she looked at Mary. 'One of the neighbors came and helped you, didn't he? And you've been protecting him.'

Let them think what they liked, she decided. 'I can't say anything more.'

'You've told the police. Right?' her son said. 'First your place is broken into, now this. The police understand what's going on, don't they?'

Mary thought of Detective Rossini and his questions. 'I believe they do,' she said, hoping the man didn't know more than he needed to. 'Now I have a question.'

'Yes, what?' Clare asked.

'May I spend the night here?'

CHAPTER THIRTY

THE NEXT MORNING, instead of going directly to the station, Jack drove through the areas of Rivershore where known gang members lived. Along the way, he stopped at a couple of repair shops and checked if anyone had brought in a black truck with damage to the right front fender. No one had. He told the shop owners to call him if anyone did bring one in, especially if there was red paint on the right front fender. Whether they would call or not was another matter.

Jack thought he might have lucked out when he saw a battered black truck parked near a double-wide. It had plenty of dents and rust, but nothing new and no signs of red paint on any of its fenders. One thing he discovered: there were a lot of black trucks in Rivershore.

He grabbed a hot coffee at McDonald's and was headed back to the station when he decided to take a side trip by Jose Rodriguez's place. Not that he expected to find the truck parked there. From what he'd discovered, Jose was too smart to let any of his gang members – especially any that might be connected to a crime – hang out at his place.

What Jack didn't expect was to see a white Impala parked just down the street from Jose's place, and although Jack hadn't memorized the license plate of so-called Agent David Burrows' rental car, he'd make a wager it was the same one.

Jack slowly drove by the Impala. As far as he could see, there was no one in the car. At the end of the block, he made a U-turn and cruised by again. Unless Burrows was lying down on the seat, the man wasn't in the car. He wasn't anywhere to be seen.

Three houses down, Jack parked his Durango.

What in the hell are you up to, Burrows?

Sitting in his car, Jack mentally rehashed exactly what had been said the night before. Burrows had wanted to know about Jose, but Jack had avoided giving the man any information and definitely hadn't told him Jose's last name. Even if Burrows had overheard Jose's last name, how did he know to come here?

And why?

To tell Jose to get his gang to lay off Mrs Harrington?

Now that wouldn't be a smart move.

Jack glanced at Jose's house. He'd love to get a peek inside. Maybe he, as a concerned officer of the law, should pay Jose a visit … just to make sure Burrows was all right.

At the same time he started to open his car door, his cellphone rang. He glanced at the ID, then took the call. 'Hey, Wally. I'll be in in a bit, I was just …'

'You need to come in right away,' Wally said. 'I think we've got a problem. I want you to check your computer.'

'My computer?'

'I have a feeling it's been compromised.'

'Compromised?' Jack almost laughed, thinking of his PC in a compromising position.

'Hacked.'

'Oh.' That was a different matter. 'Give me ten. I was just …' He glanced back at the Impala.

It was gone.

'Weird,' he said, feeling uneasy that he hadn't noticed Burrows leave Jose's house or even heard the car leave.

'It's more than weird,' Wally responded. 'All of our computers are showing the same message.'

'Which is...?'

'Beware of AntiSec.'

'AntiSec?' Jack could understand Wally's concern. They'd all seen the notices sent to law enforcement departments about the 'Anonymous'-affiliated group of hackers. These hackers were determined to embarrass and discredit police officers across the country, especially after arrests of Anonymous members.

'Why are they targeting us?' As far as Jack knew, none of their ongoing investigations involved the Internet or hackers. They certainly hadn't arrested anyone who claimed to be an Anonymous member.

'I have no idea,' Wally admitted.

'Did they deface our website?' That seemed to be a common occurrence with the group.

'The website seems to be all right,' Wally said, 'but I know you've got some pretty sensitive material on your computer.'

Generally that was the second phase of the hackers' attack. Within a short time after defacing the websites, the hackers would publish private emails and correspondence from confidential informants. Jack didn't like the idea that some of the notes he'd saved on his computer might be made public.

'Damn.' He tried to remember exactly what he had saved on his computer. 'Have you called a computer tech?'

'I called the Sheriff's Department right away, and talked to their tech. He said he'd come take a look, but it will probably be tomorrow at the earliest. He said to call if anything starts showing up on the Internet.' Wally snorted. 'That's like closing the barn door after the horse is out.'

'Maybe it was just a kid,' Jack said, trying to reassure his boss, though nowadays kids knew more about computers than Jack ever would.

'I even called the FBI,' Wally said, sounding deflated.

Jack knew that had taken a toll on Wally. It was a real put-down when the police had to call in the FBI, an admission that they had a case they couldn't solve. 'So what did they say?'

'They don't have anyone available right now either. Maybe in a couple of weeks,' Wally growled. 'In a couple of weeks the whole world may know what we had on our computers.'

'OK, calm down. I'm on my way in.' No reason to stay where he was. Burrows obviously didn't need rescuing, and without a search warrant, Jack knew he couldn't get into Jose's house. 'Five minutes, and I'll be there.'

CHAPTER THIRTY-ONE

MARY STAYED IN bed until she heard Shannon leave for school and Robby leave for work. She considered staying there until it was time to get dressed and return to her house. The idea of sitting around the breakfast table 'chatting' with her daughter-in-law had no appeal, especially since Clare had already indicated she wanted to know everything about this David Burrows.

The malicious part of her brain urged Mary to give Clare what she wanted. It would be fun to see her daughter-in-law's expression once she learned the truth about her mother-in-law's past. 'David?' she would say, pausing to take a sip of tea. 'Yes, I have known him for a while. I met him back in my twenties, when we were assigned to kill the dictator of a small country.'

Clare would frown, of course, not quite sure if she'd heard her correctly or if Mary was kidding. Clare would probably repeat the word *kill*.

'Assassinate,' Mary would say, making it sound like a correction. 'We assassinated him.'

From that point on, it would be interesting to see how Clare treated her. Maybe she would drop that condescending tone she'd been using lately, as if once a woman reached her mid-seventies she needed to be treated like a child. Or maybe she would be sure Mary was senile and making it all up.

Of course, if Mary did tell the truth and Clare did believe her, Mary would have to kill her.

And since she had no intention of doing that, she vanquished all malicious thoughts from her mind, pushed herself out of bed, and twenty minutes later, greeted her daughter-in-law with a smile and, 'Good morning, Clare.'

Clare Harrington slid her chair back from the breakfast table and stood, leaving her cup of coffee and the opened entertainment section of the newspaper. 'Oh, Mother Harrington, good morning. I was wondering if I should wake you. Did you get any sleep?'

'I slept quite well actually.'

'I don't see how.' Clare shook her head and moved over to the counter. 'Coffee? Tea?'

'Tea would be fine,' Mary said, and took the chair opposite her daughter-in-law's.

'And what would you like for breakfast?' Clare asked, placing a mug of water in the microwave to heat. 'I can fix you an egg. Or heat up one of the muffins I have in the freezer. Or...'

Mary stopped her. 'How about a slice of toast? I'm not really hungry.'

'Oh, of course not.' Clare gave her a consoling look. 'You must be so upset. What a terrible experience.' The microwave dinged, and Clare turned toward it and removed the mug of hot water. 'You're welcome to stay here as long as you like.'

'I figured I'd leave right after breakfast,' Mary said. 'I'm hoping the police have all the evidence they need, and I can get into my house. I want to see what kind of damage those kids did. Is Robby contacting the insurance company about Shannon's car?'

'He said he was going to.' Clare set the mug in front of Mary, along with a tray of assorted tea bags. 'But is it safe for you to go back to your house? What if those men come again?'

'I don't think they will,' she lied. 'They've made their point. Besides, I'm not going to let a bunch of teenagers scare me out of my house.'

'I hope you're not being foolish,' Clare said, stepping back to the counter. 'Shannon said she was terrified last night, that she thought that truck was going to drive straight into your house.'

'It was frightening seeing those headlights coming straight at the window,' Mary admitted, 'but we were still in my bedroom and wouldn't have been hit.'

'Thank goodness.' Clare gave an indulgent sigh. 'And what about that man who was visiting you? Robert said there was something about him he didn't like, something …' she seemed to grope for a word, 'something sinister.'

'Sinister?' Mary shook her head, smiled, and chose a black tea. She was going to need something strong this morning. 'Hmm, that's not how I would describe David.'

'You need to be careful, Mother. With Father Harrington gone, you're vulnerable. Probably lonely. There are people out there who would take advantage of a woman in your position … a widow with money. Robert said you helped this David fellow out years ago, when you were in Europe. Did he borrow money from you then? Ask for money last night?'

'No, David's never borrowed money from me in the past, and yesterday he just came by to say hi.' *And warn me*, she thought. *Little did he know I had more than a man from my past to worry about.*

'You need to sell that house, Mother Harrington. Move into …'

Mary stopped her from going on. 'Clare, I am not moving. Not for a while, yet.' She motioned toward the counter where she knew her daughter-in-law kept her bread. 'Do you have any whole-wheat?'

By ten o'clock that morning, Mary was on her way home, dreading what she was going to find. Cloudy gray skies didn't lighten her mood, and she groaned as she neared her house. The yellow crime-scene tape had been removed, but now, in the light of day, she could clearly see the tire tracks across her front lawn. The grass had been torn up in several places, and one of the barberry bushes near the property's edge had been crushed. Worst of all, the yews Harry had planted years ago under the living-room window were nothing more than black stumps, their needles devoured by the flames before David was able to put the fire out with the extinguisher she kept in the kitchen. The vinyl siding under the window looked as if it had melted, strips sagging downward, their edges charred. All of it would have to be replaced.

Mentally numb, Mary stared at her house until the chill of the wind permeated her windbreaker, and she began to shiver. Finally she went inside. First thing on her to-do list was call the insurance company.

Her telephone started ringing the moment she reached her kitchen. She wasn't surprised when she heard Ella's voice on the other end of the call. 'Are you all right?' her friend asked.

'Upset, but all right.' Mary made herself comfortable on the stool. The insurance agent would have to wait until after she'd talked to her neighbor.

'I was watching your house when they came down the street. I couldn't believe it when I saw that truck run up on your lawn. I called 911 right away.'

'I'm glad you did.' The fire department's quick arrival had eliminated any chance of the fire smoldering under the siding and flaring up later.

'Do the police have any leads?'

'I haven't talked to them since last night.'

'I told them all I knew,' Ella said, sounding proud that she had witnessed the event. 'I described the truck and the car, told them how many occupants I saw in each, I even gave them the exact time, just like Officer Carlson told us we should.'

'I'm glad you were watching.' Mary wondered how long Ella had been at her window, watching what went on across the street. Probably from the time David arrived. Her friend had been paranoid enough before the Neighborhood Watch meeting.

'It's a shame they ran into Shannon's car. Didn't she get that just last summer?'

Mary was sure Ella knew exactly when Robby had bought the car so Shannon could take a summer job in South Haven, but Mary told her again. 'He gave it to her in June.'

'I thought so. What are you going to do about the front of your house?'

'As soon as we finish talking I'm going to call my insurance company.'

'Oh, well then, I'll let you go. Oh, my, that white car is back. It just parked in front of your house. I think … Yes, that man from last night, the one who went into your house … he's back.'

So she wasn't the only one who didn't wait until afternoon to return.

'You didn't tell me you had a boyfriend,' Ella said, almost whispering. 'He's very good-looking.'

'He's not a boyfriend,' Mary insisted. 'Just, ah …' She wasn't quite sure how to describe her relationship with David. 'Listen, I'll talk to you later.'

Mary hung up the phone and made it to her front door just as David was about to ring the doorbell. He looked refreshed and debonair, his austere black suit of the day before replaced by tan slacks, a black turtleneck, and a tan, knee-length wool overcoat. His polished presence made her wish she'd put on more than an old pair of gray slacks and an off-white cable-knit sweater.

'Good morning,' she said, glad she'd at least applied some makeup before leaving her son's house.

David smiled. 'You saw me coming?'

'My neighbor did.'

'I wasn't sure if you'd be home yet, but I thought I'd drive by, just in case you were. Have any coffee made?'

'It will only take a second.' She headed for the kitchen. 'Did you have to stay here very long after Shannon and I left last night?'

'No, your detective buddy finally ran out of questions to ask. He's certainly curious about you.'

David settled down at her kitchen table as she turned on the coffee maker and grabbed a mug from the cupboard.

'He's been doing his best to figure out what you were doing before you moved here.'

'He told you that?' Mary asked, starting the machine.

'No.' David slipped out of his overcoat – exposing his shoulder holster and gun – stretched, and leaned back in his chair. 'But he's been looking for information about you for weeks now. His searches started after you attacked those boys.'

'I didn't attack them, they attacked me.'

'Well, you know what I mean. He even had his son looking for information about you. The son's an FBI agent, so we squelched that fast.'

She didn't ask how. She knew they had ways.

'Last night, after I left here, I had Samantha – she's our night-time IT gal – go into Rossini's computer again. Your sergeant had mentioned someone named Jose, and I wanted to find out how he was connected to those kids last night.'

'And did you find out?'

He nodded. 'Looks like the boys you tangled with are connected to an ex-con named Jose Rodriguez. According to Rossini's files, the guy has taken over a gang called the River Boyz and is using this area to transport and distribute some major drugs.'

Mary handed him his coffee, then sat down across from him. 'So why is this gang so determined to get back at me?'

'I'm not sure,' David said and paused to take a sip of the coffee before going on. 'But I paid Rodriguez a visit this morning.'

She hadn't expected that. 'And...?'

'Rossini was there, too. At least he was parked down the street from Rodriguez's place when I left.'

'So is Rodriguez dead now?'

'Not yet.' David smiled over his mug of coffee. 'I thought I'd leave that up to you.'

Mary stared at him, not quite sure what to say ... or what he was saying to her. 'How are you leaving it up to me?' she finally managed.

'I told him you were going to take him down, that those two you tangled with were just the start.'

Slowly she understood. 'So this is how you're getting rid of me.' He'd said he wouldn't push her down the stairs. He hadn't said she wouldn't die.

'It's up to you. You take him out and the gang will fall apart. Do nothing and the next attack may succeed.'

She knew he was right, but she shook her head. 'Even if I wanted to kill the man – which I don't – how could I? With one phone call you know who the gang's leader is and where he lives. I tried to get that information last week and hit a wall. Mary Smith Harrington doesn't have the same resources as Pandora Coye had, and the reality is, I'm an old lady. I lucked out the other night.'

'There is one other alternative.'

'What's that?'

'I have to get back to Washington. Those nosy senators subpoenaed me. I'm scheduled to appear before the committee next week, so come with me, Pan. Come back to work for us. I'd like you to train some of our new recruits.'

'Come back?' She stared at him.

For forty-four years, she'd been Mary, a woman who lived a quiet life, didn't get involved in causes or politics, was a good wife and mother, and carried spiders outside so she didn't have to kill them. Did she want to be Pandora again? Did she want to teach others how to kill and not care?

Slowly, she shook her head. 'No.'

'Why not? Your husband's dead, your son is all grown up and capable of taking care of himself, and your granddaughter seems to be fine. Who needs you here?'

A good question, she guessed, but not one that mattered. Whether her family needed her or not, she needed them. Again she shook her head. 'I'm not going with you.'

'Don't forget that Dubois kid is still around, Pan. I don't know exactly where he is, but Samantha tracked his computer to this area. As far as she can tell, he's about fifteen miles north of Rivershore and ten miles or more southwest of some town called Allegan.'

Mary knew approximately where that might be. 'Sounds like he's near the Allegan State Game Area.'

'They have wireless at the park?'

'No, I don't think so, but there are homes and farms in that area. Lots of them.'

David nodded. 'Then my guess is he's staying in one of those homes or farms. Which means he's probably just biding his time before he comes here.'

That made two men – or more – who wanted her dead. Maybe she wasn't going to have a choice. Maybe she should go with David, get out of town.

He seemed to sense her indecision. 'I can wait until you pack a bag,' he said. 'You wouldn't need to take a lot. Just some memorabilia. Everything else you can buy once you're in D.C.'

She thought about it, thought about all of the memories she'd be leaving behind, about never seeing her son or granddaughter again. Again she shook her head. 'I can't, David. I just can't.'

'So you're saying Pandora Coye is dead?'

The way he said 'dead' bothered Mary, but she simply nodded.

'Then I guess it's time for me to head out of here.' He put his mug down and stood. She watched him slip his overcoat back on, watched his eyes for any signs of emotion, and thought maybe she saw sadness. Or maybe not.

Mary walked with him to the front door. There he paused and touched the side of her face with the tips of his fingers. 'I loved working with you, Pan. You know that, don't you? I think we were fools. We should have had an affair.'

'Goodbye, David,' she said, knowing an affair would have meant nothing to him, that back then, just as now, he would have ultimately left her.

CHAPTER THIRTY-TWO

AT THE POLICE station, Wally and Phil were waiting for Jack's arrival. They followed him to his desk, and waited for him to remove his overcoat and sit down. The first thing he noticed was his screensaver was showing. 'We tried to log in,' Wally said. 'But I forgot where I put the list with everyone's passwords.'

'Do you think someone stole it?' Jack asked as he typed in his password.

'Well, I guess that's a possibility, but wait 'til you see what comes up.'

'If it comes up,' Phil said, edging behind Jack's chair so he could get a clear view of the monitor.

Jack didn't have to wait long to see what had Wally and Phil so upset. It only took a moment after he pressed the enter key for his monitor to turn completely black and for the sound of maniacal laughter to come out of his speakers. Almost immediately after that, the screen turned a bright red and the words 'Beware of AntiSec' appeared in black in the center.

'Yep, that's exactly what happened with ours,' Phil said and gave a deep sigh.

Jack stared at the screen. He knew how to use the computer to type up a report, gather information on the Internet, and access the few data banks his rank allowed, mainly AFIS and IAFIS. Anything beyond those tasks baffled him. It was his son, John, during one of his rare visits, who had urged Jack to use a password and helped him download an antivirus program, firewall, and anti-spyware program.

'So now what?' he asked, looking up at Phil and Wally.

'I hit the spacebar,' Phil said, 'and it went away.'

Jack hit the spacebar on his keyboard, and his screen went black again, but only for a second, and then the picture of his grand-daughter, taken when she was five, appeared, as it normally did, along with the usual icons on the side.

'I described what happened to the county's IT specialist,' Wally said. 'He suggested we keep our use of the computers to a minimum until he can look at them.'

'Oh, that's just great.' Jack stared at his granddaughter's picture. He wanted to go into his files and see if he still had his list of inform-ants, but he didn't dare.

'He asked if any of us had received any strange email messages recently,' Wally added. 'Something that didn't look quite right, but that we might have responded to. Someone asking a question, or an email that looked like the message had been sent to the wrong email address.'

Jack started to say he hadn't received anything like that, but then he remembered the message about the business in Rivershore, the one that didn't exist. 'I may have received something like that,' he said and told them about the request. 'I responded that I didn't know of such a business.'

'McDonald's Hardware?' Phil asked.

'No, King's Pharmacy,' Jack said.

Wally grunted an obscenity. 'I never even thought of that. Mine asked about Arby's Grocery.'

'And that gave them access?' Jack stared at his computer.

'I guess it's one way these hackers get in,' Wally said, 'least that's what the IT guy said. He also suggested we look into changing servers.'

'Meanwhile, are you saying everything we had on our computers will be spread across the Internet?' Jack didn't like the idea of his personal correspondence as well as his official documents being out there for anyone to see.

'I don't know,' Phil said. 'All these messages today have said "Beware of AntiSec." For all I know, this could be a test from Homeland Security, or maybe the FBI. They've been investigating this Anonymous group. And I don't think we should feel bad that this happened. My gosh, the Department of Defense and the CIA, along with other law enforcement agencies, have been hacked.'

Jack looked at Phil. He wasn't sure if the younger officer was naïve or simply hopeful, but as far as Jack was concerned, his computer had been raped. His personal information had been violated.

And, as irrational as it might be, Jack felt Agent David Burrows was somehow responsible.

Mary sat at the kitchen table staring at David's half-empty mug of coffee. *So you're saying Pandora is dead.* He'd said those words as calmly as if he'd been talking about a third person, but she'd understood the message. If those gang members wanted revenge, sooner or later they would get to her. If Pandora Coye was truly dead, it would be Mary Harrington – an elderly grandmother – facing the gang. Mary Harrington wouldn't have a chance.

And what about the boy who was now a man? If Peter Dubois *was* looking for her, when would he show up?

She doubted it would matter to him that people here in Rivershore knew her as Mary Harrington. Just as it had been with David, Peter Dubois would look at her and see Pandora Coye.

Did she really want to simply let him shoot her as she'd shot his mother so long ago?

Was she ready to die?

When Harry passed, she'd pondered that question. She'd been seventy-two then, and in her teens she'd considered that old. Really, really old. Back then she'd figured anyone who lived past fifty had had a good life and should be ready to die. She'd quickly changed her opinion about that when she reached fifty.

But for a while after Harry died, life without him hadn't seemed worth living. For several weeks she'd moped around the house, hating the silence, and wondering if she wanted to go on living without him. She wasn't quite sure when her attitude changed. Maybe when Shannon came by the house all excited because she'd passed her driving test and wanted to take her grandmother for a ride. Or maybe when she went back to exercising.

But now, would she have a choice?

Mary Harrington couldn't take out this Jose Rodriguez guy. She wasn't even sure Pandora Coye could. Oh, years ago it would have been an even match. Years ago she would have had the upper hand, but nowadays there was no way Mary or Pandora could protect herself against Jose's gang members. She might be in excellent physical condition for a woman her age, but that was the paradox. She was now seventy-four. Her joints grew stiff if she sat too long, and her body wasn't as supple as when she was in her teens and twenties. She wasn't as strong, couldn't move as fast, or hit as hard. She needed glasses to read and had tinnitus, which made hearing difficult. The agency had taught them that their survival in the field depended on relying on their senses, and more than once, when she'd been on an assignment, she'd put that lesson into practice. An almost indistinct sound, the slight movement of a hand, and she'd been ready to counter an attack.

Now...?

She got up from the table and opened the cupboard under her coffee maker. From the top shelf, she pulled out the box that held the weapons she'd brought up from the basement. She placed it on the table in front of her and slowly lifted the lid. The kubotan she'd made years before was on her keychain, and the nunchuck was gone, either already in the possession of Jose's gang or taken by the son of the woman she'd killed.

Mary checked the remaining weapons. The metal kubotan – the one the agency had given her – along with the throwing stars and fighting fans wouldn't be much help if she was attacked by more than one person. The night her car had stopped running, she'd been able to use the element of surprise to her advantage. That wouldn't happen again, and unlike fights in the movies, gangs didn't hesitate to attack *en masse*. None of this standing around as the hero fought off one attacker, then another, and then another.

If she hoped to survive, she would have to act before they knew what was happening.

Mary chuckled and picked up one of the throwing stars. Even when she'd been younger she'd had trouble throwing the stars. Since then the closest she'd come to any sort of practice was back when she used to play Frisbee with Robby.

As for a gun, Harry hadn't believed in them, and she'd never asked him to buy one. Living in Rivershore, neither Harry nor she had felt a need for a gun, and even when she'd been working for the agency, she'd rarely carried one. Her assignments had involved eliminating her targets in ways that made their deaths look like accidents or natural causes. Even on her last assignment, the gun wasn't hers. The whole idea had been to use Dario Mendez's gun so he would be blamed for his girlfriend's murder. The French police and media would have seen both of their deaths as casualties of trafficking in drugs. Too bad, so sad ... thin the herd.

And if the right woman had been murdered and the boy hadn't testified otherwise, the plan would have worked.

But of course, it didn't.

She dropped the throwing star back into the box and replaced the lid. Bringing her weapons upstairs had been a mistake. Forty-four years ago she'd put her days of killing people behind her. She wasn't going to start again. Not for David and not to save her life.

Box in hand, she hesitated at the top of the stairs to the basement, then straightened her shoulders and went on down. Being afraid of her own basement was ridiculous. There were no bogymen down there.

She had one foot on the bottom step of the steel stepstool, ready to climb up and return the box to its original spot, when she heard a crash upstairs. For a moment she stood motionless, trying to identify what had fallen and broken. And then she heard voices. Male voices. Loud and strident. Arrogant.

'Where are you, bitch?' one yelled.

'Hey, *Puta*, come get what you deserve,' another taunted.

'Bitch!' a third voice echoed.

Mary put down the box of weapons and turned toward the egress window. She could try to escape through that. Climb up on the bookcase under the window, crawl out, and run to the nearest neighbor. All she had to do was hope no one came down the stairs until she made her escape, that she could get the window open without making a sound, get herself …

A pair of jean-clad legs appeared on the other side of the egress window, ragged cuffs hanging over scuffed and worn boots. The knees bent, and outside the window she saw a tattoo covered arm and hand, then a face, scraggly black hair half-covering dark eyes. She knew the moment he saw her. A sneer curved his lips, and then the arm and face disappeared, leaving just the pant legs and boots, and she heard a muffled shout in Spanish.

'Fuck,' she mumbled. No way to escape now. No place to hide.

Her gaze shifted to the crawl space. Could she get in there before they found her? Would they think to look for her in there?

From above, she heard the shattering of glass and the crack of wood. She wasn't sure what they were breaking, but the thought of them handling her possessions, of ruining the things that held such precious memories, cleared her mind. Taking in a deep breath, she started up the stairs. The bastards had no right invading her house. Maybe she wouldn't be able to win this battle, but dammit all, she wasn't going to go down without a fight.

CHAPTER THIRTY-THREE

'HEY GUYS, DISPATCH is getting 911 calls,' Allison shouted from the front of the station. 'Something's going on over at that house that was fire-bombed last night.'

'Shit,' Jack said, pushing himself away from his computer as Wally and Phil stepped back. 'I told her they weren't going to let this drop.'

'We're all going,' Wally called back to Allison, and headed for his office.

'My cruiser's right out back,' Phil said, leading the way to that door. 'You can ride with me, Jack.'

It seemed the best idea, and Jack slid in on the passenger's side of the police car as Phil started the engine. Siren blaring, the drive to Maple Street took less than five minutes, and both he and Phil were out of the cruiser, Glocks drawn, before Jack had time to come up with a plan of action. Wally pulled his car up right behind them.

Two boys peeled out of the back door, and Phil took off after them, Wally trailing at a slower pace. Jack headed for the front door, ready to stop anyone who attempted to escape that way. When no one did, he tried the door. A turn of the knob, and he knew it was still locked.

Gun at the ready, he worked his way around the opposite side of the house, looking for the point of entry. A broken window by the back door answered that question. He could also see Phil and Wally had the two escapees down, spreadeagled on the ground. 'I'm going in,' he yelled to the two.

Broken glass crunched under his feet as Jack entered the back room. From somewhere near the middle of the house, he heard a high-pitched scream. Male? Female? He couldn't really tell and cautiously hurried that direction, fearing the worst.

Through an open door next to the stairway that led to the second floor, Jack could see the top of the stairs that led down to the basement. Another yell – deeper and more guttural – came from that area, then a crash and a thump.

'Mary?' Jack yelled.

'Yeah?' came back at him from the basement, the voice a little shaky.

'You OK?'

She didn't answer, and he hurried to the stairway.

He couldn't make out the sounds he heard, but by the time he'd gone far enough down the steps to see, Mary was setting a fallen stepstool back up. 'Hey,' he said and repeated his question. 'You OK?'

She looked up at him, smiled, and brushed her hands together. 'I've had better days.'

Behind her, scrunched up against a metal shelf, a cardboard box shoved next to him, was Jose Rodriguez himself. His right arm was at an odd angle and blood trickled down from a gash on his forehead. Although a knife on the floor had no signs of blood, Jack knew the crowbar by the stepstool could be lethal. 'Is he dead?'

'No, just unconscious. What about the others?'

'We've got them,' he said, and then heard Wally, from somewhere above him, shout, 'Stop where you are!'

Jack rushed back up the stairs. Wally had his gun pointed at a dark-skinned teenager who had started down the upstairs stairway. The boy gave a quick glance Jack's way, looked back at Wally, and then sunk down on the middle step and raised his arms up in defeat.

'The woman...?' Wally asked, never taking his gaze off the boy.

'Fine.' Jack laughed and walked up the steps to where the teenager sat. 'You guys picked on the wrong old lady.'

The kid frowned as Jack pulled him to his feet. 'But Jose, he say this the one.'

'Oh, she's the one, all right,' Jack said and cuffed the boy. 'She's just not a defenseless old lady. Your fearless leader is now going back to jail.' He jerked on the boy's arm, causing him to stumble down the stairs. 'But don't worry. So are you.'

'She took him out?' Wally said, the shake of his head expressing his disbelief.

'Anyone going to call an ambulance?' Mary asked, appearing at the top of the stairs. 'The guy down there is going to be in a lot of pain when he comes to.'

Jack stared at her. In his thirty-four years of police work, both in Chicago and on the Rivershore police force, he'd never seen a potential victim so calm after a break-in and attempted murder.

Mary had to admit, she felt damned proud of herself. Halfway up the stairs, she'd decided she needed a weapon. Although she would have preferred using her nunchuck, with it gone she'd decided on a more conventional weapon and went back for the crowbar hanging by the furnace.

Next trick was to conceal her intentions. Carl always said, 'Catch your target off guard, and you'll have the advantage.'

'Help,' she yelled, knowing that would bring the enemy to her.

Within seconds, a man started down the stairs.

By then she'd moved the stepstool closer to the bottom steps and positioned herself beside it. She had a feeling the man was surprised to find her looking up at him, smiling.

'Looking for me?' she said as sweetly as she could manage with her heart thudding like a jackhammer.

'*Puta*,' he growled, a dark scowl narrowing his almost-black eyes and drawing thick, bushy eyebrows together.

'*Puta*?' she repeated, hoping she looked confused. 'I don't understand.'

He paused, his frown deepening. His hesitation gave her time to assess her adversary. A gray hoodie covered all but a lock of his dark hair and created an oval frame around his face. His features were Hispanic, his skin swarthy. He wasn't very tall, but she had a feeling there was a lot of strength in his lean frame. The denims hugging his hips and legs looked fairly new and expensive, as did the leather boots on his feet. He looked older than the boys who had attacked her the night her car stopped running, but she doubted he'd reached his thirtieth birthday.

'Bitch,' he growled and held up a knife with a blade long enough to easily slash a tire or puncture a lung and heart.

'Now, son, what did I ever do to you?'

'I ain't your son.' His nostrils dilated as he slowly proceeded down the steps, his gaze locked on her face, and his movements reminding her of a cat on the prowl.

She edged closer to the stepstool, as if retreating in fear, all the while using the stool and her body to hide what she held in her right hand.

He smiled.

She leaned to the side, using the stool's top step for balance, and tilted her head up to watch him.

He reached the basement floor, his gaze focused on her face.

Mary held her breath. Move too soon and she would lose her advantage; too late and he would overpower her.

His eyes, along with the tightening of the muscles around his mouth, relayed his intentions. As he made a slashing lunge with the knife, aiming for her neck, she leaned her head and shoulders back, out of range, and rotated to the left. In one smooth motion, she swung the crowbar up and around in an arc in front of her.

His arm and her crowbar collided, opposing actions doubling the force. A keening sound came from deep within him, the knife flying out of his hand and falling onto the concrete with a clatter.

Mouth open, he staggered back, clutching his right arm with his left hand, until he bumped against the bookshelf under the egress window, jarring books and knick-knacks to the floor. For a moment he stared at her, a mixture of pain and anger giving his eyes a wild, unfocused look, then he gave another yell, this one deeper and more guttural. Again he lunged forward.

As she'd been taught so many years before, she pivoted out of range. He saw the stepstool too late to stop his forward momentum and hit it full-force. The stepstool went over, taking him with it, and throwing him into the metal shelving unit. His head hit an edge with a thud, and he dropped to the floor like a bag of dirt.

Mary heard her name called from somewhere up above and called back, somewhat surprised by how shaky her voice sounded. She started for the stairs, but then, from behind her, she heard a grunt.

She stopped where she was and turned to look back. Blood poured from a gash on her attacker's forehead, and his eyes had a dazed, crazed look. His lips contorted into a snarl as he struggled to his feet. She waited until he was standing before she moved.

Rather than retreat, she surged toward him. She used the side of an open hand to hit the pressure point at the side of his neck. He had no chance to react, and, although she would have liked it to be a killing blow, she held back, satisfied when his legs collapsed under him, and he slid back down the shelving unit to a seated position on the floor.

He would have toppled over, but she quickly shifted a fallen box of books under his side to prop him up. She then picked up the fallen stepstool and set it back on its legs. That was when Sergeant Rossini came into view.

CHAPTER THIRTY-FOUR

THE THREE MOBILE gang members were taken to the County Jail in Paw Paw. Phil volunteered to do the initial paperwork on them. Wally accompanied Jose Rodriguez in his ambulance ride to the hospital, and Jack stayed at the house. He kept Mary isolated in her bedroom while the county's Crime Scene Unit gathered evidence of the break-in. Other than a few general questions, he didn't ask her for a step-by-step description of what had happened. He wanted to leave that interview until everyone had left and just the two of them remained.

Once the house was cleared, he opened the bedroom door and told her to come on out. 'Want some tea?' he asked, leading the way to the kitchen and going directly to her coffee maker.

'Sure,' she said and sat down at the table.

'You were lucky,' he said, refilling the water reservoir. 'They knocked this over, but it didn't break.'

Mary said nothing, but as she absently rubbed the side of her right hand, she looked around her kitchen and into the living-room area. Jack knew she was taking in the damage the gang had done: the broken window, shattered glassware and dishes, emptied drawers, and knocked-over lamps.

As soon as the water heated, he prepared a mug of tea for her and a coffee for himself; then he sat opposite her. She still hadn't said anything, and her silence bothered him. For the first time since they'd met, she looked all of her seventy-four years.

'You OK?' he asked, wondering if she might be in shock and if he should take her to the hospital ... or call an ambulance.

'I guess so.'

'You want to talk about what happened here?'

That brought a small chuckle ... and a 'No.'

'Well, I do.' He didn't pull out a notebook. He wanted her to see this as a friendly conversation. 'Do you realize you just put a gang leader ... an ex-con and probable drug pusher ... in the hospital?'

'So that was Rodriguez?' She shook her head. 'When he came down those stairs, I had no idea who he was.'

'Being involved in a hit isn't his style. Normally he lets others do the dirty work for him, makes sure he isn't connected. I don't understand why, personally, he was after you.'

'My charming personality?'

She said it with a fake smile, which irritated Jack. 'Don't be coy, Mrs Harrington, or whatever your real name is. Something's going on that's bigger than a gang looking for revenge. Did you know your friend Burrows was at Rodriguez's house this morning?'

'That's what he told me.'

'So he was here? You talked to him this morning?'

She nodded. 'He came to say goodbye. He's flying back to Washington D.C.'

Jack hated to admit that was a relief. He still didn't under-stand why Burrows made him so nervous. 'Did he warn you that Rodriguez might come after you?'

'In a way.'

She was still being evasive, which irked Jack. 'Come on, Mary. Why did Rodriguez come here specifically for you?'

'Why?' She leaned back in her chair. 'Because that's the way David works. If you want someone dead, you make it look like someone else did it.'

Her calm accusation surprised Jack. 'Burrows wants you dead? But why?'

She gave a small laugh. 'I can't tell you, Detective, or he'll have to kill you, too.'

'He's not going to kill me.'

'I wouldn't be so sure about that.' Mary lifted her mug of tea, but before she took a sip, she added, 'We have our ways.'

Jack noticed the 'We.' He also heard the pride in her voice, and he wondered if she might be right. Hadn't he already sensed something very dangerous about David Burrows?

'How's he going to know you told me?'

'You'll put something in one of your reports, or you'll start doing some checking on the Internet, to see if what I told you was correct. He'll know.'

Her confidence explained a lot. 'He hacked into our computers, didn't he? That message we all found this morning, he did that, didn't he?'

'I don't know what message you mean, but yes, your computers have been hacked into. He needed to know what you'd discovered about me. He also found out about that gang from your computer.'

'And the box the crime-scene boys found on the floor down in your basement,' Jack said, 'the one with the martial arts weapons. That's yours, isn't it?'

For a moment he thought she would deny it, then she gave a slight shrug. 'I should have gotten rid of those weapons years ago. They certainly didn't help me today.'

'You said you'd never had any martial arts training.' He remembered that clearly.

'I said I hadn't taken any classes since moving to Rivershore. Actually, I never took any classes. It was simply part of my training.'

Training she hadn't forgotten, from what Jack could tell. 'Training for what?'

'For ways to kill people.' She closed her eyes and shook her head. 'I'm telling you too much.'

As far as he was concerned, she wasn't telling him enough. 'What people?'

'Back then?' She looked at him again and shrugged. 'Spies. Political leaders. People the government couldn't legitimately touch.'

'You worked for the CIA?'

'No. Even back then they had limits on what they could do.' She pushed her chair away from the table and stood. 'You know what, Sergeant? I'm hungry. All I've had today is a piece of toast. What about you? Hungry?'

She walked over to her refrigerator and opened it. Once again, her calm amazed him. 'I wasn't finished, Mrs Harrington.'

'I have some leftover chicken. Or I could fix an omelet.'

181

'Mrs Harrington, we need to talk.'

'OK.' She closed the refrigerator door and came back to the table, holding a chicken drumstick. 'What do you want to talk about?' She sat back down. 'What happened today? It's simple. Four guys – who evidently belong to a gang – broke into my house. I suppose they planned on robbing me. Their leader, this Jose Rodriguez, tripped going down the stairs, hit his head, and broke his arm. I was very lucky that the police arrived when they did.' She took a bite of chicken, chewed it for a moment, then asked, 'Why did you arrive when you did?'

'Your neighbor called 911.'

She smiled. 'Good for Ella. She called here right after the ambulance left. I told her I'd call her back as soon as I could.'

Mary looked over at the telephone, and Jack was afraid she'd get up and make that call before they were finished. 'You can call her after I leave,' he said, hoping she took that as an order.

To his surprise, she didn't argue, simply took another bite of chicken. He kept talking. 'We actually received several 911 calls. According to the dispatcher, the first one came from a man who hung up right after giving your address. She couldn't trace the number and wasn't sure if it was a prank or not ... but then the call from Mrs Williams came in.'

Mary frowned. 'I thought you could always trace 911 calls.'

'It could have been from one of those throwaway phones.'

'Maybe I'm wrong, then.' She put the drumstick down and smiled. 'Maybe he's not trying to kill me.'

'Rodriguez?'

'No, David.'

Knowing David hadn't totally thrown her to the wolves – or in this case, to Jose Rodriguez – made Mary feel better. Actually, it made sense. David didn't want her dead, he wanted her back in the agency. And what better way to convince her to return than to force her to use her training. If she'd killed Rodriguez, she wouldn't have been able to stay in Rivershore.

Too bad for David his plan didn't work. She hadn't killed Rodriguez, and so far only Rossini knew anything about her past.

And just a little at that. If she could keep him on her side, Mary Harrington had a future.

New energy in her step, she carried her empty tea mug to the sink and dumped the chicken drumstick in the garbage. 'David said you've been having trouble with this gang. You need to get a warrant, and check out Mr Rodriguez's place.'

'You're now dictating police business?'

He sounded a bit miffed. Not a good way to keep him on her side. She softened her suggestion. 'Didn't I hear Rodriguez was in jail and only released a couple years ago? Wouldn't he now be on parole?'

She could tell from his look that Rossini understood what she was saying; nevertheless, she added, 'Does this county have any drug-sniffing dogs?'

Rossini frowned. 'If Burrows planted drugs, we won't get a conviction.'

'I don't know if David planted any drugs, but he doesn't make mistakes. If you find drugs, you'll get your conviction.'

Once Rodriguez was back in jail, she doubted if any of that gang would bother her again. She'd also bet a search of Rodriguez's home would reveal the whereabouts of her nunchuck, but she wasn't sure how to ask Rossini to give it back. Which was really a shame.

'Now, is there anything else?' she asked.

'We're not through,' he grumbled, but he did get up. 'I'm going to question those three boys and Rodriguez. Something's going on that you're not telling me.'

'I doubt they know anything.' She smiled and headed for her front door. 'You're the one who knows more than you should.'

One down, and one to go, Mary thought as she watched Rossini get into a police car and drive off. Now all she had to do was figure out where Peter Dubois was staying.

CHAPTER THIRTY-FIVE

AT THE HOSPITAL, Jack found Wally standing in the hallway outside of Rodriguez's room. 'Your car's parked outside,' Jack said, stopping beside the chief. 'You talked to him yet?'

'I have.' Wally smiled. 'He's saying she lured him to her house, and then she got him down in her basement, and started hitting him with a crowbar.'

'How's he explain the broken window near her back door, or the knife we found on the basement floor?'

'Says they thought she was in trouble and broke in to help her. As for the knife ...' Wally chuckled. 'He says he had that for protection.'

'Didn't do him much good.' Jack waited for a nurse to walk by before going on. 'You heard from Phil? What are those guys saying?'

'Haven't heard a word.' Wally pointed at a sign down the hall on the wall. 'No cellphones allowed. I'll step outside and call him in a bit, but I'm waiting for the doctor to come back with the initial tox screen. I'm pretty sure the knife Rodriguez was carrying is a violation of his parole, but if he's also using, maybe we can tie him to that delivery we stopped. I'd sure like to find some drugs in his house.'

'Mary thinks we should check the house right away.'

'Mary?' Wally gave him a sideways look.

'Mrs Harrington.' Jack shook his head. Even he couldn't believe he was taking advice from a citizen. 'She seemed to feel we'd find something, especially if we had a drug-sniffing dog; but we'd better act fast.'

'She know something we don't?'

'Not that she would admit, but that friend of hers, Burrows, was at Rodriguez's house this morning.'

'Think he planted something?'

'I don't know.'

'Well, only way we will know is if we look.' Wally pointed toward the front of the hospital. 'Take my car and head over to

Paw Paw, find out who Rodriguez's parole officer is, tell him what's up and what we need. Once you have a search warrant, grab Phil, Mendoza, and VanDerwell. Have them go with you to Rodriguez's place.'

Ella called almost immediately after Sergeant Rossini drove off. Mary didn't really want to talk to her friend, not right then, but considering the fact that Ella had probably saved her life, Mary resigned herself to a long conversation.

'Thank you,' she said, over and over. And she meant it. Sure, she'd taken care of the Rodriguez guy, but she might not have been as lucky with the remaining three gang members. No telling how long they could have kept her trapped in the basement, or what might have happened if all three had come down those steps at once.

'You know, I wasn't the only one who called 911.'

'So I've heard.'

'Our Neighborhood Watch is working.'

'Thank goodness.' Mary meant it. She considered herself lucky. Sure, the survival training she'd received so many years before and the fact that she went to the gym on a regular schedule had helped, but if she hadn't kept a crowbar in the basement, and the guy Rossini called Rodriguez hadn't been so cocksure he could take her with that knife, their confrontation might have turned out differently.

'I heard you clobbered one of them,' Ella said.

'He fell down the stairs.' Mary wanted that version told, and knowing Ella, it would be repeated to anyone who asked – and even those who didn't ask. 'Broke his arm and knocked himself out.'

'I know how much you dislike going down to the basement,' Ella said. 'Did they force you down there?'

'No, I was putting something away.' Something she no longer had. Mary had wanted to tell the crime-scene people the box was hers, but she'd remained silent as they carried it to their van. Much good her silence had done. Rossini knew the weapons were hers.

Damn, she'd said too much to him. Blame it on shock … and anger. She'd nearly spilled the beans, told him everything. Thank goodness she came to her senses in time.

'I can't believe how calm you sound.' Ella seemed surprised by that. 'I'd be a basket case if someone broke into my house.'

'It all happened so fast, and with you calling 911 ...' Mary let her words trail off. David had also called 911, but it was Ella's call that got action. 'Thank you,' she said again.

'I'm just glad I saw them sneaking around your back yard. They must have parked on the other street and cut through your neighbor's to get to your place.'

That made sense. 'I didn't have any idea what was up until I heard them break the laundry room window.' Even then she hadn't been sure what was going on.

'Are you going back to your son's house tonight?'

Mary hadn't thought about that. Did she want to spend the night in her house, all alone? Anyone or anything could climb through the laundry room window while she was sleeping. But go back to Robby's house? Spend more time with Clare? That morning her daughter-in-law had once again asked Mary if she'd found the information Clare would need to trace the Smith's family tree. The woman just wouldn't let that subject be.

'No, I'll be here,' she said. At the moment she had the door to that back room closed, blocking off the cold air coming through the broken window, but she needed to get the glass replaced or something covering the opening before dark.

'You could spend the night here,' Ella offered. 'I have that extra bedroom, if you don't mind sharing it with the cats.'

Mary did mind sharing it, and it wasn't just the number of cats that Ella owned that bothered her. Even with two litter boxes, the smell in the house – especially in that room – was overpowering.

'Thanks for offering,' she said. 'I'll stay here. But I do need to call someone about the broken window, so if you don't mind, I'm going to hang up now.'

'Oh, sure ... certainly.' Ella sounded disappointed. 'I understand. I'm glad you're all right.'

Another thank-you, and Mary was finally able to hang up. She'd just started to get up to find her phone book so she could look up a glass repair shop when the phone rang again. She hoped it wasn't another neighbor calling. If so, she'd have to be polite and once again explain what happened, and she might never get that window fixed.

But it wasn't a neighbor on the phone. It was her daughter-in-law. 'Oh, thank God, you're finally off the phone. Mother Harrington, is Shannon there?'

CHAPTER THIRTY-SIX

IT TOOK JACK an hour to contact Andy Crouse, Rodriguez's parole officer, and another hour before they had a judge's signature on a search warrant, but by mid-afternoon a convoy of Rivershore police cars was heading for Jose Rodriguez's house, followed by one parole officer and one assistant district attorney.

No drug-sniffing dogs were available.

Neither Todd Mickelson, the assistant DA who had insisted on coming along to oversee the operation – which, in Jack's opinion, meant he was along to make sure they didn't screw up – nor Andy Crouse were to enter the premises until Jack and the other officers were sure the house was clear. And, just in case one of Rodriguez's gang members showed up unexpectedly, Mickelson and Crouse were to wear bulletproof vests, just like the rest of them.

They arrived at Rodriguez's house without lights or sirens and parked down the street. One by one, they moved into position, Jack taking the front door, while Officers Mendoza, VanDerwell, and Carlson covered the sides and back.

When a knock produced no response, Jack tried the doorknob. To his surprise, the door was unlocked. He let the others know the situation and then entered the house, calling out his presence. Quickly he cleared the single-level ranch-style house. Finding no one inside, he opened the back door and let Officers Mendoza and VanDerwell in and then signaled for Mickelson and Crouse to join them.

Room by room they went through the house, looking through cabinets and drawers, tearing the couch and chairs apart, cutting open the mattresses. At first Jack was glad they didn't find anything too easily. He didn't want Rodriguez yelling it was a set-up, that drugs had been planted by the Rivershore Police Department. But after forty-five minutes of searching with no results, Jack began to fear they'd find nothing at all.

The look the assistant DA gave him didn't help. Mickelson wasn't saying anything, but it was clear he thought the search was a bust. And then Officer Mendoza called them into the master bedroom and pointed out how one of the drawers in the dresser didn't seem as deep as the others. They found several bags of weed under the false bottom, but Jack wanted more than a few bags of marijuana, and urged them all to keep looking.

It was Mickelson who discovered the hidden storage area under the living-room floorboards, probably because the man weighed over three hundred pounds. Mickelson had basically called it a day, and was waddling toward the front door, ready to get in his car and drive back to his office, when Jack heard a board creak under Mickelson's leather shoes. Jack didn't mind that the assistant DA received the credit for finding the cocaine. Considering the way the drugs were concealed, Jack was also pretty sure David Burrows hadn't planted that evidence.

All in all, they found twenty pounds of cocaine, nine bags of marijuana, and two hundred grams of crack cocaine. Jack was smiling when he called the chief. Rodriguez wouldn't be coming back to Rivershore for a long time.

'Was Shannon supposed to come here?' Mary asked her daughter-in-law.

'No. I mean, I thought one of her friends was driving her home, but DeeDee said Shannon never showed up at her car after school. So I thought maybe she got a ride to your place. You know, so she could see her car again.'

'Give me a minute,' Mary said and put down the phone. She walked over and looked out the front window. Shannon's car was still parked in the driveway, its tail light and back fender hanging at an odd angle. If Shannon had come to the house, she hadn't driven off in her car.

As she stared at the Fusion, a sickening sensation twisted through

Mary. What if her granddaughter did come to check on her car? What if she arrived when those gang members were breaking in?

But no, she told herself. *That would have been too early.* Rodriguez and his boys had hit her place close to the lunch hour, way before school let out.

Mary started back to the phone, then stopped. They were assuming Shannon disappeared after school. What if she did get someone to drive her over during her lunch hour? What if she was at the house when Rodriguez and his boys arrived?

Mary knew the police had taken the four away. Could there have been a fifth gang member? One who grabbed Shannon?

One person might know.

Mary hurried back to the phone. 'Clare, I'm going to hang up and call a neighbor. I'll call you right back.'

She didn't give her daughter-in-law a chance to object. A click of a button and the press of another made the disconnect and automated the call to Ella Williams. As soon as Ella answered, Mary asked her question. 'While you were watching my house today, did you see Shannon? Did you see anyone grab Shannon?'

'No. I haven't seen her since last night. Why, what happened?'

Mary wasn't sure what had happened. That was the problem. 'You said you saw those boys sneaking around my house. How many did you see?'

'I don't know. Didn't they take three away in a police car and one in the ambulance?'

'Could there have been another one?'

Ella hesitated before answering. 'I ... I'm not sure. I don't think so.'

'But you're sure you didn't see Shannon?'

Again Ella hesitated before she spoke. 'I did go to the bathroom,' she admitted. 'I'd already called 911, and I took the phone with me, but I just couldn't hold it anymore. I just had to pee, so I wasn't away from the window all that long. If she came while I was in there, I guess I could have missed her. Why? What's wrong?'

'She didn't go home,' Mary said, not sure what to think. 'Clare's all worried. She thought maybe she came here, but if you didn't see her ...'

'If she came while I was in the bathroom ...' Ella didn't finish. 'I'm sorry.'

'It's not your fault.' Mary didn't want her friend blaming herself. 'She probably never came here. She's probably over at another friend's house, or maybe she went to see Robby. He said he'd get her car fixed as soon as possible. She probably went to see him, to make sure he was doing that.'

It sounded logical, yet it didn't sound like something Shannon would do ... go see her dad without telling her mother. And how would she have gotten there?

'I'm going to call Clare back,' Mary said. 'Maybe Shannon's home by now.' She certainly hoped so. 'Again, thanks for your help earlier.'

'I'm sorry,' Ella repeated. 'I shouldn't have gone to the bathroom.'

'It's not your fault,' Mary assured her, eager to get off the phone. 'I'll talk to you later.'

She called her daughter-in-law back as soon as she'd hung up on Ella. 'Still no Shannon?' she asked.

'No.' Clare sounded tense. 'I've called all of her friends. I even called Robert. No one has seen or heard from her.'

Darn, Mary had hoped her granddaughter and son were together. 'Well, I don't think she came here. We had a little excitement earlier today, and I'm sure someone would have seen her if she'd been around.'

'What do you mean, "a little excitement"? What's going on, Mother Harrington?'

Mary knew she might as well tell Clare exactly what had happened. Although she doubted the break-in would be on TV, she was sure something about it would be in the weekly paper. 'Some kids broke into my house.' she said. 'The police were here. I'm sure, if Shannon had come by, she would have come inside to see what was going on.' Unless she came before the police arrived. 'Do you know if Shannon attended her afternoon classes?'

'Of course she attended them. They had testing all day. Besides, my daughter does not skip classes.'

Mary rolled her eyes. She had a feeling Clare didn't know half of what Shannon did. 'What about her boyfriend?'

'Oh, they broke up. Would you believe, he had some wild idea about the two of them traveling through Europe for a year or two. We told Shannon there was no way we were going to allow that, and she might as well forget him.'

'Call him,' Mary ordered, knowing Shannon hadn't forgotten the boy. 'I'll bet she's there.'

'Why would she...? We told her ... Oh, all right.'

'Then call me back and let me know she's safe.' Mary knew she wouldn't relax until she knew Shannon was OK, until she was sure one of those gang members hadn't grabbed her.

Less than two minutes passed from the time Mary hung up until the telephone rang again. She'd barely had time to grab the telephone book and turn to the yellow pages section for glass repair. Clare started talking immediately. 'She's not there. He said he hasn't seen her since last hour of class.'

So Shannon was in school through that last hour. That more or less eliminated one of the gang members grabbing her.

'He said she got a ride with someone driving a black car,' Clare said. 'He couldn't tell who was driving, just that Shannon got into the car on her own.'

A *black car*. Mary tensed. Shannon had seen a black car driving up and down Maple on Halloween night. Both of them had seen it. And the car was back the next day, parked just down the street. Maybe it belonged to one of the gang members. Maybe they did have Shannon after all.

'Clare, I think you'd better call the police. Ask for Sergeant Rossini.'

By the time Jack returned to the police station all he wanted to do was write up his report and head to the Shores for a cold beer. Allison had already left for the day, but she'd been busy while everyone was searching Rodriguez's house. A pile of 'While You Were Out' slips sat on his desk, all marked 'Urgent.'

The moment Jack saw the names of the callers and their messages, he knew it would be a while before he got that beer. Allison had taken the last message just before leaving the station, so Jack chose that number to call first. 'Mr Harrington,' he said. 'This is

Sergeant Rossini.'

'About time,' the man on the other end of the line snapped. 'Do you realize how many times I've called?'

'I'm sorry, sir. What seems to be the problem?'

'Problem? My daughter is missing, that's the problem. You won't answer my calls. The state police are giving me the runaround, and the FBI won't do anything. That's the problem.'

He was nearly shouting, but Jack understood the man's frustration ... and fear. In response, Jack kept his voice level, hoping to calm the man. 'When did you realize your daughter was missing?'

'This afternoon. Hours ago. My wife has called you. So has my mother.'

'Is your mother Mary Harrington?' Jack asked, though he was sure she had to be Robert Harrington's mother.

'Yes. She told us to ask for you specifically. She said you've met Shannon.'

Of course, Jack realized. *The teenager from the night before, the one with the red Fusion.* That they were talking about an older child, not a young one, eased some of Jack's concern and gave a possible reason for the girl's disappearance. 'I have met her,' he said. 'She's a lovely girl. Why do you think she ran away?'

'She hasn't run away,' Harrington shouted. 'She's been kidnapped.'

'And why do you think that?'

'Why? Because her boyfriend ... that is, one of her friends saw her get into a car, and no one's seen her since.'

That didn't sound like a kidnapping, but Jack didn't say so. 'Have you been contacted about a ransom?'

'No.' Robert Harrington hesitated. 'Not yet. But my mother said that car has been over by her house, was there the night Shannon helped her give out trick-or-treat candy.'

A stalker? Jack didn't like the sound of that. 'Tell me everything you know,' he said, pulling out a pen and pad of paper.

CHAPTER THIRTY-SEVEN

MARY STARED AT the clock. Hours had passed since Clare's first phone call. Hours of waiting, wondering, and fretting. She'd called Rossini's cellphone number twice. In each case she'd ended up leaving a message. She'd called the station directly. Same result.

She wanted to drive over to Robby's, but she didn't want to leave her house, just in case Shannon showed up there. Every time the phone rang, her stomach churned and her heart raced. She'd hold her breath when the voice on the other end of the line turned out to be Robby or Clare. No news became good news, at least better than some of the scenarios playing through her head.

Was it a kidnapping? Did one of the gang members have Shannon? Were they going to use her granddaughter to punish her?

Mary kept hoping for the best. Maybe this black car had nothing to do with the black car both she and Shannon had seen hanging around the neighborhood. Maybe this black car was driven by a friend of Shannon's, someone Shannon hadn't mentioned before, someone who showed up unexpectedly and suggest they go for a ride.

At this very moment Shannon might be in Grand Rapids or Kalamazoo having a blast. Maybe she was at a movie or a concert, eating dinner, or dancing. Maybe, maybe, maybe …

Mary didn't want to think of other possibilities, but the thoughts kept slipping into her head. Shannon was a beautiful girl, friendly and sweet. A little naïve. No, very naïve. She could easily be duped into offering to help a stranger. Once in his car …

The doorbell rang.

For a moment Mary didn't move, then slowly she pushed herself to her feet.

Again the doorbell.

'I'm coming,' she called, her voice sounding weaker than she wanted. Older. More feeble.

At the door she hesitated. The racing of her heart made her light-headed, a mixture of dread and excitement stalling her hand. And then she released the chain and turned the knob.

'Sergeant,' she said the moment she realized who it was.

'May I come in?'

He looked tired, his eyes bloodshot and a stubble of beard covering his normally smooth cheeks and chin. His overcoat was unbuttoned, as if thrown on as a last thought.

'My granddaughter. Is she...?' Mary didn't want to say the word.

'I have no idea,' he said and nodded toward her kitchen. 'I need a coffee.'

'I'll fix one.'

He walked by her, heading for the kitchen. She looked up and down the street, half-expecting to see a black car. Wishing she would.

A street light illuminated the SUV parked in front of her house, otherwise the street was empty, houses mere silhouettes under the street lights.

She closed the door and went into the kitchen.

'I gather you got my message,' she said as she placed a single-cup container into the coffee maker.

'I didn't see the ones on my cellphone until just a while ago. I'd had it on mute, so I never heard those calls, but I saw you'd called the station. Your son did, too.'

'You've talked to him?'

'I have. The other night you said you'd seen a black car hanging around here. Can you describe it?'

She shook her head and grabbed a clean mug from the cupboard. 'Black. Four doors. Otherwise looked like half of the cars on the road.'

'Did you ever see the driver?'

'Not really.' She pushed the button to start the coffee. 'I think it was a man, but I couldn't be sure. Shannon said the car went by several times Halloween night, and then I thought I saw it following me another day.'

As soon as the machine spat out the last of the coffee, she handed Rossini the mug, then sat down across from him. 'I don't even know if that car has anything to do with Shannon's disappearance, but the moment Clare said someone had seen Shannon get into a black car, I thought of that one.'

Cradling the mug in his hands, he took a sip of the coffee, then a long gulp. When he set the mug down, he gave a slight nod and a sigh before giving her his full attention. 'Are you sure your granddaughter has actually disappeared? Maybe this black car belongs to one of her friends. Maybe she's just off doing her own thing.'

'That's what I'm hoping,' Mary said. 'But Clare – my daughter-in-law – said she's called all of Shannon's friends. Not one knows where she is, not even her boyfriend. Besides, this isn't like Shannon. She doesn't just disappear without telling anyone.'

'You're sure?' His tone expressed his disbelief. 'We parents think we know everything our kids do, but I've learned that's not always true.'

Mary wanted to argue that Shannon wasn't like that, but she remembered the discussion they'd had about a trip to Europe. Shannon had kept that plan a secret from her parents for a long time. Even now Clare and Robby thought Shannon had broken up with her boyfriend. Mary doubted that was true.

'Besides,' Sergeant Rossini added, 'officially, at her age, your granddaughter is under no obligation to tell anyone where she's going.'

Mary had thought of that, too. An eighteen-year-old was an adult according to the law. Shannon might still be living with her mom and dad and still be in high school, but legally she was responsible for her own actions.

'Does that mean you're not going to do anything?' Mary knew if he wasn't, she was. She wasn't sure what, but she couldn't just sit around waiting.

'I didn't say that.' He took another gulp of coffee, then pushed himself back from the table. 'I'll go talk to your son and daughter-in-law, see if they can give me any additional information. I'll get a picture of your granddaughter. Maybe talk to this friend who saw your granddaughter get into the car.'

He didn't sound hopeful. Mostly he sounded tired, and Mary felt a measure of compassion for the man. He'd evidently had a long day, which made her ask, 'Did you search that Rodriguez guy's house?'

'We did.' He shook his head, but he also smiled. 'After all, you told me we should.'

'And?'

Rossini's smile was bigger, more natural. 'If your friend planted those drugs, I don't want to know, but if everything holds up in court, Rodriguez will be out of here for a long, long time.'

'If you found a lot of drugs, they weren't planted by David.' That wasn't how they worked, at least not when she was a part of the agency. 'My guess is one of those gang members gave him all the information he needed, someone who's now decided he doesn't want to live in Rivershore any longer.'

'You guys don't exactly work within the law, do you?'

She wasn't sure how to answer. The ringing of the phone eliminated the need. 'Let me get that,' Mary said. 'Maybe Shannon's home.'

It wasn't Shannon on the phone. Nor Robby or Clare. Ella's voice was high-pitched and excited. 'There's a man at your car, Mary.'

'There's someone at my car,' Mary repeated for Rossini and waved her hand toward the front window.

'Or maybe it's a boy,' Ella continued, and Mary could picture her neighbor at her living-room window, watching all this. 'He's wearing one of those hooded sweatshirts, so I can't really tell. Oh, he put something in your car.'

'He's putting ...'

Mary didn't finish. Rossini was already at her front door, pulling it open.

CHAPTER THIRTY-EIGHT

JACK RAN, BUT he wasn't fast enough to catch the man – or teenager – before the guy reached the black sedan parked behind Mary's car, got in, and pulled away. Cursing too many beers and hamburgers, along with age, Jack went to his SUV.

By the time he had his Durango in gear, the sedan had turned the corner at the end of the block. He keyed his radio and put out a call. Jennifer Mendoza responded first. He gave her a quick rundown on what was happening. 'Car's a Nissan,' he said. 'I only got part of the license plate. Mud covered the rest, but it starts with a ZYK. Get back with me as soon as you have something.'

She promised she would, and he caught sight of the sedan two blocks ahead, as it turned onto Main.

He didn't stick his light on the roof. He hadn't seen the girl in the car and didn't want to panic the guy. 'Lead me to her,' he muttered and pulled out his cellphone.

He punched in Mary Harrington's number, waited through seven rings, then dropped the phone on the passenger's seat. He could talk to her later. Right now he needed to figure out where the car ahead of him was going and what he wanted to do.

He could pull the car over, tell the driver he was conducting a safety check, but if the car and driver were connected to Shannon Harrington's disappearance, that might panic the guy. Better to give the driver a little leeway, see where he went.

Again he tried Mary's number.

Still no answer.

The black car left the downtown area and crossed the river, heading north. Only a few cars were on the road ahead, and Jack eased his Durango farther back. If the sedan's driver knew he was being followed, he wasn't in any hurry to get away.

The ring of his cellphone interrupted his concentration. He didn't recognize the number, but the moment he clicked 'accept' he recognized Mary's voice. 'Have you got him yet?' she asked.

'Not yet, but I'm following him. He's just up ahead. What did he do to your car?'

'He left something on the seat. A pin I gave Shannon for her birthday.'

Which meant the bastard had the girl. 'Any note?'

'Not exactly.'

He wasn't in the mood for games. 'Come on, Mary, what did he leave?'

'An article. A copy of an old newspaper article. Where are you?'

'North of town, near the Hill and Dale Vineyard.' Aptly named for the rolling hills and valleys where grape vineyards flourished. 'What's the article about?'

'Something that happened in the past.'

'Your past?'

He noticed the hesitation before she answered. 'It was a mistake. A terrible mistake.'

'What kind of a mistake?' If this guy had left the article in her car, it had to have something to do with her.

'I can't tell you.'

'Dammit, Mary, do you want to find your granddaughter or not?' He was tired of all her secrets.

'Yes, I want to find her, but you need to stop following him. Go back to the police station, or home, or wherever you would have gone after leaving my house.'

'I am not going home.'

'Are you near the Allegan State Forest?'

'Yes.' An occasional sign posted on the trees on his right identified the land as state-owned and open to hunting. 'Why?' Even as he asked the question, he knew why she'd asked. 'Where are you, Mary?'

'I'm just now turning onto Main.'

'Turn around and go back home,' he ordered. He didn't need a civilian involved in a police chase. 'Let us take care of this.'

'This man wants me.'

'All the more reason for you to go back.'

'No. Once he has me, I'm sure he'll let Shannon go.'

'We're not making any trades. Whoa!' Jack slammed on his brakes.

'What? What's going on?'

'A deer just darted out in front of my car. I nearly ... Oh, damn.'

'Now what?'

Jack stared at the empty road ahead. 'Nothing. Go back home. I'll call you when I know more.'

He didn't want to tell her he'd lost the car. Hell, there was no way he could have lost the sedan. He'd been watching it while talking. There was no other traffic, coming or going. No crossroads. He would have seen if the car had turned in at one of the farmhouses they'd passed, and there was no way the rows of grapevines on his left would conceal a car. The woods on his right were the only alternative. Somehow, somewhere that black sedan had turned into those woods without him seeing it.

He turned on his emergency flashers and kept his speed below twenty. For a half-mile he crept along, looking in all directions; nevertheless, he almost missed the two-track. He drove past it before it registered that the opening between the trees was wider than normal. He stopped the Durango, backed up, and stopped again.

He could just barely see the rear end of the car, its dark color blending in with the shadowy tree trunks and brush. It wasn't more than a few hundred feet off the main road.

Jack pulled his Durango over to the side and off the road, then called Mendoza.

'Get me some backup,' he said and gave her his location. 'State or county, I don't care.'

He knew he should wait for assistance, but he wasn't sure where the two-track led. He'd thought he was hanging far enough back not to alert the guy, but maybe the driver realized he was being followed and panicked. If he had the girl with him, he may have decided it was time to get rid of her. In that case, waiting could be a fatal mistake.

Jack grabbed the flashlight he kept in his glove compartment, and took out his Glock. He eased himself out of the warmth of the Durango, and into the cold of the night, slowly closing the SUV's door so he didn't make a lot of noise. From the road's gravel shoulder, he progressed along the two-track, clumps of grass and stunted brush rubbing against his pant legs.

Step by step he neared the car, listening for the slightest noise as he moved deeper into the woods. When he heard the snap of a branch, he quickly turned to his left.

But not in time.

Something solid hit the side of his head.

Mary cussed the car in front of her. 'The light is green,' she growled through her windshield. 'You go when it's green, so move it, buddy.'

Slowly the car in front of her moved through the intersection.

She didn't like that Rossini had hung up on her. Something was wrong, and she didn't think it had anything to do with a deer. She needed to find him, to catch up with the man who had left the pin and article in her car. She had to catch up with Peter Dubois.

He had Shannon, but he wanted her. Wanted Pandora Coye, the woman who murdered his mother. To make sure she understood his message, he'd underlined the end of the article where the six-year-old boy had sworn, '*Un jour je la trouverai.*' Someday I will find her.

Her cellphone rang just as she crossed the river and headed north out of town. 'What did you see?' she demanded.

'Pan, where are you?'

'David?' He was the last person she'd expected to hear from.

'I just heard your granddaughter's missing.'

'He's here, David. Peter Dubois is here.'

'I told you I thought he'd find you.'

'He left a copy of the news article from forty-four years ago in my car ... and the Pandora pin.'

'Again, where are you?'

'Just leaving town. Sergeant Rossini's been following Dubois' car. I know they were as far north as the Allegan State Park, but I haven't talked to him for the last ten minutes.'

'All right, keep me posted with what you find. By the way, nice job handling that gang leader.'

'No thanks to you.' She wasn't about to tell him she knew he'd called the police and alerted them to the gang's invasion.

'I knew you could do it. Just like I'm sure you'll find your granddaughter. Once an ADEC assassin, always an assassin. But if you need any help, give me a call.'

'And what, you'll fly back from D.C.?'

He chuckled. 'No, I'm still here in Michigan. You should've known I wouldn't be able to leave until after this Dubois situation was taken care of. Just call this number back if you figure out where Dubois has taken your granddaughter.'

'And what, you'll come to my rescue? Her rescue?'

'I'll be there.'

He ended the called abruptly, and she dropped the phone onto the passenger's seat. *I'll be there.* Ha. Like he was there when that gang invaded her house?

She glanced in the rear-view mirror. Headlights indicated a car following her.

Maybe he would be there when she found Shannon. If his 911 call earlier that day was any indication, he'd been keeping an eye on her for some time.

'OK, David,' she said to the reflection in the mirror, 'let's go get 'em.'

Mary clicked on her brights and brought the Chevy up to sixty. She kept her gaze on the road ahead, scanning the edges for deer. Rossini had nearly hit one. She didn't need to.

Two cars passed, heading the opposite direction, back to Rivershore. The car behind her had dropped back some. Otherwise, there were no cars on the road.

She whizzed by the Hill and Dale Vineyard, passed farmhouses, and fields of grapevines. Clouds covered the moon and stars, her headlights illuminating a limited arc of road and roadside ahead.

She didn't see the flashing red and blue lights behind her or hear the siren until the car was almost on her tail. A quick glance at the speedometer brought a groan. Sixty-five. Ten miles faster than the speed limit. She didn't need this. Not now.

Mary eased her foot off the accelerator, ready to pull over to the side of the road. Her mind raced for excuses. Sergeant Rossini had asked her to come? To hurry? She didn't realize how fast she was going?

That was the truth.

She thought ...

The need for an excuse ended the moment the sheriff's car flew past her, lights flashing and siren blaring. A sickening sensation invaded Mary's stomach as she watched the patrol car speed on ahead. Something had happened. Something bad.

To Rossini?

To Shannon?

Again, Mary stepped on the gas, following the lights of the patrol car and praying the Sheriff's Department had been called out for something totally unrelated.

201

Wishful thinking, she realized, the moment she saw Rossini's Durango by the side of the road, the sheriff's car – lights still flashing – pulled up behind it.

She stopped next to Rossini's SUV and rolled down the passenger window to see into the car.

'Keep going,' a deputy yelled, getting out of his cruiser.

'What happened?' she yelled back.

'Keep going,' the deputy repeated, coming up between her car and Rossini's.

'I was talking to him just minutes ago,' she said. 'He was trailing a car.'

'Ma'am, either move your car or I'm going to arrest you.'

She moved her car.

Mary pulled over in front of Rossini's SUV, but she left the Chevy's engine running. The moment the deputy realized she'd gotten out of her car, he switched the beam of his flashlight from the interior of Rossini's Durango to her face. 'Ma'am, I told you to keep moving. Get back in your car.'

She shielded her eyes with her arm and glanced at the Durango, and then to her left at the woods.

Another car passed, heading north. For a moment she thought it was David, but the car traveled on. And it wasn't a white Impala.

'Ma'am, are you listening?'

She looked back at the woods. Though she couldn't see clearly, the distance between the trees was wide enough for a driveway. A two-track? Had Rossini stopped because the black sedan pulled in there?

'Ma'am!'

Her gaze went back to the deputy. His stern look and posture reminded her of a cartoon character. She could almost see the smoke coming out of his ears.

'No sign of him in the car?' she asked, keeping her voice as calm as possible.

'This is the last time I warn you,' he growled, but he switched the beam of the flashlight to the Durango's interior, as if assuring himself no one was in the SUV.

'We need to look for them in there,' she said and started for the two-track that led into the woods.

'In where?' The deputy swung his light beam toward the trees. 'Ma'am, come back here.'

Mary ignored his demand and hurried down the barely discernible driveway. She was actually pleased the deputy ran after her. His flashlight gave her enough illumination to see where she was going and after less than a minute, to know neither Rossini nor Dubois were ahead of her. The way the grass was pressed flat, both going forward and slightly off to the side, told the story of a car that had gone down the two-track only so far and then backed up.

'They're not here,' she said, stopping abruptly.

The deputy ran into her, nearly knocking her down. 'Ma'am,' he repeated, stumbling to catch his balance.

Mary had a feeling the deputy might try to arrest her, or at least detain her. To make sure he did neither, she side-swiped his legs, completely taking him off balance and dropping him to the ground.

'Sorry,' she said, already heading back to the road. 'I've got to find them.'

By the time the deputy caught up with her, she'd slid back behind the steering wheel of the Chevy. He reached for her door handle as she stepped on the gas. Gravel kicked out from under her tires, and though the flashing lights of his patrol car made it difficult to see, she had a feeling he gave her the one-finger salute.

'Damn you, Dubois,' she muttered as she drove away from Rossini's SUV.

At least she hadn't seen a body lying along the two-track, but she hadn't spent enough time looking to be sure Dubois hadn't stashed Rossini's body in the woods. She didn't want anything to have happened to the sergeant. He was a nosy pest, but a concerned pest. A nice guy. She never meant to get him involved in this mess. Never meant to get her granddaughter involved.

Mary blinked back tears and slowed her car.

Where to now? How was she supposed to find Dubois? The note he left in her car didn't give a clue. The only thing she knew was the man drove a black sedan and was last seen heading down this road. Could be he knew Rossini was following him and came this way simply to trap the sergeant. Once he eliminated Rossini, Dubois could have doubled back, could have gone a different direction.

But no. Hadn't David said they'd tracked Dubois to some place north of Rivershore and southwest of Allegan? That would put him right in this area.

But where?

She looked in her rear-view mirror. In the distance she could see the flashing lights of the deputy's car dropping farther and farther back. At least he wasn't coming after her. She slowed her Chevy and tried to think.

One thing about rural areas: people noticed things. People talked to each other. Strangers stood out. If Dubois was staying anywhere around here, someone would have noticed.

Most of the houses and farms she passed were set back from the road, and she wasn't eager to pull into one this late at night. It would take too long to explain who she was looking for and why, and if Dubois was at one, the moment she drove up, he'd know, making her vulnerable.

A crossroad up ahead and a store on the corner gave her an alternative solution. An 'open' sign just below an ad for beer blinked on and off. One car sat in front of the store, another parked by the back. Mary stopped her Chevy near the door.

'Greetings,' the dark-skinned man behind the counter said the moment she stepped inside. 'How may I be of service?'

'I'm looking for someone,' she said, noticing another man back by the coolers, just his head and shoulders visible above a shelving unit filled with chips and non-perishable grocery items. A baseball cap covered thick gray hair and wide red suspenders crisscrossed a blue-and-gray plaid flannel shirt.

'What kinda someone?' the guy with suspenders asked, coming around the end of the shelves carrying a twelve-pack of beer.

'Someone who drives a black sedan,' Mary said. 'He may have driven by here just a while ago. He'd be new to the area. Arrived just a few weeks ago.'

Suspenders looked at the Indian clerk, then back at her. 'Any particular reason you're lookin' for this guy?'

'I think he may have my granddaughter with him.' Let them think what they liked. She didn't want to go into a long explanation.

Suspenders made a face. 'One I'm thinkin' of's pretty old. Maybe sixty or so. Wouldn't be your husband, would it?'

'No, he's not my husband.' And Dubois wouldn't be in his sixties, but some people looked older than they were. 'This man's kidnapped my granddaughter.' And may have killed a police officer, she feared, but no need to add that. 'You know where he lives?'

Again Suspenders looked at the clerk. 'That city-slicker ever tell you where he was staying?'

'Not me.' The clerk emphatically shook his head and rang up Suspenders' beer. 'He scared the shit out of me.' He looked at Mary, his eyes widening, and he put his fingers up to his mouth. 'Oh, pardon, ma'am. I mean he frighten me.'

City-slicker. Scary. Mary was getting an image. 'And this man drove a black car?'

'Yes, ma'am. Black with four doors.'

'I think it might have been a rental,' Suspenders said. 'Day him and I was both in here, he was complaining about the heater. Said it were the worst rental he'd ever driven.'

'He was in here more than once?' That would mean he was staying somewhere close by.

'Yes, ma'am,' the clerk said. 'Many times. Usually he buys ice, but first time he stops here, he wants to know if we sell lanterns.'

'Did you happen to notice which way he went when he left here after buying ice?'

'I saw him go that way,' Suspenders said, pointing out the window at the road heading west.

Mary felt she was getting closer. 'Any houses that way recently been sold or rented?'

'Not that I've heard of,' Suspenders said and looked at the clerk. 'What about you, Rashe? They didn't sell the old Springer farm, did they? I saw a car there last week.' He glanced at Mary. 'Farm's been abandoned for over a year. Car I saw was white, though, not black.'

'Where exactly is this Springer farm?'

CHAPTER THIRTY-NINE

JACK'S HEAD THROBBED and his shoulders ached. With his arms wrapped around the four-by-six behind his back and his wrists tied together, he could barely move. Roughly eight feet away, Mary Harrington's granddaughter was in a similar position, seated on the cold cement of the barn floor, tied to what might have been a support beam for a stall that never was finished. On the other side of the barn, Agent David Burrows stood near his white Impala, swinging a pair of short wooden rods attached by a chain. As he rotated his wrist in a circle, the two rods appeared as one, the palm-wide chain no longer visible.

Jack had seen the weapon used in martial arts demonstrations and in Bruce Lee movies, and he knew a well-placed strike could break a block of wood, shatter an arm, or crush a skull. Burrows seemed to be having trouble controlling the two rods. He missed a catch, and the rods and chain clattered onto the cement floor. Then he nearly hit himself with an attempted switch-up. Each time he made a mistake, he glared over at Jack, daring him to say anything. Jack knew better. The lump on his head and the ropes around his wrists put him in a vulnerable position, and this man was too dangerous to irritate.

But when Burrows put a dent in the Impala's fender with a miscalculated strike, Mary's granddaughter yelled at him, 'Way to go, you bastard. You're sure no James Bond. I doubt you're even an agent, least not for any *real* government agency. Bet you made everything up, even that bit about my grandmother. You're just a creepy old man, and if you don't let us go, you're gonna be in a lot of trouble.'

Still holding the two rods clasped together so they were barely visible, Burrows strolled over to stand in front of Shannon Harrington. 'And just who is going to give me trouble, missy? You?'

'No, my dad,' she said, glaring up at Burrows. 'I bet he has the police out looking for me now.'

'Here's your policeman.'

Jack grimaced when Burrows motioned toward him. Some policeman. He'd walked right into Burrows' trap. Jack had no idea what Burrows hit him with, but he was already hogtied and lying across the back seat of the sedan by the time he came to.

Jack wasn't sure how long he'd been out. All Burrows said when Jack groaned was, 'Welcome to the party, Sergeant,' and then he backed the black sedan out of the woods and drove a short distance to the farm they were now at.

For Jack, the most deflating aspect of the whole ordeal was how easily Burrows had managed to get him out of the car and into the barn. Mary's granddaughter was wrong. Burrows might be in his late sixties, but he was still strong as an ox, and the hold he'd put on Jack's arm was painful. Now here he was, tied up and helpless. Maybe it was time for him to retire.

If he lived through the night.

'My dad will have the *whole* police force out. The FBI. Everyone,' Shannon Harrington threatened.

Burrows laughed. 'The only one I want to find you is your grandmother.'

'Why?' she asked, voicing Jack's same question. 'I thought she was your friend.'

'We have no friends,' Burrows said. 'Your grandmother broke a promise and can no longer be trusted.'

'What promise?' Jack asked the same time the girl did.

Burrows looked over at him. 'To keep a low profile. To never do anything that would draw attention to the agency.' He walked over to stand by Jack. 'You're the reason I'm here, Sergeant Rossini. You and Pan. She had to go and get her picture in the paper, go and beat up those boys, and you had to start nosing around. You and your son.' Burrows grunted. 'Now I'm going to have to eliminate him, too. Too bad. You shouldn't have asked him to look into Pandora's past.'

The thought of John being killed sent a chill through Jack. 'Leave my son out of this.'

'It'll probably be a car accident,' Burrows said. 'We often use that as a means of eliminating problems. He'll be driving home and bam, something will happen. He'll suddenly feel dizzy and drive into the path of an oncoming car. Or maybe the brakes won't work, and he'll drive into a tree. Driving can be very dangerous.'

Burrows grinned, and Jack strained against the ropes binding his wrists, willing his arms to pull the fibers apart, just as all the superheroes managed in the movies. But the ropes didn't loosen, didn't slide off. The only outcome of his efforts was an increased pounding in his head.

'Why me?' Shannon asked, her voice small and plaintive. 'Why am I here?'

Again Burrows turned toward her. 'Because she'll come for you. I just hope she's still sharp enough to follow my clues.'

'Did she really work with you?' Shannon asked. 'Did she really kill people?'

'Oh yes, and she was good at it.' Burrows' expression softened and took on a look of longing. 'She was beautiful back then. Absolutely stunning. And such a lovely voice. That lady could sweet-talk any man into taking her home with them, or off to a deserted isle. It didn't matter if he was Russian, German, or French, Pandora Coye could converse in multiple languages, could make a man think he was the center of her world.'

He looked at Jack and chuckled. 'She could get them to tell her secrets. Pillow talk. It's a man's downfall.'

'She slept with them?' Shannon said. 'With lots of men?'

Burrows shrugged, his attention going back to the girl. 'I don't know how many, but from what I heard, she was a whore before Carl brought her into the agency.'

'You're a liar,' Shannon shouted, her voice taking on a hysterical edge. 'A liar, and a … a terrible man, and …' she started crying. 'I wanna go home.'

Jack hated to admit it, but he felt the same way. He was tired, his head and body ached, the cement he was sitting on was cold, and he didn't see a good ending to this situation. He wanted to close his eyes and fall asleep, to wake up in the morning in his own bed, to find this was all a bad dream.

But he knew that wasn't going to happen.

His best hope was Jennifer Mendoza. She'd said she'd send backup.

But what good was backup if the officers didn't know where he was? He certainly didn't know where he was, other than in a musty-smelling barn that had cobwebs hanging from the rafters and looked as if it hadn't been used in years. Lanterns sitting on the cement and hanging from several beams supplied some dim lighting, but Jack doubted much would be visible from the outside. Not with the big sliding barn-door closed, and years of dust covering the side door's window as well as the two narrow translucent panels up near the roofline. Burrows had even brought his car inside the barn, so it wouldn't be visible from the road.

Jack thought about that. The white Impala was parked over by the side door, but he'd been following a black Nissan.

'You have two cars,' he said, looking at Burrows.

'Smart boy.'

'You've been spying on her for some time,' Jack said, remembering that Mary had complained about a black sedan driving up and down Maple on Halloween night. 'You were in Rivershore even before I started checking up on her.'

'As I said, she shouldn't have gotten her picture in the paper. No telling when someone from her past might have recognized her. I've got enough problems with Congress. I don't need her popping up, telling that subcommittee what we did in the past, or suggesting we might still be operating outside of the law.'

'I saw you,' Shannon said, sniffing back tears. 'That night, while I was giving out candy, I saw you.'

'I know.'

Burrows smiled, and Jack understood why the girl had been taken. The man wasn't going to leave any witnesses. 'So we're here to lure her to you so you can kill her, then us. And after that? Once our bodies are found, you know others will start probing into her past. I've got a file about her in my computer. When ...'

He didn't get a chance to finish. Burrows shook his head. 'That file no longer exists, Sergeant. I guess that Anonymous group is still up to its old tricks, breaking into law enforcement files and eliminating certain information. At least that's what your buddies are going to think when they go into your computer. As for your bodies ...' He glanced over at a stack of bags. 'I doubt they'll be found. I'm not sure who lived at this farm in the past, but he was kind enough to leave several bags of lime. And there's a nice pit out back where he used to dump his horse and cow manure. I've already prepared a spot for the three of you. A little lime on top of your bodies will reduce the smell, and once the composted manure is back in place, who's to know you ever were here?'

'So what kind of clues did you leave for Mary?' Jack hoped whatever those clues were they'd also bring Mendoza and other officers.

'Little ones, so if you're hoping the cavalry will come and save you, I wouldn't hold your breath.'

'He doesn't need the cavalry, David. I'm here.'

'Grandma,' Shannon cried.

Both Jack and Burrows looked toward the Impala.

CHAPTER FORTY

MARY HOPED HERS wasn't an empty boast. She'd found them, but now what? She'd picked up a pitchfork that was leaning against the side door of the barn, but what good would that be against David's gun?

'I thought he was your friend,' Shannon said, her voice cracking. 'I wouldn't have gotten into his car if I'd known.'

'Not your fault, honey.' Mary understood how David had tricked the girl. The agency taught them to deceive, and they did it well.

David stepped away from Rossini, smiling as he slapped his left palm with a short stick. 'Took you long enough to get here.'

'I'm an old lady, remember? Not as fast as I used to be.'

As he drew closer, she realized he held two wooden sticks, not one, the chain connecting them barely visible. 'So you took it.' She nodded toward the nunchuck he held. 'Not Dubois or that gang.'

David smiled. 'You know, I have absolutely no idea where Peter Dubois might be or if he's even alive.'

'So he never moved to Florida, never saw my picture in the paper.'

'Not that I'm aware of, but using his name was a good idea, don't you think? Kept you off guard.'

David released one of the sticks, holding the remaining one up near the chain end. 'It's been a while since I've used one of these. I figured, in case someone did find your bodies under that compost, blunt force trauma would be harder to trace than a bullet, especially if this was found next to your body.'

He began spinning the nunchuck so it flared out, appearing to be one long stick. 'If it's even important, time of death will be identical for the three of you. You first, of course.'

Mary watched as he neared, knowing she couldn't make her move too soon. 'So that's why you kept them alive?' she said, staying close to the Impala.

'That and so I could tell them all about your glorious past.'

She glanced at her granddaughter. 'What did you tell her?'

David made two diagonal strokes with the nunchuck, one from his upper right to his lower left, then a switch. Mary didn't move. She knew he was too far away for the stick to hit her. He was taunting her, showing her his prowess with the nunchuck, and trying to goad her into revealing her defense.

'I told her you were a whore, that her saintly grandmother slept with men then killed them. Are you going to deny that?'

She wanted to, but she couldn't. 'You've turned into a nasty person, David.'

'You always said I enjoyed my work too much.'

'You're such a liar, who can believe anything you say?' Rossini shouted from where he sat, tied to a post.

David turned toward the sergeant, halting the rotating motion of his hand. The end rod stopped spinning and dropped down, swinging back to hit his arm. He flinched, and Mary moved. Pitchfork held waist high, she bolted forward, driving the tines into his side.

His coat stopped the pointed ends from penetrating his flesh, but the force of her thrust caused him to drop the nunchuck and step back. A look of surprise crossed his face, then one of anger. He knocked the pitchfork away from his side and out of her hands, and reached inside his coat for his gun.

Mary didn't wait for him to pull the gun from his shoulder

holster. Using the full force of her weight, she slammed into his side.

Together they fell to the cement floor, Mary on top. She immediately rolled off and to the side, rising up on her knees. Four and a half decades before they'd sparred on mats in ADEC's workout room. They'd both been in their twenties then, supple and full of energy. Ultimately David always won, his strength dominating her skills, but she'd made him work for those wins.

Today she couldn't let him win.

She reached for the fallen nunchuck. He pushed himself up to a seated position and again went for his gun. She swung the wooden weapon up using a backhand stroke just as he aimed his Glock at her. The gun blast and his scream overlapped. She heard the bullet hit the Impala, and saw the gun leave his hand. His wrist hung at an odd angle.

For a moment he stared at her, eyes wide with both pain and surprise, and then he looked over to where the gun lay on the cement, not far from Rossini.

'Leave it,' she ordered.

'You broke my wrist,' he growled, the fury in his words warning her he wasn't through fighting.

Cradling his right arm to his chest, he scrambled to his feet. She tried to stand before he did, but in spite of his injury, the six-year difference in their ages gave him the advantage. He delivered a side-kick before she had her balance. The blow sent her sprawling.

She lost her grip on the nunchuck when her hand hit the cement, the wooden rods sliding out of her reach. The pitchfork lay closer, and she started for it, only to see David coming at her. She rolled onto her back and grabbed his leg as he kicked at her side. The toe of his shoe hit her ribs, taking her breath away and sending a jolt of pain through her body, but she didn't let go. Forcing herself to ignore the pain, she did a sit-up, rising to the side just enough to press her weight against his leg.

Caught off balance, he fell backwards and onto his side, jarring his body and forcing out another cry of pain. In his eyes, she saw the fury of a wounded animal and knew she'd merely increased his desire to kill her.

She gritted her teeth and moved, ignoring the pain as bruised or broken ribs protested her action. Scooting along the cement toward the pitchfork, she put as much distance between them as she could before he was on his feet. She managed to get to her knees and grab the pitchfork before he took a step closer. One glance at the pitchfork and he stopped, smiled, and took a step back.

She wasn't quite sure how to interpret his retreat until he took another step back, then another, and another, each bringing him closer to where his Glock lay on the cement. He didn't look at the gun but kept his gaze on her.

She could see Rossini behind David. Although the sergeant's arms were tied behind his back and around a board that went from the rafters to the floor, he was stretching out his body, trying to reach the gun with his foot. She didn't want David to notice, so she groaned and set the pitchfork back down. She brought one hand to her side, about where he'd kicked her, and let the fingers of her other hand touch the cement. She hoped Rossini would notice how she was sweeping her fingertips toward her and would get the message.

She also hoped David wouldn't notice.

'Ah, did I hurt you?' David taunted and grinned.

'Like you care.' She gave a slight nod and tensed her muscles, ready to move.

Rossini moved his right leg, sweeping it along the cement floor, the toe of his shoe pointing at the Glock. David heard the movement and looked behind him, immediately understanding what Rossini was attempting to do.

The tip of Rossini's shoe caught the Glock near the grip and propelled the gun away from David's feet. If they'd been on a smooth surface – a polished hardwood floor or ceramic tile – the gun might have slid into Mary's hands, but the rough surface of the cement slowed its forward motion.

Mary lunged forward, and David swooped down. She grabbed the grip with her right hand and pulled the Glock closer. David slapped his uninjured hand over hers, the weight of his body stopping her from moving the gun any farther.

An involuntary cry of pain accompanied the thud when his shoulder, then hip, hit the cement. She had a feeling the groan she heard as she tried to scoot back and away came from her. The pain in her side brought tears to her eyes, but she didn't let go of her hold on the gun.

'Give it to me!' David snarled, his face only inches from hers.

'No,' she yelled, though she wondered how long she could counter his strength.

'Give it!' He squeezed his fingers around hers, pressing her hand into the frame of the gun.

She could feel him lifting both her hand and the gun, and she knew once he had enough room, he would twist her wrist until she had to release her hold. After that, it would be over. He would have the gun, and she would be dead, along with Shannon and Rossini.

'No!' she yelled again, and countered his lift by raising her hand even higher and rolling to her side.

The twist of her body turned her hand slightly to the side, and she clasped her fingers around the gun's grip, her index finger reaching the trigger. The deafening bang when the gun went off was matched by the recoil, slamming her back against the cement. She saw David coming down on her, saw the look of anger in his eyes, then the surprise.

'Damn,' he growled, falling on top of her.

Trapped beneath him, the gun and her hand now squeezed between them, Mary waited for his next move. She could feel the rise and fall of his chest, the rhythm uneven, and for a moment she thought he was breathing hard. Then he coughed and tried to push himself off, and she realized he wasn't going for the gun.

'David?' she said cautiously, using her free hand against his shoulder to push him to the side.

'Damn you,' he gritted through clenched teeth.

'Mary, are you all right?' Rossini called from behind David's feet.

'Grandma?'

'David?' she repeated, inching away from his body.

She could see the blood now, pooling beneath his side. He simply looked at her.

'Mary, cut me loose before the police arrive,' Rossini yelled.

In the distance she could hear sirens.

214

It took her a moment to understand. Finally, she slowly rose to her feet, still holding the gun. 'I called 911 before I came in here.'

'Cut me loose and give me the gun,' Rossini ordered. 'You don't want to be holding that gun when they arrive.'

She looked over at Rossini, and then back down at David. He was still alive, but barely, his breathing shallow.

'Grandma, is he dead?' Shannon asked, her voice shaky.

'No, not yet.' She looked back at Rossini, then left David's side and went to the sergeant.

'Hurry,' he ordered. 'Check my right pant pocket. I think I still have my jackknife in there.'

CHAPTER FORTY-ONE

'THANK GOODNESS YOU'RE here,' Jack said, the moment Jennifer Mendoza entered the barn, her weapon drawn. 'Call an ambulance.'

Gun still drawn, Jennifer stood where she was, her gaze moving from where Jack knelt beside David Burrows' body, to where Mary Harrington was cutting the rope holding her granddaughter's arms behind her, to the Impala, and then back to Jack. 'What happened?'

'We were struggling with the gun, and it went off.' Jack touched the side of Burrows' neck, waited a few seconds to make sure he didn't feel a pulse, then shook his head. 'Never mind calling the ambulance. We'll need the county M.E.'

Frowning, Jennifer holstered her weapon and pulled out her cell-phone. 'Is that Agent Burrows?'

'It is.' Jack rose to his feet and took the Glock over to Jennifer, handing it to her butt first.

'I thought he was with law enforcement. The other night ... when those boys fire-bombed her house ...'

'He had us all fooled,' Jack said, knowing he should have trusted his gut feelings about the guy. 'He kidnapped the girl, then grabbed me when I followed him out of town.'

'But why?'

That was going to be the difficult part to explain, at least without revealing Mary Harrington's role in the situation. Jack looked back at Burrows' body. 'I guess that's something we'll never completely understand.'

'This isn't your weapon,' Jennifer said, carefully handling the Glock he'd handed her.

'No. I'm not sure where mine is.' Last Jack remembered he'd had it in his hand as he approached the back of the black car. 'Maybe in the woods ... or maybe in his other car.'

'There's a black Nissan parked outside and a gray Chevy.'

'The Chevy's mine,' Mary said.

Jack looked her way. Mary Harrington was standing, her left hand pressed against her right side, while her granddaughter remained seated, rubbing her wrists and flexing her shoulders. 'You two all right?' he asked, knowing how sore his shoulders felt from having his arms tied behind his back, and how painful a kick to the side could feel, especially if Burrows had broken any of Mary Harrington's ribs.

'Yes, thanks to you.' Moving slowly, Mary Harrington left her granddaughter's side and came over to where they stood 'Thank you, Sergeant.'

'You're the one who called 911, aren't you?' Jennifer said.

'I did. I—'

Jack interrupted her. 'I was at Mrs Harrington's house when Burrows came over, driving that black car. He was putting something in her car when he saw me and took off. She followed me, saw what was going on, and tried to rescue us, but he got the drop on her, too. It wasn't until he cut me loose that I was able to catch him off guard. We were struggling with the gun when it went off.'

Again Officer Mendoza looked at the gun he'd given her. 'Wow, sounds like you were lucky.'

'Very lucky,' he agreed.

Sirens could be heard in the distance. Officer Jennifer Mendoza glanced that way. 'Dispatcher put out an "all units" call. Others should be showing up soon.'

Jack turned to Mary. 'Why don't we step outside for a minute so you can call your son and daughter-in-law and let them know their daughter is all right.' He looked at Jennifer. 'If that's all right with you?'

She hesitated, then shrugged. 'I guess so.'

Jack knew he was playing on Jennifer's lack of experience, but he wanted to talk to Mary and her granddaughter before others arrived. 'Come with us,' he motioned to the girl. 'We need to call your parents.'

'Shannon,' Jack said as soon as the three of them were outside of the barn. 'Your grandmother does not want others to know what she did in the past or what she's capable of doing. Do you think you can keep what you heard and saw today to yourself?'

'At least until I decide what to do next,' Mary added.

'I ... I guess so.' The girl looked at her grandmother as if she'd never seen her before.

'In that case, we need to make sure our stories are the same.' He pointed at Mary. 'You came in with the pitchfork. Poked him in the side. That will explain any tine marks they find on his jacket. He knocked you down and kicked you. Then he cut me loose. He was going to take us outside and shoot us, but I managed to get hold of the gun, we struggled, and he ended up being shot.'

'Grandma broke his arm,' Shannon said. 'How are you going to explain that?'

Jack looked at the girl. He certainly couldn't tell Wally or others that he broke the guy's wrist using the nunchuck. It wouldn't take long to prove he had no idea how to handle one of those. 'He fell on his hand?'

'Tell them you have no idea how he did that,' Mary said and put a hand in her pocket and pulled the nunchuck out so both he and her granddaughter could see the tops of the two rods and the chain holding them together. 'I picked it up before I released Shannon. Without the weapon, they'll just be guessing how David's wrist was broken.'

Jack noticed one other weakness in their story. 'You have some blood on the front of your jacket.'

'He was a friend of mine,' Mary said. 'After he was shot, I went over to see if I could help him. I must have gotten some blood on me at that time.'

The sirens were coming closer, and they could see the flashing lights and headlights of the cars as they neared the farm. 'So we're agreed?' Jack asked.

Both Mary and Shannon nodded.

'For tonight we keep your past a secret, but Mary, if Burrows didn't want you talking, how long before someone else connected with the agency shows up to keep you quiet? You need to tell that congressional committee what's going on.'

'But I haven't been with them for over forty years,' she said. 'What can I tell anyone?'

'That it exists.'

She said nothing for a moment, then nodded. 'I'll think about it.'

CHAPTER FORTY-TWO

IN ADDITION TO Officer Mendoza, two more Rivershore police officers showed up at the barn, along with deputies from the Van Buren Sheriff's Department and officers from the Michigan State Police. Mary was separated from Shannon and Rossini. She hoped their three descriptions of what had happened in the barn would be close enough to be believable but not so close they seemed prepared.

The paramedics checked out her ribs and told her they couldn't tell if they were broken without an X-ray, but when they suggested taking her to the hospital, she refused. 'I'll see how I feel tomorrow,' she told them and signed the release.

It was after eleven o'clock when she was told that she and Shannon could leave. She knew Robby and Clare would still be up. When Shannon had called them earlier, she had said, over and over, 'I'm fine,' but Mary knew Robby and Clare would want to see for themselves.

Standing around, talking to one officer after another, there were moments when Mary wished she had taken the paramedics up on their offer to transport her to a hospital. Once in her car, she decided sitting wasn't going to be much better. Every inch of her body was beginning to hurt. She had the car started before she realized Shannon still hadn't gotten in.

Passenger door open, Shannon stood next to the car without moving.

Mary hoped there wasn't going to be a problem. 'Get in,' she urged. 'We need to get you home.'

'I ...' Shannon shook her head.

'I'm not going to bite.' Mary had no idea what her granddaughter thought of her after what she'd heard from David, but they'd have to deal with that later.

'I know. I didn't think ...' Shannon sniffed and looked at her. 'I wet my pants, Grandma. I was so scared, I peed all over myself. If I get in, I'll get the seat wet. All smelly.'

'Oh, hell.' Mary started to laugh, then stopped herself at a warning stab of pain. 'Don't you worry about the seat, Shannon. Your dad's right. It's time I got a new car.'

With her granddaughter in the car, Mary headed back to Rivershore. She drove as fast as she could within the speed limit, but every bump and jolt in the road caused a pain in her side. She didn't realize how often she gasped until Shannon said, 'Are you OK, Grandma?'

'I've definitely had better days.'

'So have I.'

Mary looked at her granddaughter. 'I'm so sorry, honey,' she said. 'I never thought he would kidnap you, that he'd use you to get to me.'

'He was so nice at first, said he wanted to talk to me about you, that he was worried about you and wanted my opinion.' She shuddered. 'And then he got nasty and pulled out that gun.'

'Did he do anything to you? I mean, besides tie you up?' That was one thing they hadn't discussed before the police arrived, and Mary had no idea what Shannon had told the police who interviewed her.

'You mean like rape me? No. But he was mean. He wouldn't let me go to the bathroom, wouldn't give me anything to eat. I'm starving.'

Mary glanced over at her granddaughter, amazed by the girl's resilience and relieved that food was Shannon's main concern at the moment. 'I'm afraid you'll have to wait until you get home to get something to eat.'

'Yeah, I figured as much.'

Mary wasn't sure what to say next, or how to broach the subject of what David had said. Shannon resolved the problem. 'He said a lot of nasty things about you, Grandma. How you were the director's favorite and that's why you were allowed to leave the agency. Did you really kill people?'

Mary hesitated, and then nodded. 'All but one were people who deserved to die, but I guess that doesn't really make it right.'

'He said you both worked for a secret agency, one I wouldn't have heard of.'

'I doubt if more than a handful of people know of its existence.'

'Why did you quit?'

'Because the agency made a mistake, and I killed the wrong person. And I think I was getting scared. You can only live on adrenaline for so long. I knew, sooner or later, one of my marks would figure out I wasn't who I said I was, and I'd be the one who died.'

'You slept with them?'

Mary wished David hadn't told Shannon that, but she wasn't going to lie to the girl. 'With some.'

'Do Mom and Dad know about your past?'

'No, and I'd hoped they'd never find out, that you'd never find out.' But that wasn't to be.

Shannon reached over and gave Mary's leg a light pat. 'Don't be embarrassed. I think it's kinda awesome.'

'Awesome?' Mary again glanced her way.

'Not everyone has a secret agent for a grandmother. And the way you broke his arm with that stick and knocked him down. In a way, it's not fair that Sergeant Rossini gets all the credit.'

'I'm perfectly happy to let him take the credit.'

'My grandma's a secret agent.'

She said it so proudly, almost like a chant, and that scared Mary. 'Shannon, that isn't something I want known. I did what I thought was right at the time, but when I moved here, I wanted to forget that life. I don't want people looking at me and seeing some sort of James Bond figure.'

'Yeah, well, maybe, but I think Sergeant Rossini is right, you should tell people about the agency. I mean, if you don't, someone else might try to kill you.'

For the first time, Mary heard a note of fear in her grand-daughter's voice. When she looked over, she saw tears sliding down Shannon's cheeks.

'I don't want anyone to kill you, Grandma.' The girl's voice trembled. 'They might come after me, too, just like he did. I don't want to die.'

'Oh, Shannon, honey.' Mary pulled over to the side of the road. 'Come here.'

In spite of the pain in her side, Mary drew her granddaughter closer and kissed her forehead. 'I am so sorry you had to go through this. I never thought David would do such a thing, and I promise you, I'll do everything I need to do to make sure no one ever comes after you.'

'Or you?' Shannon sniffed.

'Or me.' Mary gave her granddaughter's shoulders a squeeze. 'Now, let's get you home.' The pain in her side made her grit her teeth. 'And then I think I'm going to go visit the emergency room.'

'Dad's going to wonder what happened to you.'

Mary chuckled and pulled back onto the road. 'We'll tell him I ran into something.'

CHAPTER FORTY-THREE

CHRISTMAS BREAK WAS over, and life in Washington D.C. was back to its normal, frenzied pace. Snow had fallen the night before, the outside temperature hovering around twenty degrees, so no one paid much attention when a white-haired woman entered the Russell Senate Office Building wearing a hooded, calf-length wool coat.

221

The two senators who accompanied her hustled her through security and into one of the staffrooms. Once they were sure someone would bring her a cup of hot tea and were assured she was comfortable, they scurried off to find the remaining three senators on their committee.

No recording devices were evident. No TV cameras or reporters. When her lawyer had contacted the committee and explained there was a witness who could provide a substantial amount of information about the agency they were investigating, he'd set the parameters for her testimony. She would tell what she knew. After that it would be up to members of the committee to verify or dismiss her information.

The five senators entered the small room, some frowning, some grumbling when they saw her. She didn't care. She would agree with them that her information was outdated, but one person had considered her a threat to the agency. She hoped what she told these senators would be enough to keep anyone else from bothering her.

'Good morning, gentlemen,' she began. 'I'm here today because for thirteen years I was an agent with America's Department of Environmental Control, otherwise known as ADEC. During those thirteen years, I participated in the elimination of twenty men and women considered threats to this country. In other words, I helped control the environment we now live in. If you have any questions …'

The phone rang, and Jack looked at the clock. It wasn't quite 4.15.

Mary? She'd said she'd call and let him know how this first day of testimony went.

He hoped everything was OK. The week before, when they'd had dinner at the Shores, they'd talked about what she was going to say. He knew she would have preferred to put her past behind her, to forget she was ever known as Pandora Coye. But as he'd reminded her, she didn't really have a choice if she didn't want another ADEC agent showing up in Rivershore.

From what she'd told him over dinner, her granddaughter was doing well, had seen a trauma specialist a few times, and didn't seem the worse for her experience. Shannon had vowed to keep her grandmother's past a secret, but Jack was still surprised that Mary's son and daughter-in-law had no idea what actually went down in that barn. The day Jack talked to Robert Harrington, telling the man he was putting the final touches on his report about the abduction, he'd nearly laughed when Harrington expressed his concern about his mother's welfare. It had taken Jack all of his self-control to simply say he thought Mary Harrington would be all right living alone in her home, and that he didn't think she'd be bothered by any gang members in the future.

The phone rang again, and he answered, 'Hello.'

It wasn't Mary.

'Hey, Dad, you're a grandpa again.'

'Angie had the baby?'

'Jaxson Rossini – that's Jax with an x – entered the world at 2.25 p.m. Eight pounds, five ounces and twenty-one inches.'

'He's a big one. How's Angie?'

'Doing all right. I just left her. She's a little groggy from the shot they gave her. She did want me to ask if you thought you could get time off and come here next month. She'd like to get Jaxson christened when he's a month old.'

'Actually, I'm scheduled to fly into D.C. tomorrow. I have a friend who may need a little moral support. I'd like you to meet her, but if that would be too much ...'

'No. No, that would be great, Dad.' His son gave a chuckle. 'You are full of surprises.'

'I've been learning from a pro.'